the
GALLUCCI
GALLERY

Grandeur Publishing
400 E. Station Avenue #110
Coopersburg, PA. 18036
www.grandeurpublishing.com

Printed in the United States of America
First Printing, 2021

To the individuals who have been abused

and must live with mental illness

the
GALLUCCI
GALLERY

K.B. RICHARDS

GRANDEUR PUBLISHING

1

What a
Wonderful World

I GREW TROUBLED, JUGGLING the authenticity of my reality. I pinched myself, hoping the life I lead wasn't a dream. The mess I made humbled me, allowing me to remove the rose-tinted glasses. There's no cure for what I am, and who I've become. People tell each other they should embrace who they are––that they should live their truth. My truth compelled me to stare into the mirror every single day, facing the ugliness which once laid dormant. Must I espouse the destructive side I possess? Society will never accept who I am once they learn of my interior nature. I will be rejected and shunned to a place distant from their inner social circle. They can't feel my pain. They don't understand my deep-rooted trauma and remorse brimming from the surface of my core.

I hated my husband and wanted him to suffer. He would become an afterthought someday and acknowledge the anguish he rained on me for the rest of his life. Revenge still isn't enough. I wondered if my children would cope without their father around.

Will they despise me one day? Will they act out, due to his absence? People say, "The apple doesn't fall far from the tree." I hoped to God my son wouldn't turn out like his father. Worse, I hoped my daughter wouldn't inherit my illness. My transgressions are etched into the universe's book of karma, but when it came to protecting my kids, I chose to endure any punishment. I would sacrifice my life for their happiness and safety. I would do anything necessary.

A pair of bloody scissors resided in my hand while I contemplated my life and illegal action. And as I departed from the space I created in my head, I fumbled necessity and my sanity, hand in hand.

Oh, God, what have I done? A sliver of guilt migrated from hell and forced its way into my derailed mind. I stood in my gallery comprehending my crime while my victim's blood crept toward my feet like cough medicine crawling out of an open, toppled bottle. *Step back.* I dropped a .38 revolver from my hand while holding scissors in the other. Blood proceeded to claim the marble floor, following me. My thoughts whirled into a scattered frenzy. My cuticles dampened and my clenched grip, unable to release my scissors. They bonded to my hand—tethered by the crimson saturating my pores. *Take a deep breath, Bianca.* My heart slammed against my ribs. A devilish chill conjured its way to my skin's surface, skewing my grip on reality and immobilizing my legs. Nothing but time could stop my unnerved, bloody hand from shaking and drops claiming the floor.

My intermittent, pounding chest forced me to my knees. The adrenaline surged through my veins and a feverish sweat claimed every inch of my face, neck, and forearm. *Breathe, Bianca, breathe.* The shock alone restricted my movements until I was capable of uncurling my fingers. I stared at my hand with a catatonic glare, as if afflicted with Locked-in syndrome. Nausea surfaced while I conceded second-degree murder. My eyes drowned in regret, knowing the likelihood of prison. No forced entry and or signs of a struggle. My prints resided on the gun and scissors. *I had motive.* I allowed the scissors to fall to the floor and acknowledged blood splatter on my gray shirt—the one I deemed worn-out and old. I rubbed it with the cuff of my sleeve, eager to vanquish the undeniable proof. *What am I doing? It's getting worse.* I contemplated my situation while wiping my cheek, smearing blood on my face.

Think, Bianca. Think. Calm down. Rationalize your thoughts. A small sense of relief permeated the air while I justified my actions. "I did it for the kids," I kept telling myself until I gained the strength to stand. My arms rested by my side while my victim surveyed my presence with furrowed brows. Although she didn't say anything, her eyes spoke to me. They displayed emotions of regret and sorrow, asking for forgiveness. No one witnessed my crime. *No one needs to know. Don't freak out, Bianca. Don't freak out. Think. Think. Think.* No alibi. No one to corroborate my story. *Did anyone see her enter?*

She tried speaking with an abundance of blood flowing out of her mouth. Her body sat upright a few feet from me, as I paced back and forth. I was afraid to touch her, petrified to dial the authorities, and terrified to leave. *I need to call for help. Oh God, where's my phone?* I searched the front desk after scouring my office and found it in the wastebasket. 'What a Wonderful World' played through the speakers overhead.

A familiar apparition merged into my body. My pounding heart accelerated before slowing down, and I existed in a world of complete peace while listening to the melody. *This song—oh, I love this song.* The music grew faint, dissipating with every note that followed. I smiled, closing my eyes—ready to bask in the ambiance of my surroundings.

The walk back to my victim appeared timeless, and the closer I got, the more I enjoyed watching death devour her. I smiled while kneeling to caress her pale, saddened face. Her breathing labored.

"You deserve this. You should've stayed away. Now, you'll be gone forever. Time to clean you up," I said. I elevated to a superior version of myself. Rejuvenated. Renewed.

"I promised to keep Bianca and the twins safe, and that's what I'm going to do. She *will not* rot in prison because of you. We're ready to do what's necessary," I said.

I knelt over her almost-dead body, placing one hand over her mouth while my other pinched her nostrils. It was only a matter of time until she stopped struggling. She convulsed. *Shh. Be still. It'll be over soon.* She ceased to budge, and the power I possessed from taking her life exalted my superiority. She was no more.

The radio continued playing in the background, cradling my core while I sat next to her lifeless body. I contemplated disposal of her corpse and to finish my painting. The hint of red I desired laid within my reach, and I fell intrigued by the color before me.

I dipped my brush into the pool of blood, smearing it onto the canvas. *There. Perfect.* The mixture of her blood and the paints gave it an astonishing, robust hue. *Beautiful.* One hour turned into two, as I created a masterpiece. *Hide the evidence in plain sight. No one would be suspicious.*

My victim's body and work of art sat side by side. My adrenaline wore off, and I grabbed an opened bottle of wine, sat down on the floor, and gestured a toast to myself. My eyelids grew heavy, consumed by sleep. *I'll deal with the corpse soon.*

2

He's Dead

I HELD AN INTERVIEW a few weeks prior. All was well with the world, but I needed an assistant to help run my gallery. A mother of two can only do so much on her own in a twelve-to fourteen-hour day. My husband, Lucas Pope helped on the weekends. Forty-eight hours wasn't enough for quality family time. I sat at my desk in a pencil skirt and blouse with a notepad and pen in front of me. My interviewee sat across the table, wearing a similar style of clothing. She complimented my shoes before crossing her legs and interlacing her fingers.

"Hi, Makaela. It's so nice to meet you. I'm glad you were able to be here, today," I said. "Thank you for having me, Ms. Gallucci!" She was a confident girl, asking all the right questions with all the right credentials under her belt. Beautiful, too. She appeared to be smart, capable, competent, and what I searched for in a perfect candidate. I navigated toward my computer to refer to her resume. We hit it off, and her widespread knowledge of art impressed me. Besides that, she also acquired solid recommendations from past employers. I wanted to hire her before she walked through my door, but I needed to examine her mannerism before making a concrete decision. I listened to the way she spoke as she answered my questions.

"Tell me a little about yourself," I said. She was careful with her words, and there might've been some nervousness on her part, but I was fond of her. The more comfortable she became, the more she rambled, but I didn't mind. She was expressive, captivating, and articulate. I admired her passion for art. After some more questions, her time was drawing to a close. *Yes, she's the one.*

"So, anything else you'd like to ask?" I said. She peered with inquisition before asking me a borderline-private question about my past, a few about my kids, and the establishment of the gallery. Our interview transitioned into an old-fashioned conversation filled with rapport and personal connection. We spoke of many subjects such as my childhood in Italy, the crazy motorcycle story Lucas and I experienced when he and I first met, and my sister's memorial. Speaking with her was easy. She didn't over-complicate anything, and I could've spent the entire afternoon chatting, but work needed to be done.

"So, you kept the Gallucci name alive. I find that honorable," she said.

"Family first," I said.

"Yeah, I see how important that is."

"So the job is yours if you want."

"It would be my pleasure," she said.

I had a good feeling about her, and I extended my hand to shake hers.

"Makaela, welcome to my Gallery. Any more questions for me?"

"No, I don't think so."

"Let's give you the tour and introduce you to some of my staff."

She marveled at the interior of my office, admiring the decor, quotes, artwork, and pictures before leaving. One particular portrait caught her eye.

"Is that your family?"

"Oh, yes—my husband and the twins."

"Beautiful! Not every woman is as lucky as you."

"Thank you! That's sweet of you to say."

"How'd you two meet, if you don't mind me asking? I'm sorry, I'm a sucker for stories about how couples meet, especially the relationships that last for decades."

"Oh, okay. Well, since you ask. We were young when we met in Naples, and I was a little bit of a pick-pocket, back in the day. Oh, my God, I'm embarrassed to admit, but my family was poor, and we had to eat, you know? Anyway, I stole his wallet and he caught me red-handed. To make a long story short...well, he took me to dinner instead of the police. I fell in love with him since that day."

"Aww, that's so sweet. Thank you for sharing that with me.

She smiled at me, at stared at the photograph while I walked away from my desk. I paused, cleared my throat, and gazed at her with a slight raise of my eyebrow. She delivered a sharp exhale and blinked more times than I could count.

"Oh, I'm so sorry. I don't mean to be rude. I just—my contact lens is getting old. Time for new ones."

"Those things are so bothersome. I don't know how you deal with them."

Her hand raced to her eye, moving the lens around before retrieving a bottle of eye drops from her purse. I handed her a tissue after she glanced at the stationary items near my family photo.

"Are you sure you're okay?" I asked.

"Yes. I'm fine. I'm ready," she said.

I moved from around the desk while she got herself situated. "This way, please," I said. We walked through the door and continued down the hallway as I gave her a small lesson in the professional structure and setting of my gallery. We soon set foot in the showroom where all the paintings hung on the walls. Each piece of art had its spotlight cascading upon it.

"I house some of the most popular and most obscure art. This is where some of the starving artists get discovered, and I'm proud to house their work."

Makaela appeared to be enjoying the tour, and paused a moment, staring at one of New York's highly-regarded artists.

"This is—no way!"

"Yes. Robert LaRue. His work is remarkable."
Makaela sauntered about, walking past my artwork hanging next to LaRue's with only a subtle glance. My current assistant approached us.

"Bianca," he said.

"Peter. You're back! Did everything go well with delivering those packages?"

"Yes, here's the receipt," he said.

He handed me a slip of paper. I grew engulfed in the detailed receipt, forgetting Makaela lingered in our presence.

"Oh, forgive me, Makaela. Peter, this is Makaela, your replacement. He's relocating to California for a new position. I'm sad he's leaving, but he'll show you the ropes and start training you tomorrow, perhaps?"

"Uh, yeah, tomorrow will be great!"

"Could you come in at 11:00?"

"I'll be here."

"Okay, good! I'm sorry I have to leave you, but I must make a few phone calls. Please excuse me."

"Oh, no, it isn't a problem. Thank you, again."

"Sure thing. I'm glad to have you onboard."

I walked away, leaving her with Peter while they commenced their chat. He appeared to be a little shy at first and blushed as she stared at him. I was sure it did more good than harm to have some eye candy around the gallery. I was content in my decision, and I smiled as I sauntered along the long, narrow hallway back to my office. The short story I told Makaela about my family made me reflect and treasure everything I had in my life. I took a minute to appreciate my family and to admire my fruitful career. I extended my hand, barely touching the wall, and adorned the beauty of my accomplishments before stepping foot into my office. There was work to do. And as soon as I was done with my calls, I handled a couple of issues before departing for lunch.

***

I gathered my belongings and headed toward the entrance. To my surprise, a suspicious-looking man—a stranger stood outside the gallery window, staring in with a bleak, sinister presence. I couldn't move. I was too fearful and rendered powerless, as I tried moving my feet to walk away. He gazed at me, and I returned the gesture, observing his appearance. Something about him was unsettling—unnerving, as he stood motionless. His height was... about six feet (1.83 m) —and he just... looking inside with his hands in his pockets. My experience with weirdos in New York was deemed mundane, but my curious nature sensed something different about him. His beard was visible, but his large fedora covered his eyes and most of his face. Fearful, yet interested, I wanted to know his identity.

"Peter, can you come a moment, please?" I said. "Peter, can you hurry up? Come quick!"

He jogged toward me, furrowing his eyebrows, and by the time he was by my side, the stranger disappeared.

"What's wrong? Are you alright?"

"Umm, have you seen any strange men come around or wander in here?"

"Um... no, I haven't."

"Oh... okay. My mind must be playing tricks on me or something. I'm going out to lunch. I'll be back in an hour or so."

"Alright, enjoy."

A gust of wind guided me in the direction I intended the second I walked out the door, swaddled in apprehension. It was brisk outside, and I tried to forget about the mysterious man while I enjoyed the sun and chilled air. I kept my wits about me, checking over my shoulder in recurrence like a paranoid maniac who's lost their mind. The illusion of safety grew, as long as I felt like I wasn't being followed.

***

I arrived at my favorite restaurant to meet my best friend, Claire Benoit. We were great friends, like sisters who looked after one another. When she needed me during her divorce, I was there to console her—help her out with whatever she desired. She and I were as 'thick as thieves,' as the phrase goes. Claire is a charming French woman who couldn't leave her accent at home, like me and possessed the cutest attitude. Her hair was short, curly, blonde, and her eyes, a mesmerizing blue—constantly attracting men.

"Oh, you caught me off guard! I didn't see you there," I said.

"Ah, you look more beautiful every time I see you, Bianca!" she said.

She was standing on the street corner in front of the Empire Diner with a cigarette in her hand—her lighter returning to her purse. Her embrace and warm personality discarded the chill in the air as we hugged and kissed each other on the cheek.

"Claire, it's *so* good to see you!"

We entered the restaurant—escorted by Leo, the host and long-time acquaintance who had always been so genuine to me and my family whenever we dined. We had much to catch up on.

"You look fantastic, Claire! How long's it been?" I said.

"I... think about... three months, yes?" she said.

"Yeah, I think so."

"So tell me. How are my beautiful babies doing?"

"Oh, forget about it. Every two seconds it's, 'mommy this and mom that'."

They're growing up so fast, though. The both of them are always telling me something new they've learned in school—and that's the least of it. Isabelle has a new best friend almost every week! You know what it's like at that age. I love them so much, though."

"Aw, they're so adorable I could steal them from you, and hug and kiss them till they become sick of me! I miss them a lot, Bea. I can't wait to see them!"

"Yes, they're going to be *so* happy to see their Aunt Claire."

"How's Lucas doing?"

"Oh, he's well, and busier than ever. Work's good, too. He's working on expanding his medical practice."

"Oh, wow. What wonderful news. Congratulations to you both!"

"It's great, yes, but I don't get to see much of him anymore. He's been *so* busy working, but I wish he was around more to spend time with the kids."

"That's got to be tough on you."

"It is sometimes, but I manage. How about you—any *lovers* in your life, yet?"

"Um, yeah, actually, I do!"

"Uh–oh, here comes a husband and children in your future."

"Oh, stop it. A husband, someday? Yeah, maybe. Children? I don't have to tell you how f**ked up my insides are, thanks to my military accident. *Anyway*, he has two ki—"

"*No*, don't say that, hon. We have modern science these days… and miracles happen all the time. So, what's this lucky guy's na—"

I couldn't believe my eyes and stopped mid-sentence, peering out the window. Fear immobilized me. Somehow, I couldn't help to look away. I stared in disbelief.

"Bianca, what's the matter?" she asked.

I didn't respond. My eyes fixated on the huddle of people walking by. Claire also looked and touched my hand, diverting my attention.

"Bea? What's wrong? What are you looking at?" she asked.

"Oh my God. It's... it's him again," I said.

"What? It's who? *Who are you looking at?*"

"It's the man. The man from earlier."

"What man are you talking about?"

He drifted along the sidewalk near the window within an intermittent throng of strangers. He was the same as earlier—hands in pocket and head held down in black attire. The nearer he got, the more nervous I became—the more recognizable he became.

"What man are you looking at, Bea?"

I took my time scrutinizing as he got closer, but it was so damn hard to get a glimpse of his face with his eyes hidden under the fedora. He took his time lifting his head, allowing me to view his eyes and his long, intentional stare. Such a leer burned a hole through my soul while he walked by.

The mystery man's eyes were full of malevolence, and I somehow unveiled his true character. It was like a transference—

an instant, confirmed knowledge of his authenticity. *No, this can't be happening!* I couldn't *believe* what I was seeing! He held a strong, striking resemblance to my father! He never broke eye contact and stared at me until I was no longer within his field of vision. An internal heat arose in my chest, crawling up my neck. Tears ran down my face and into my cup of tea, as I bowed my head in disbelief. Staring at him awakened images of my past.

"Honey, are you alright? Talk to me. What's going on?"

She handed me a tissue from her purse and begged me to verbalize my thoughts.

"Did you see him... the man in black? You *had to* have seen him."

"I—I didn't get a good look at who you're talking abo—"

"That man that walked so close to the window looking *right* at me! The one with the hat! You didn't see him?" I said.

"Bea, I saw a lot of people in that crowd. I'm not sure who you're talking about."

"It was him! My father. Oh, my God, how is he still alive?"

"Bea, that's not possible. It's been 32 years. He's dead."

"I know! I watched him die," I said. I got up from the table and rushing outside.

"Wait. Where are you going?"

"I need to know that what I saw was real."

"Bea? Bea, wait!"

I scurried out of the restaurant and stood out front, hoping to spot the stranger I believed to be real. I couldn't spot him. It's like he vanished into thin air!

"Wait, where'd he go? I'm not crazy. I know what I saw."

Claire lingered at the door, leaving it halfway opened.

"Bianca. Bea! Come back inside," she said.

"It *has* to be him. It looks *so much* like him, Claire. I mean, he's older, but... his eyes. A person's eyes don't change much as they age. I *know* those eyes!"

"*Bea*, come in and sit down. Let's talk about this."

There wasn't much I could do. I was anxious, uneasy, helpless, and confused. Keeping my legs from fidgeting was impossible while Claire tried consoling me.

"Bea, calm down, please. Take a deep breath," she said. Her hand rested on mine.

"I *am* taking a deep breath. He just needs to stay away from me! That's it, okay? That's all I want! I *will* call the police if I see him again."

"And what will you tell them if you see him again, *huh*? Honey, you're not even sure it was him. Bea, look at me. Are you *positive* it was him?"

"...I'm ninety-five percent sure, but I had a dreadful sensation the moment I laid eyes on him. You *had* to see the evil in his eyes, Claire. You *don't* forget eyes like his. Fathers aren't supposed to rape their daughters!"

The instant those eyes met mine, a flashback of my past overwhelmed my mind. The mere thought of him imprisoned me––shackled by his dominance, and noosed with terror. I don't want him near my children.

"You've told me everything before, and no child should have to go through that. I understand why you're so scared, but sometimes our minds play tricks on us and..."

"And what? Were you about to say I need to visit a shrink or increase my medication? That would be hypocritical. You *know* me better than anyone. You know I don't see things."

"And that is why I'm concerned. I looked right out that window and didn't see anyone staring at you. You know I love you and would do anything for you. My shrink helped me years ago, and I'm just looking out for my best friend. I think I've earned the right to give sincere advice."

She showed genuine concern, but I couldn't shake the image of the stranger's face.

"Perhaps you should give my cousin a call or visit him at his office. I'm sure he wouldn't mind. He's always happy to see you," she said.

I dunno. Maybe I should visit Dr. Summers again.

3

The Box

"ALRIGHT, I'LL CONSIDER SEEING FRANCIS. Oh, my, God, look at the time. I gotta go. I forgot the kids get out of school a little earlier than usual, today—some sort of teacher's conference this afternoon. I'm so sorry to cut our lunch short, Claire. Would you like to come with me?"

"Oh, honey I wish I could, but I've got a business meeting to attend, and I'm flying out to France tonight. I'll be in Paris a couple of days, but I'll be back to spend time with you, Lucas, and the twins on the weekend—Friday night. You won't be disappearing to the Poconos again without me, now, will you?"

"No, we're not going on vacation anytime soon. We could pick you up at the airport, and the children will have fun. I think they'd enjoy the surprise."

"Oh, you are too kind... and that's why I love you."

"Send me your flight itinerary, and we'll see you then!"

"Bea, everything will be alright, hon."

We kissed each other on the cheek, hugged, and parted ways. The wind died, but the air still possessed a raw, unsettling chill. My hustle back to my gallery appeared to be longer than usual, as I kept my eyes peeled for the man from earlier. I imagined him watching my every move—following me—hiding in plain sight. An imagination like mine wasn't easy to ignore, and I prayed that seeing him was all but a trick of the mind. It was time for me to take my medicine—the small bottle of pills I searched for within my shoulder bag. I swallowed one and washed it down with some water before arriving at the gallery. Peter was talking to a customer while I made my way to my office. I opened the door to discover mail on my desk. Among the letters, I received a small red box. An elegant white bow sat on top. *Well, what do we have here? Aw, Peter didn't have to give me a present.* I pulled the ribbon apart with curiosity—opening the light-weighted box with excitement.

I looked inside, and my eyes rested upon a sleek, gold card, resembling a hotel key. *Hmm, no physical black strip like a credit card. No numbers or inscriptions.* I assumed the gift was from Peter, but I grew skeptical. Lucas wouldn't send me unmarked gifts. No return address. I flipped the box over, searching every corner for anything I might've missed. I found a small piece of paper—a note taped to the underside of the lid. The half-folded note read, "Your secret is no longer your own. 332." My heart pounded harder, and my thoughts scattered about. *Who sent this? 332? Is this a key to a hotel room? It's possible. What hotel does it belong to?*

I stormed out of my office toward Peter in search of answers. He sat at the front desk reading a novel entitled, 'The End of May.'

"Peter, where did this box come from? Who gave it to you?" I said. I extended my arm, holding it at his eye level. His eyes left his page, furrowing his brows.

"The mailman. It came with the rest of the mail."

"Are you *sure*?" I asked. His eyes widened before he reclined in his chair.

"Yeah... the same one as always. He handed it to me, and I put it on your desk right away. Is everything alright?"

"That man—the one I felt unsettled about earlier. Have you noticed anyone out of place? Anyone sort of... *odd* while I went out?"

He shrugged his shoulders. "Yes. Every day. Almost everyone here in the city is odd in some way or another," he said.

"No, I mean... did you see a suspicious-looking man in all black? He would've been wearing a black hat as well. A fedora."

"No one like that, here. I had a few people come in to look around, but that was all. Everyone seemed pretty *normal* to me. I set your mail on your desk and closed your door behind me...and then came back out here," he said. "Are you alright? Is someone harassing you—sending you weird gifts or something? Your security system is good, but maybe you should consider upgrading if you're threatened in any way?"

"Don't worry about it. I'm fine. Everything's fine. Never mind that I said anything, okay? I have to leave and pick up my kids. You'll take care of things for me the rest of the day, yes?"

"I got this."

I walked back into my office for my coat and purse. Taking the card along crossed my mind. My curiosity peaked, wondering where the clues would lead. I placed the card in my purse, put my jacket back on, and traversed toward the front door.

"Take care, Peter. I'll see you tomorrow morning." He waved goodbye while I walked out the front door, and made my way halfway around the block in haste. I arrived at the local garage to retrieve my Audi and gave the attendant, Elias my ticket.

"Hey, Eli. Today's a good day for you, no?"

"Same sh*t. Different day," he said. He walked away grinning before returning with my car.

"Thank you, Eli," I said. He handed me my keys.

"You have a good day, now, Mrs. Gallucci!"

He waved and smiled while holding the twenty-dollar tip in his other hand as I pulled away. I smiled, climbed into the driver's seat, and navigated to Isabelle and Michael's school—heading north on the West Side Highway along the Hudson River. The sunshine gleamed through the trees' branches and intensified the colors of the almost-fallen leaves.

My daily commute was always a beautiful sight. My favorite. As twelve-thirty approached, the traffic started increasing—getting somewhat congested. Arriving at the Calhoun

School didn't take long, and a parking spot in front of the school's entrance turned out to be my luck. The car ran idle while I leaned against the passenger door—responding to unanswered emails. *The kids should be bursting through the doors, running into my arms any minute.* I put my phone away, closed my eyes, and thought of the rough morning I experienced, shoving its existence under the car's rug. The wind increased, and I found a moment of tranquility while I stood, listening to the rustled leaves scrape against the cement. I also enjoyed watching them dance about in the harsh, brisk breeze. The front door of the building swung open, and a wave of adrenaline-filled children ran out laughing and shouting. There they were—my two angels.

"Mom!" said Michael. His math teacher stood in front of the door, and I gave her a short-handed wave, making my presence known. Isabelle followed, and they came running down into my arms as if they didn't see me in ages. Their embrace calmed my nerves, allowing me to forget my awkward morning—and their seven-year-old smiles filled me with joy while they spoke over each other, telling me about their day.

"Alright, alright. Come. Let's get in, buckle up, and then you can tell me *all* about your day." They complied before I pulled off, drove around the block—navigating back on to the West Side Highway, heading south.

"Mom, I'm hungry," said Isabelle.

"Pizza! Pizza," said Michael.

"We have pizza at home. I'll pop it in the oven as soon as we get there, okay?"

"Okay," they said.

Isabelle went on and on about her day at school while Michael continued to play with his new Transformer toy.

***

We arrived home twenty minutes later, and I parked the car in the garage across the street. The kids were full of energy and ran to the front door of our building after I gave them the okay to cross.

"Hey, kids! How was school, today?" said Christian, the building attendant. He extended his hand for a high-five.

"Eh, it was kinda fun," said Michael.

"How've you been, Mrs. G?"

"Oh, busy as ever. *These two* are to blame."

He chuckled and I smiled. As usual, Michael and Isabelle would run to the elevator, competing to press the 5th-floor button first.

"This never gets old, Chris. I'll see you later, okay?"

"You enjoy your evening, Bea," he said. I shuffled off to catch up with the kids. The elevator took its time.

The twins paced, slouching their posture and jostling about the corridor before the door parted. We arrived upstairs and as I opened the front door to our condo, they dashed past me, running toward the living room.

"Hey, munchkins! Put your backpacks away and wash your hands. Pizza will be ready soon, okay?"

"Mom, can we watch TV while we eat?" said Michael. I relished family time, so eating in front of the television was a restriction. However, I made an exception.

"You can watch TV for one hour, okay? I'm sure you have homework to do," I said.

Taking advantage of the temporary silence allowed me to assess my thoughts at the dining table with a glass of wine. I reached into my shoulder bag to examine the item I received earlier. *What the hell could this belong to?* There was no doubt the stranger and card were connected. All I wanted was to protect my children—and I experienced a sudden flashback of the stranger's eyes while my mind wandered.

***

Their food was ready, and they ate while I washed my hands. My phone rang. Isabelle turned around, eyeballing it on the counter.

"You can get it, honey," I said. She sprung off the chair, racing to it.

"Hi, daddy!" she said. She jumped up and down—thrilled about their short-lived conversation. They hung up moments later, and she had much to tell.

"Daddy's on his way home!" she said.

"Great, sweetie!"

"He said to tell you he's gonna be home soon."

"Good—just in time for dinner."

It was rare Lucas was home early, but tremendous, knowing he was willing to make an extra effort to spend time with us. The kids were ecstatic. They raced to him the moment he opened the door. He showered them with affection before diverting his attention to me—and he wrapped his arms around my waist while my body faced the sink. His endearing kiss on my exposed neck ignited an amorous flame.

"*Mm*. Hi, hon. Did you enjoy your day?" he said.

"Uh... yeah. I met with Claire, today. It was...refreshing, spending time with her."

"Oh, that's terrific. She gonna come by for dinner tonight?"

"No, she's on her way to Paris for a couple of days, but she'll be back Friday night. She says, "hello" by the way. The kids and I are gonna pick her up. They'd like the surprise. Anyway, food's ready!"

I wanted to tell Lucas about the events of my day, but not in front of the kids at the dinner table. The skies grew darker a lot earlier. Daylight savings took effect. The children's bedtime was at 8:30 pm, and I kissed them on their foreheads, pacifying their upbeat energy.

"Buona Notte, my loves."

The evening was a success, and my constant yawning steered me to exit. I left their room, sauntering to mine. Lucas was in the bathroom, showering, and I entered to brush my teeth. He rambled about a patient who suffered from a paralytic he administered called 'succinylcholine.' I soon zoned out and stared into the mirror, replaying the events that took place earlier, trying to level my mental energy. He stepped out of the shower and grabbed a towel off the hook by the door. My arms hung by my side, wondering if what I experienced was a trick of the mind.

"Honey, what's wrong? You okay?" he said.

"Something strange happened today."

"Strange? How so?"

"Earlier this afternoon before I met with Claire at a restaurant, a weird man was lurking outside the gallery, and then ran into him again, somehow! He never approached me, nor did

he say anything. But when I saw his eyes, they terrified me."
Lucas filled the gap in between us before caressing my neck.

"What? Someone's stalking you? Wait, what's so significant about his eyes?"

"I don't know how to explain it, but it looked like pure evil, you know? Like, he could see right through me—but wait, before you pass judgment on me, you *know* my treatment was successful, right?"

"*Yes.*"

"And I've never come across as crazy to you, right?"

"*Yes...*"

He squinted, anticipating that I finish my sentence.

"*Okay, yes?* So who was the guy? Did you recognize him?"

He was more curious than ever.

"... My father."

He sighed, scratched his head, and walked away before taking a seat on the bed.

"...*Your father?* That's impossible, hon. He's dead."

"I know he's dead! I know it sounds crazy, but I saw him with my own eyes—older, yes, but I saw him. I swear it's him!"

"Well, did Claire see him, too?"

"Well, no. She couldn't see him because of where she was sitti—look, never mind. Forget I said anything about it." He exhaled with frustration written all over his face.

"No. Don't do that. Don't look at me like that, Lucas."

"*Like what?*"

"Like I'm making sh*t up! I *know* what I saw, today."

"No. I'm not saying you're crazy, hon!"

"You're not saying that I'm crazy, but you're not saying you believe me either!"

Not having anyone believe me was one of the worst feelings in the world. The loneliness in that matter encapsulated me.

"Hon, I'm not saying it *wasn't* him. It could've been someone else—a doppelganger, maybe?"

"His eyes were the same as I remember. The *exact* same, Lucas. Anyone can get plastic surgery and change whatever they want, but a person's eyes won't change, Lucas—even as they get older. You *know* that to be true."

"Look, all I'm saying is you could be wrong. There are ten million people in the city—odds are someone's gonna look like someone you know. I'm only asking you to consider other explanations."

I realized I couldn't change his mind. He wasn't there. Persuading him to regard my point of view and believe me was a challenge. *Francis will listen to me. He'll believe me.*

"Fine. Whatever. I won't mention it again."

I got into bed, turned my lamp off, and laid on my side, facing the window. Lucas didn't say another word. The night's sky poured into the room, and I stared into the distance, thinking about Francis. I needed professional advice and decided to make an appointment with him as soon as possible. My rampant thoughts eluded me as I fell asleep and awoke the next morning to the aroma of coffee. Lucas woke up earlier than me to leave for work. He left a note near the pot that read, "Had to go. See you later," and I got the kids ready for school.

***

The next couple of days went by without a wrinkle. Enigmatic, unwanted guests didn't come strolling by, and I didn't go anywhere without looking over my shoulder twice. God knows I did my best, keeping myself occupied with business calls. *I'll call Francis and talk to him before I go out for lunch.* I closed the door to my office while searching my contact list for his number. It rang a few times before he answered his phone.

"Hello?"

"Francis, hi. It's Bianca... Gallucci."

My eyes wandered into space as I waited for his response.

"Oh, Bianca! What a pleasant surprise! It's so good to hear from you! How are you doing these days?"

A big part of me just wanted to cut the small talk and address the point, but I knew that would've been rude.

"I'm well, Francis. I hope all is well with you, too?"

"Yes, yes. No complaints."

"I hope you don't mind me calling you on your personal line."

"No, not at all. You're family to me. Is everything okay, Bea?" I paused, wanting to choose the right words.

"Bianca? Are you there?"

"Yes. Uh, yes and no. I mean... there's something I need to discuss with you," I said. "It isn't anything alarming. It's just something I'd like to get your opinion on. Can I make an appointment with you?"

"Sure. When are you available?" he said.

"Um, can I see you Monday?"

"I'm booked with appointments that day. Tell you what— come during my lunch break. I'll let my receptionist, Grace know that you're coming. How's eleven-thirty in the morning, sound?"

"Yeah, works for me. I'll see you then!"

I went about the rest of my day, and the kids were home from school around 3:30 pm. I received an email while I was doing my chores, and it was an alert regarding Claire's flight. She was due to land ahead of schedule.

***

The children and I got into the car and headed to the Airport. As usual, Isabelle and Michael fought in the car, and the ridiculous traffic before the Hugh L. Carey Tunnel made their bickering a little unbearable. It was a Friday night after all, and my trip to JFK should've taken only thirty minutes. It took us an hour to arrive.

"We're here, guys!"

"Mom, why are we at the airport?" asked Isabelle.

"You'll see, honey."

We exited the car, moving toward the inside terminal, awaiting Claire's arrival. It took about ten minutes to spot her while we waited—and they ran toward her with exhilaration.

"Aunt Claire!" Michael and Isabelle shouted.

They tackled her with hugs and kisses, and it appeared that her love for them illuminated their lives. She and I greeted each other before heading back to the car.

"So, tell me. How was Paris?"

"Beautiful as always—all work no play, though. Perhaps we can go for a short vacation—just you and me."

"Are you serious?"

"*Yes*, of course. We can go in the spring—just us. Lucas can stay home with the kids for a couple of days, no?"

"He wouldn't know what to do with them," I said.

"I'm sure we'll figure it out when the time is right. So, what have you been up to while I was away?" she asked.

"Nothing much, really—same old."

I told her about my fight with Lucas, and she agreed he was being stubborn. Unlike Lucas, she was able to understand my point of view and listen to my tirade.

"Well, did you call Francis and tell him you wanted to see him?" she asked.

"Yes, I'm meeting him Monday."

"You'll be fine, love. Everything will work out."

She rested her hand on mine to console me in a way that said, "I'm here for you. I've got your back no matter the outcome."

I counted on her to be there for me, and also counted on Lucas, too, for emotional support. But it appeared he had grown distant, lately—especially after our last disagreement. Maybe the stress from work disheveled him. In all transparency, he and I changed in some way over the years, but we still loved each other. That part didn't alter.

"Aunt Claire, are you staying with us tonight?" asked Isabelle.

"Well, I was planning to go home, sweetie."

"No, you can stay the night if you'd like," I said.

"Are you sure?"

"Yeah. Lucas is away for the weekend again, and I can use the company."

"Okay. I can stay, but I'm going to have to sleep in Isabelle's bed!" she said. She smiled, looking back at her. Isabelle smiled and nodded.

"So, how's the new assistant so far?" said Claire.

"Oh, Makaela Cooper? She's working out, thank God. She's doing well and catching on quick."

"Good! I'm glad things are working out for you, Bea."

"You haven't seen that weird man around again, right?"

"Nope, and I'm relieved. I know *you* didn't see him, but I know what I saw, and I can't let it go. I've tried, but I just *can't*—especially not after what he did to me as a child."

***

By the time we got home, the kids were sleepy, staggering to the door like zombies. Claire and I continued our conversation after tucking them into bed.

"I'm going to make a cup of tea. Want one?"

"That sounds perfect right about now. Thank you, love."

I took my time prepping some chamomile tea and felt it was the right time to tell her about the unmarked card.

"Hey, remember the day we had lunch?"

"Yeah."

"Well, I went back to the gallery to find a box sitting on my desk with a gold card in it."

She appeared perplexed—lost for words—just as I was. She also found it creepy, as did I.

"Where is it? Do you still have it?"

"Yeah, it's in my bag. Inner pocket."

I showed her, and she held it in her hand without flipping it over. Her eyes widened.

"I know what this is!" she said.

"You *know* what it is?"

"This is definitely a hotel key card... to the St. Regis Hotel. I've seen very few executives flash it around. It's like a premiere access card of sorts—kinda like a special privilege thing."

"Why the anonymity, though?"

"I dunno. Perhaps someone wants you to find something."

I couldn't think of anything anyone wanted me to discover in that room—if that was their goal. Claire and I stared at each other like illusionists do, who pretend to read people's minds.

"Maybe it's not *something*. Maybe it's *someone*. If they wanted me to find something they would've sent it to my office or home. I'm sure this person already knows where I live.

"Maybe you should go to the police, after all."

"And what would I tell them, Claire? It would look like a silly prank."

"I know that look in your eye, Bea. You're *going* to the St. Regis, aren't you? I should come with you just in case."

I paused a moment. My curiosity peaked, but I didn't realize she was waiting for a confirmed response. She knew me too well. She knew I couldn't let it go.

"It has to be him."

"Him, who?"

"The man I saw. It's no coincidence *this card* shows up the same day he appears!"

"Bianca, promise me you won't go by yourself."

"Yes. Yes, I promise. I'll let you know when I plan on going. It'll probably be sometime next week."

"Don't you *dare* go by yourself," she said.

Truth is, some part of me wanted to venture alone. Another part of me didn't. The mere thought of being in the same room as him petrified me. But there was no doubt in my mind our paths would cross again, and I prayed it didn't occur in the presence of my children.

4

Elizabeth, Reborn

THE WEEKEND ENDED, and I settled into my weekly routine. My morning regimen didn't change much except for Monday— the day I planned to visit Dr. Summers. Not only was he my therapist, but he was also a close family friend. I made tremendous progress with him in the past and trusted his expertise. My morning at the gallery went well, and Makaela appeared quite comfortable managing the place by herself.

"Hey, I'm going out for lunch. Will you be okay by yourself?" I said.

"I'm fine. Everything's under control here, Ms. Gallucci. You have nothing to worry about," she said.

"Oh, just 'Bea' is fine. I'll see you later."

Francis' office was in midtown—42nd and 3rd Ave— about twenty minutes away. His receptionist, Grace, sat at her desk outside his door, greeting me with a smile. I didn't recognize her. *She's definitely a new hire.* Although I hadn't visited Francis in a while, his reception area didn't change. Everything remained the same.

"Hi, there. How may I help you?"

"I have an appointment with Francis at 11:30—Bianca Gallucci."

Grace paged him and asked me to fill out a form before I sat down in the waiting room. I tried my best to avoid fidgeting.

"He'll see you in a few minutes, Ms. Gallucci."

"Okay. Thank you."

***

Five minutes passed and Francis exited his office, greeting me with a hug. Nervousness almost got the best of me while I returned the gesture.

"Bea! It's *so* good to see you, again."

"Please come in. Here, let me take your coat."

We walked into his office where I gave him my coat and scarf.

"Oh wow. I like the new furniture."

"Thank you. Adjustments were needed—more-so in here, I suppose."

Like always, he dwelled in comfort. The distant city noise and sub-volume music in the corner near the window swelled with an invitation of warmth.

"Make yourself at home, Bea," he said. He poured a glass of water.

"Would you like some water?"

"Oh, no thank you, Francis. I'm alright."

"Okay, so tell me. How's the family doing? I haven't seen the twins in ages! I bet they're growing faster than ever."

"Everyone's doing great! Zero complaints in that department."

"Splendid. That's wonderful to hear... and what about you? How are you doing?"

"Well, I'm okay, but I experienced something... peculiar... about a week ago."

Francis positioned himself on his leather chair across from me, leaning forward. My fingers pranced upon my bicep while my arms remained folded. I grew reluctant to tell him what was on my mind, but I knew I had to. I needed answers.

"To be honest, I'm here because Claire suggested I see you, and I'm hoping you can help shed some light on something."

"Please... speak freely... as you always have—and as you're aware, everything you tell me stays enclosed within these walls."

My heart clobbered against my ribs. The words wanted to slide off my tongue, but my head wouldn't allow it. I guess it was due to fear of being judged, but I found the courage to blurt out my concern—much to Francis' surprise.

"I saw my father last week!"

"You saw your father? I don't follow. Didn't he die when you were a child?"

I trembled as if the thermostat read thirty degrees in his office, but it was only my overactive nerves taking over. My body temperature rose the instant a flashback of my past manifested.

"Yes, but I have no idea why I'm seeing him. He's real, Francis. I told Lucas and Claire, but they don't believe me. Claire was with me when I saw him, but she didn't see him. Francis, I know I'm not seeing things. I actually watched my Father die."

"Hmm. This is quite puzzling—being you're so certain. You had a traumatic past, which obviously affected you—and it's a little early to draw any conclusions. Bianca, the things that happen to us in our past don't define us. They shape us. But what you claim to have seen has some sort of delayed manifestation. Perhaps you didn't deal with your past in full or perhaps this is your mind's way of identifying what you dread most."

He grew pensive and wrote down a few more notes before getting up, walking over to his desk in search of his digital recorder. He raised it at eye level, muttering a few words, and smirked, asking, "Is it okay I record our conversation?"

"Yeah, I don't mind."

"Okay, one moment while I turn the music off."

"No, leave it. It's helping me stay calm."

"As you wish. Let's begin, shall we?"

He sat in his chair, and I nodded, anticipating that he could confirm I wasn't a complete nut-job.

"Have you been extra stressed lately? Or maybe... Bea, what's wrong? Why are you holding your head?"

An acute head-throb commenced. I closed my eyes in hopes it would dissipate, but it grew with a gradual intensity while I cringed in discomfort.

"Turn the music off. I can't stand it."

"The music? I can barely hear it."

"Francis, turn the music off!"

He rushed to his desk to turn it off. Silence filled every corner of the room. I opened my eyes, and he was mouthing the words, "Bianca, what's wrong?" but I couldn't hear a thing. I had no idea what was happening to me. I had gone one hundred percent deaf for a few moments before I could hear his muffled voice with ease.

"The song that was just playing—Louis Armstrong's, 'What a Wonderful World.' I remember it as a child. Such a beautiful song, Doctor."

"What a Wonderf—What are you talking about? Bea, we've known each other a long time and you've never referred to me as "Doctor," before. What's going on?"

I stared at him with a smirk, observing his body language while he studied me. However, I could see the fear in his eyes, the confusion in his eyebrows, and the uncertainty in his movements, as he repositioned himself on his chair.

"Louis Armstrong was just playing. You didn't hear it, doctor?"

"Bianca, please listen to me. You weren't coherent a moment ago. Tell me what you're feeling now."

"You're wasting your time. I'm not Bianca. My name is Elizabeth."

5

Elizabeth Revealed

I PERCEIVED HIM AS INFERIOR and knew he was about to start with his mumbo jumbo doctor bullsh*t. He gave me his undivided attention and approached me, sauntering with caution.

"Elizabeth. I need to speak to Bianca, please. It's me... Francis."

"I *know* who you are, doctor... and no you may *not* speak with her. You can speak to me. I'll tell her all about our conversation."

"Fine. Let's talk, then. What do you desire, Elizabeth?"

"I want what we all want—to be in control."

"To be in control of Bianca? What did you do with her? I need to speak with her."

"She's... in here." I pointed to my head.

"Absolutely remarkable," he said. He took a step forward. "It's very important I speak with your sister."

"No, you don't want to speak to her. You just want to get rid of me."

"That's not true. I want to get to know you. I swear."

"You can't separate us, doctor. You see, we have a particular bond, Bianca and me. You can't separate blood."

"Elizabeth, Bianca told me so much about you, and I have no ill intentions. You have my word."

I didn't like him knowing me. However, my contempt and disdain were enough to keep him at arm's length.

"So what are you going to say next, huh?... that you want to help me? You can't. You know, I wanted to reveal myself during Bianca's first couple of visits, but it wasn't the right time. Even I'm surprised I survived your *boring* sessions."

My display of dominance and pride solidified my authority as I sat on his couch with my legs crossed and chin raised. I observed his demeanor and admired his poise. He was tall, bald, and somewhat attractive. His eyes—ice blue and judgmental, embodied an austere presence.

"I know how you feel toward Bianca, doctor. Your pupils dilate every time you look at her."

"I beg your pardon?"

"*I beg your pardon,*" I said. "So... 'British' of you." He tried concealing his expression. His denial would've presumed him foolish. "Oh, playing dumb doesn't suit you, doctor. No need to be shy."

I uncrossed my legs and bit my bottom lip as he peered into my incarnate soul. Clearing his throat and furrowing his eyebrows indicated the feelings he kept buried inside, as I ambled towards him, standing inches from his face with his back toward his desk. He grabbed my wrist, removing my hand from his ridiculous-looking, silk tie.

"Don't ever touch me without my permission. Do you understand?" he said.

A smirk seemed well-suited as a response to his reaction. He removed himself from my personal space and sat at his desk as though I didn't exist. I couldn't tell what he was thinking nor could I read his body language.

"I want to speak to Bianca," he said.

"No."

"Why not?"

"Because she doesn't need to talk to you. She's fine."

"I remember Bianca telling me that you became aggressive when you two were kids. You weren't always that way, though, right?"

I didn't care to answer him because *I* was the one in possession of the 'gavel' in that room. He was trying to get into my head and get Bianca back, but I didn't want that. I wanted to stay. He stood to his feet, leaning forward with closed fists against the desk's surface. The challenge—thrilling as ever.

"Tell me... *Lizzy*. How did your father do it, huh?" he said.

"I *hated* when he called me that," I said.

"Why, because it made you seem insignificant? How did it feel when he hit you…when he touched you?"

"Stop it!"

"How did it feel when he tossed you around and bruised your face?"

"No! You need to stop, now!"

"How'd it feel to be helpless, Lizzy?"

"Stop. *Stop talking* about him!"

I couldn't bear it anymore and wanted him to stop. My breathing increased, and I walked away from his desk as fast as I could. He kept talking—going on and on about my past.

"Tell me. How did it feel to be completely helpless while you and Bianca were in separate rooms after he locked the door behind him each night?"

"*Stop!* I can't take it anymore!" I covered my ears and hummed a song as loud as possible.

"Do you *really* want me to stop?"

"*Yes! Yes!*"

"Then let me speak to Bianca!"

"*No!*"

"*Why* not? Is it because you're selfish? Arrogant? Manipulative? Or is it because *you're* weak?"

"S*he's* the weak one! *I'm* the reason she's alive, today. *I'm* the stronger one! *I'm* the one who watched that lowlife a**hole father die, and I would've killed him if I had the chance."

***

If fire and ash manifested as a result of my rage, his office would've been engulfed in flames. I'd never been more alive, reveling in my superiority. Another headache befell me, and I struggled to maintain my balance. Dizziness commenced before I could make sense of my surroundings. I lost my balance, falling to the floor.

6

Identity

"GRACE! HURRY!" SAID Francis. I contemplated why he called out to her while I laid on the floor in his arms. But of more importance, I wondered why I was looking up at him in the first place! I was in a situation I never expected.

"What's going on? Why am I on your floor?"

"Bea, is it you?"

"Why are you asking me that? Of course, it's me."

"Oh, good. You're back."

"What happened? How did I end up on the floor?"

"You had an episode. I'll explain everything to you in a moment, but first, how do you feel? Are you alright?"

"My head hurts a little, but I'm fine."

He helped me sit upright against the sofa. Grace dashed into the room with bottled water and a damp towel.

"Can someone *please* explain to me what's going on?" I asked.

She handed him the items and sauntered out, closing the door. Francis knelt in front of me.

"We had a breakthrough. This might be a bit much for you to handle or believe."

"Okay... what is it. Tell me."

"You don't recall anything that happened in the last ten minutes or so?"

"Uh, I remember sitting down for our session, and then I started getting a headache. The next thing I knew, I'm on the—"

"—I just met Elizabeth," he said.

"What? What do you mean? My sister's dead. She's been dead a long time. You know this, already."

"Yes, but I'm afraid she's very much alive...*within* you."

"I'm not sure what you're insinuating."

"Okay, let me explain. You had something awful and traumatic happen to you when you were a child, and when it happened, it affected you *so* much, your brain flipped a switch. I know how close you were with Elizabeth, but in your mind, deep down inside, she never left. You've adopted her personality. Bianca, you blacked out and *became* Elizabeth."

My heart trembled. I didn't want to believe him, but his explanation made complete sense. I wondered what the rest of my life would've been like carrying her around inside of me—to the grocery store—around my kids—or even waking up in a mental institute one day. Yes, these thoughts flooded my mind in the span of a few seconds.

"I do feel a little weird... or a little strange, Francis."

"What you're feeling is normal, and you were pretty... *intense*, so your headache might linger. You should know Elizabeth is *extremely* aggressive. I have proof of the recording."

"I don't want to hear it. I'm not ready for... look, I should go home."

"Lucas is on his way, Bianca. I can't let you leave in this condition by yourself, and he should be here within the hour. You can stay as long as you'd like.

"Oh, that wasn't necessary."

"He's your emergency contact. I'm sorry.

I had no—"

"—It's okay. Not to worry. Thanks for calling him. I'm sure he'll believe me this ti—Wait.... I've changed my mind. I wanna listen to the recording. I need to know what I'm dealing with."

He played it back, starting it from the beginning. I *couldn't believe* what I heard. *Oh, my God.* It was *me,* but then again... it *wasn't.* I had goosebumps all over my arms, and the fear I experienced rippled from my core, expanding into every inch of my body. *The aggression. The anger. The seduction.* Utter *disgust* in her voice made my stomach turn sour. Francis' eyes were full of pity while I struggled to listen to the rest of the recording. Lucas rushed into the room. Francis paused the recorder.

"Honey, are you alright?"

He dashed over to me and held my head close to his chest. I nodded while my tears and mascara blotted my white shirt.

"Yeah, I'm okay."

"Francis, what happened to her?"

"Please, be seated—both of you."

"Lucas, Bianca just had what is called a 'switch' in personality. You might know it as 'D.I. D,' Dissociative Identity Disorder. Bianca, most people call it Multiple Personality Disorder. However, D.I.D is a *severe* form of dissociation. To make it simple, you disconnected—became *separate* from yourself. This is a mental process that produces a lack of connection in a person's thoughts, memories, feelings, actions, or sense of identity. In your case, D.I.D derives from the trauma you experienced as a child, and *any* future trauma can still trigger an episode. Lucas, as we've discussed in the past—in the few sessions you attended with Bianca, she's had some distress she was dealing with. She didn't show *any* signs of D.I.D. None... ever.... until she mentioned seeing her dead father."

Lucas' jaw dropped open before pacing about. He stared at me, furrowing his eyebrows. An epiphany draped his face. Confirmation settled into his eyes.

"Okay, so you're saying she has more than one personality. What's this persona like, sound like, or whatever?"

"Bianca, is it okay I re-play the recording?"

I nodded, knowing the shame would be difficult to bear. I didn't want Lucas to perceive me as someone different, but he needed to understand that Elizabeth was alive. The clicking of those buttons on the recorder couldn't be any louder, as I sat on the sofa, *hoping* I wouldn't be judged. What a terrible thing to be ridiculed—to either accept or deny someone's raw opinions and assessments of us. But he played the recording, and I cringed, as I sloped down in my seat. Francis pointed out that Elizabeth emerged after hearing the song, 'What a Wonderful World.' Lucas exhaled, covering his mouth with his hand, and I avoided eye contact as much as possible. I could feel his stare, as he asked the haunting, yet mortifying question.

"Hon, was that *you*? Wait, and what's the whole thing about *dilated* pupils? Francis… *do you have a thing for my wife?*"

"Whoa, whoa, whoa. I run a professional office, here. Lucas, I can assure you I *do not* hold feelings for Bianca. Her other personality is *powerful,* manipulative, and will say *anything* to obtain what she wants. Lucas. Bianca. We've been friends a long time, now, and feelings aren't the issue, here. *Elizabeth* is, and I promise you I can help. Bianca, I suggest starting weekly sessions right away. I also want to refer you to a hypnotherapist. Her name is Dr. Miranda Clifton, and she's a colleague—also one of the *best* hypnotherapists in the city. I used to practice hypnosis but transitioned into something more satisfying. This is an important part of treatment which can open another gateway as a remedy."

Lucas let his guard down, apologized to Francis, and shook his hand. Francis wrote a prescription and explained my dosage and side effects before we left.

"Bianca, I'd like to start seeing you some time at the end of this week. I can fit you in my schedule somewhere, okay?"

"Thank you. I appreciate this so much."

"Grace will take care of everything for you—pencil you in."

I left Lucas' side to hug Francis in gratitude for agreeing to help. *There's no way I could turn into Elizabeth around the kids.*

"Stay hopeful. Try getting some rest. Do things that relax you and keep you at ease. *Don't* hesitate to call me if you lay eyes on that man again, alright?"

We left his office and hailed a cab. I tried regaining my poise, but as much as I wished Elizabeth never manifested, her tone replayed in my brain like a looped recording. My 'episode' was a monumental moment in my life. However, I found the courage to continue with my day and did my best to retain a sound mindset before calling Makaela.

"Hi, Makaela. It's Bianca. I'm aware you'll be leaving soon, but can you stay a little longer to lock up? I have a bit of an emergency."

"Sure, not a problem. Is everything okay?"

"Oh, yeah, everything will be fine. Thanks for asking."

"No need to worry. I've got everything under control, here."

"Thank you so much. Enjoy the rest of the day. Bye." I turned my attention toward Lucas.

"Hon, can you get the kids from school today, or do you need to return to work?"

"I'd love to pick them up, but I've *gotta* get back to the office. There was an issue I was in the mid—"

"Forget it. It's alright, I'll call Claire."

He sighed, stared out the window, and ran his fingers through his hair. I wanted his help—and rare that I asked for it, but needed it more than ever. However, I didn't possess the energy to start a heated discussion. All I needed was to relax and contact Claire. Her line rang a few times before she picked up.

"Hi, Bea."

"Hey, love. How are you?"

"I'm good. I'm just here at work, finishing up a little early and heading to the gallery to see you in a bit. Are you there, now?

"No, I'm home and was wondering if you could do me a favor. Could you pick the kids up from school for me? They get out at two-thirty."

"Oh, absolutely. No problem at all. Is everything okay?"

"I'll be fine. I went to visit Francis, today. Don't worry. Nothing serious. I'll tell you all about it when you get here."

"Okay. See ya later."

7

Room 332

HAVE YOU EVER LOVED SOMETHING so much it became your saving grace? Perhaps it drowned out the noise in the world, allowing you to regain your sanity. I think we all have that "one thing"—whatever it may be, making all things right in our minds. Francis said I needed to rest—to take it easy, but I craved creativity, as well as the need to get my hands messy. My heart embodied a burning desire for liberation—an exhibition of my emotions—one I couldn't verbalize. Art is a way of expressing oneself. It's a voicing of feelings translated onto a medium. It had been a while since I painted something, and I was ready, but not without my cup of chamomile tea—something to soothe my soul. I needed my atmosphere to be quiet so I could listen to my inner self. Silence has a voice—a whisper that appears in the dungeon of our thoughts. Peace resides within silence, and within that peace was the whisper inside me—the one clawing at the inner walls of my core.

The time read one o'clock in the afternoon when darkness emerged inside me. Somehow, as satisfying as it was, it was more than solely a whisper. Like, goosebumps it grew on the surface of my arm, traveling across my chest before dissipating from my left hand.

My wrist swiveled before making my first deliberate stroke of the paintbrush. A compelling unity of hand and brush was sustained. I had no image in mind—nothing specific I wanted to convey. A single, smeared stroke of black paint stretched from one side of the '4 x 6' canvas to another as I kept the brushstrokes fluent in motion. All my worries of the morning had dissolved, and I experienced a moment of clarity I didn't recognize. The only sublet voice I heard was my thoughts, but my heart guided my hand in a creative collaboration of feelings and movement. I knew at that moment—at the first stroke that my work was going to be a projection of my soul's deepest, darkest desires. One satisfying brushstroke lead to another. I was entranced—on a mission to create something masterful. I took heed to my heart's call to action, mixing colors without reason. The need to express my emotions in that instant was important to me but held no bearing. Without intent, my work began taking form. I reacted, acting upon my impulses, and gave into its beacon call before I realized the mess I made. Soon enough, my new piece of art stood complete, exhibiting a personality of its own. I laid my arms to rest at my side, took a few steps back, and stared at my new creation. If you'd seen me you would've called me a nutcase, but I experienced a creative advancement. *All* the great minds in history have had some sort of 'breakthrough.' Einstein, Newton, Poe, and so on, right? Their works of art changed the world, but my art changed the way I saw *my* world. I deemed lost in my creation, enthralled by its essence and consumed by its nature. Michael, Isabelle, and Claire walked in through the front door. Startled, the kids ran toward me with open arms.

"Oh, Claire! Kids! What are you doing back so early from school? What time is it?"

"Early? It's four o'clock. I took them to the diner right after picking them up."

"Four PM already? I swear it feels like only fifteen minutes went by."

She peered at me with unmoved eyebrows. I remained drifted—somewhat confused, staring at my painting without a flicker of emotion.

"Whoa! So cool! What are you painting, mom?" said Michael.

"Oh, no. Not for you guys. Grown-up stuff. Go change your clothes, and then you can go play video games or watch TV while we get cleaned up, okay?"

Michael didn't hesitate. Isabelle drifted toward the door but eventually followed.

"Go on sweetie. Aunty Claire and I need a moment. I'll come see you soon."

Claire walked over to me in my studio before Isabelle intersected her path.

"Are you okay?" she said.

"I feel amazing... but different. It's hard to explain, but I never felt this way before!"

She peered at me with a smidgen of worry in her eyes. *Something's wrong.*

"What? What's the matter?" I said.

"I called you like, four times before I took the kids to the diner. I didn't know if you had food prepared."

"You did? I didn't even hear my phone ring. Where is it, by the way? Oh, there it is on my desk. Check it for me, please? My hands are covered in paint."

"Yeah. Are you *sure* you're okay, Bea?"

I walked away from my painting and headed to the sink to wash my hands. Reliving my experience from earlier wasn't something I wanted to do, so I stretched my silence for as long as possible. I took a deep breath, swallowed my pride, and explained my horrendous occurrence.

"What happened at Francis' office, Bea? Bianca, would you *please* tell me what's going on?" she said.

"I have multiple personality disorder, Francis believes. And I had a sort of... *episode* where he witnessed me as my sister. Elizabeth."

"*What*?"

"Yeah, I went to tell him about the guy that looks like my father. One minute I was on the couch, telling him about what I had seen, and then minutes later I was on the floor with a headache. He recorded the whole thing with his digital recorder and played it back. Elizabeth was *terrifying*. Her voice looped in my head until I got here. Claire, I couldn't believe it was me."

"You know, Liz said she watched our dad die. Come to think of it, I never saw my father take his last breath. I remember seeing his dead body, but I don't recall what happened. Hmm— funny how I swore I saw him die in front of me. I remember seeing a lot of blood in the living room, but I don't know the details of his death—so after all that commotion I wanted to be home. I needed to get my head straight, and that's when I asked you to get the kids. A distraction was needed, so I began painting. The next thing I knew, you and the kids arrived. I swear I didn't even hear the phone ring. Ever since I saw that man in front of my gallery, weird things have happened, Claire. Francis believes my memory suppressed itself and went into hiding for a long time. For me, there's no other explanation. It's plausible," I said.

"Oh, you poor thing. So what's next? Treatment?" she asked.

"Yeah, I guess. There's a possibility I'll be seeing a hypnotherapist on Friday."

"I think that might be good for you... and I'm not being cruel here, but this is the *most intriguing, yet* disturbing painting you've ever created."

She was right. It was quite disturbing, and I had no idea what came over me.

"My life was perfect last week, Claire. Today, it somersaulted out of control."

"Well, I'm glad you're getting help. You need to get a grip on this because it's not going to go away on its own."

The weight of the truth slid right off her tongue. Its solidity benchmarked my life, and I accepted her authenticity. We both stared at my painting. I believed it was good enough to be sold in my gallery. She gazed at it with great curiosity and admiration despite its disturbance.

"Wow, it's so edgy. You *do* like it, right? I mean, it's like you projected a lifetime of pain into it," she said.

"Yeah, I guess I do like it."

I *did* like my panting. I adored it more as time went by. Claire followed me out of the studio and into the kitchen where she poured us both a glass of wine.

"Thank you."

"Bea, I've been thinking about that gold card you showed me. With everything going on, maybe we should back off a little while, no? I think it's a good idea you sort things out with Francis first... and *then* we could explore the meaning of that card."

I had no intention of putting things on hold.

"I don't know. Maybe finding out what's behind "door number one" might unravel some important things for me."

"I don't have good vibes about this."

"I think everything will be okay. We'll be careful, hon, and if things get out of hand, we'll leave."

"Does Lucas know about this?"

"Not at all. I didn't tell him because he didn't believe me when I told him I saw my dad. He's been too busy and seems very distracted, lately."

***

The evening transitioned into a night of wine and conversation as she and I talked more before the kids went to bed. It was about ten o'clock, and she grew tired. I arranged for an Uber to pick her up. We said our goodbyes moments later, and I got ready for bed. Lucas arrived the same time she left. He appeared tired, kissed me, and headed toward the kid's room to kiss them goodnight before crawling into bed with me.

"How are you feeling?" he said. I told him about my new painting and Claire's visit. "I'm glad you feel much better."

I dared not tell him about the discussion she and I had, but I thought about my painting. I dwelt on the feelings, and no matter what I did, sleep didn't commence—for a while, at least. I was restless, reminiscing the events of my day, but for some reason, I couldn't stop thinking about the card. Determination adjudged me to be relentless in my pursuit of unraveling its purpose.

***

I woke up the next day—Tuesday, to be exact, weary and fatigued. Yesterday was a day to remember—a day I kept replaying Elizabeth's vocal tone in my head while I drove before arriving to work.

"Makaela. Good morning. How are you?"

"I'm fine. No complaints here. How are you? Is everything okay?" she asked. I walked past her desk.

"Everything is just wonderful," I said.

Everything *wasn't* wonderful, though, but I guess we say such things to guard ourselves. The time was about nine o'clock in the morning. I walked to my office with a cup of coffee in hand and placed my coat, scarf, and purse on my chair before heading back to the front desk.

"Makaela, did any packages arrive for me?" She set her phone down and scrambled, getting the mail she put aside.

"No, sorry. Just this."

"Hmm. No strange boxes or letters, right?"

"No, nothing of that sort. Oh, wait, there was a letter addressed to you, but no return address. I always think of those as fishy."

I was more curious than ever to view its contents and walked away as if curiosity wasn't a factor at all. Consider my actions an avoidance of creating panic in front of her. I waited till I got into my office to tear it open. Inside the envelope was a sheet of paper with a location, date, and time: "*Go to the St. Regis Hotel for the truth. 10:00 am.*" I read that note at around nine o' clock. *Oh my God! Claire was right.* I didn't hesitate to grab my coat and dashed out of the gallery without saying anything to Makaela. I hailed a cab I discovered traveling toward me. "55th and 5th please," I said.

I know I promised Claire a call before I planned on going to the hotel, but I couldn't delay, much less ignore it. *Fine, I'll call her.* My calls went unanswered. I tried twice and didn't bother leaving a voicemail. A part of me wanted to play detective. I felt somewhat confident and kept reminding myself that 'everything would be okay,' while I sat in traffic. There was always so much congestion traveling up Madison Ave., but the closer I got to my destination, the more adrenaline circulated throughout my body. No turning back.

I glanced at my phone multiple times. Still, no call or text from Claire while I waited, sitting in a pool of anxiety. *Oh well. I tried. She's probably busy.* I was only a few blocks away from my destination, and I *couldn't* handle sitting in traffic anymore.

"Driver, I'm getting out here. How much I owe you?"

"The screen in front of yo—

"Oh, yeah. Here. Keep the change."

I gave him thirty dollars and got out. Paranoia settled into me as I continued walking through the crowd toward the hotel.

I shouldn't be doing this on my own, but what the hell. I'm here. This is happening. My paranoia didn't flat-line, and I scanned my surroundings, scrutinizing everyone within arm's length. I had to get there soon—only fifteen minutes to spare. My phone rang from inside my purse. Claire was returning my call.

"Where are you?" I said.

"I'm at work. You're out of breath. What's the matter?"

"I'm a block away from the St. Regis."

"What are you doing there? We agreed to—"

"*I know.* I know, but I received detailed instructions to meet at the St. Regis. I *need* to find out what's going on."

"Don't move. I'll be there as soon as I can. Bianca, *do not* go into that room without me."

"I gotta go."

"Bianc—"

I no longer wanted to listen to her, so I ended the call, and switched my phone setting to airplane mode. As rude as that was, I didn't have the time nor the patience to argue. I bustled down the street until I was able to see the hotel halfway down the block. *Phew! I made it on time.* I hustled up the stairs and bumped into a man before reaching into my purse.

"Anton? Oh, hi. How are you?"

"Bianca, what a pleasant surprise!" Anton Sydney was an art expert and auctioneer—a business acquaintance I knew for many years.

"What are you doing here?" he asked.

"Uh, meeting my husband," I said. "I'm so sorry, Anton, but I must go. I'm running late. So good to see you, though! I'll call you."

I left him and walked past the front desk without a hiccup in my step. My heart pounded faster than ever, and my impulsive need to run didn't take control. I didn't want to raise a concern or call attention to myself. The front desk staff smiled after I flashed my gold key card, making my way to the elevator. I pressed the call button numerous times, hoping it would descend faster. *Ding!*

The doors parted. I entered, and a lovely couple walked in afterward, delivering a warm smile. I remained inexpressive, maintaining my focus. They got off on the second floor, and I was anxious to get off on the third.

Ding! The door opened once again and I panicked— unable to move, and unable to dry my clammy hands. They dampened with fear, as I inched forward. Placing one foot in front of the other had never been difficult before. My legs grew weak while 'the unknown' was just a couple of doors down. Every door I walked past was a step closer to the truth. There it was—room 332. *Be brave, Bianca. Be brave.* I stood in front of the door and experienced the smallest inclination to walk away, but decided to turn the door handle, not knowing what awaited me on the other side.

8

Unveiled

I COULDN'T HELP THE TREMBLING in my voice as I asked, "hello?" while peeking inside. Not a soul in sight—only a handgun and a sheet of paper on the bed. The note read, "It's time you learn the truth." The only truth I needed to reveal was unveiling the sketchy-looking man and why he had been following me. If anything, it was frustrating and a dead-end to the mystery that brought me here. I refrained from touching the gun. I used one before at a shooting range with a friend years ago, and I hadn't been fond of them since. Hopelessness surrounded me, but I soon heard a beep coming from the front door. Whomever it was, they had been granted access, and I trembled, hoping to God it was only housekeeping. The handle turned slowly—counter-clockwise. My initial instinct was to protect myself—to point the gun at the door. Fear consumed my body while I placed my finger on the trigger. The door creaked opened, and the anticipation grew unbearable while I stood by the edge of the bed.

It was him—the man who had been following me! I stood trembling, unnerved by his sudden presence. He plodded in, showing half his face before closing the door—and he spoke, revealing his raspy, breathy voice.

"Please don't scream," he said. I tried calming myself down to control the situation.

"You've been *following* me and *sending* me gifts! Who are you, and why did you send me that card?"

"My name is Vincenzo Gallucci, but people call me "Pascal." I brought you here... because you deserve to know the truths.

"*Gallucci*? That can't be. They're all dead and buried."

"Then you must have known my brother."

"My father sure as hell didn't have a brother, so who are you and what do you want with me? Why were you following me?"

I did my best to minimize the shaking in my sweaty hands where I possessed the power to end his life if he assaulted me. All I wanted were answers.

"Stay where you are and don't try anything stupid. Just answer my question."

"As you wish. I *am* your father's brother."

"You're a liar. My father was an only child."

"He lied to you his whole life. We're identical, and if he was alive today, standing right next to me, you would believe me. We got separated at a young age. He never told you because he grew jealous of me—of my success. After being split up so long, we reunited on our twenty-second birthday and worked together years before he died. Twins run in the family. Am I right?"

He had a point and *did* look like my father, but I wasn't one hundred percent convinced.

"May I put my hands down, now?" I nodded, allowing him to continue his explanation. "I tried finding you so many times, but every time I got close you disappeared like a ghost in the wind—and when I got the news that your mother, father, and sister died in that fire, I did my utmost to get in touch with you. All I wanted was for you to understand was that you weren't alone. And after all my efforts, here you stand in front of me. Things were different in the early days. Information was easy to misplace. Today, all you need to do is Google someone and you'll find *all* you need. Look, I understand we know nothing of each other, but I'm not here to cause you any more pain. Your father did unspeakable acts to you and Elizabeth—even I am ashamed to be acknowledged as his brother, but I don't want you to re-live every moment of your childhood whenever you see my face."

"How could you know that?"

"Small town. Your mother went to the police, but they didn't do anything about it. Your father was a convincing man."

"If you are who you say you are, then show me proof that you're my uncle."

"It's right there on the desk in that envelope."

I opened the envelope and viewed his birth certificate, a DNA siblings test results, and a DNA swab kit. It was conclusive, but I still had my doubts.

"This could've been faked. How am I to know it's real?"

"All you need to do is use the kit and send it to any doctor you trust."

His body language and facial expressions didn't contradict each other. His nonchalant behavior inclined me to believe it was possible he told the truth. He was right, regarding my former life, and it was too late for me. I embodied the infliction of past anger and sexual abuse I had suffered. The father I had was equivalent to the devil.

I put the gun down, allowing the safety to remain disengaged just in case he got out of hand. He approached me, ambled toward the desk, removed his hat and coat, and proceeded to the minibar where he retrieved two small bottles of rum.

"You said, 'truths' earlier. You deserve to know the truths." What do you mean by this? What else is being kept from me?" I asked. He didn't utter a word, as he opened the bottles before handing me one.

"I don't drink liquor," I said.

"You will after you listen to what I'm about to tell you."

He rolled up his sleeves, and I discovered a scar on his right arm before he took a sip of his Jim Bean. "I come from a world where I deal with a lot of... 'business transactions' and these transactions made me a wealthy man over the years—illegal, yes, but I'm sure you understand. Years ago, there was a heist in London. I'm sure you read about it. I tried keeping it under the radar as much as possible, but the news traveled like wildfire.

However, whoever orchestrated it stole something sentimental to me." He smiled and eyeballed me, standing inches from my face. I stared back with an unchanged expression.

"Now, I searched everywhere for my painting—the one missing from my collection. It's worth a great deal. The Sea of Galilee. I don't care about the money or the few jewels taken as well. Those are worthless to me. Replaceable. But I do want my Rembrandt, and I'm *going* to get it back. You see, whoever took it left me a fake—a duplicate of the original, and the thief made it look like they were after jewelry. I *want* it back," he said. The temperature in the room spiked, as I witnessed the anger and irritation in his eyes.

"You're not suggesting tha—"

"Don't you dare play dumb with me."

His unexpected, malicious tone stunned me. "You think I'm unaware of your illegal art dealings and how you use your gallery as a cover? You replaced my art with a fake. What brave soul did you hire? C'mon spit it out. Tell me where my painting is, and I'll leave you and your family alone."

"Look, I don't have your painting."

"Bullsh*t. I have proof you took it. Don't insult my intelligence. I'm gonna give you one more chance to tell me the truth, okay? Where is it?"

"I swear I don't know what you're—"

Whap! The full force of his open palm across my face rendered me confused. An unexpected hit like that forced a flashback into my mind. I leered into his eyes with hate in my heart, and he glared into mine, waiting for a confession. I refused to say a word—that is until he crossed the line."

"Your children, Michael and Isabelle are so—."

"Don't you *dare* mention their names. Do you hear me?" I said. I stood in haste. "My kids have *nothing* to do with your painting!"

I wanted to rip his vocal cord out of his neck. He knew more about me than I thought, and he remained motionless— unafraid of my reaction—unmoved by my rage. He exhibited a grin, though—one that deemed sadistic, and I was confident he possessed such a nature. Pascal was kind and caring one minute— —the next—aggressive, compulsive, and extreme.

"Look, I don't know you. Yes, you look like my father, but *many* people could look like him. I don't know anything about this painting you're looking for!"

"I figured you'd say 'anyone could look like him' so I brought you this." He leaned toward me and handed me an old photograph of two little shirtless boys standing side by side. He reclined in his chair, and took another sip of his drink, swallowing its contents while I swallowed the truth. My father had a birthmark on his shoulder—not too big, but visible when he wore a tank top. Both of them possessed the same blemish in the photo, and if Pascal had it too, then he had proved himself to be my relative. I asked him to show me his, and he did so without a fuss.

"Wow, I guess I now have an uncle... but regarding your painting, I swear I don't have it. You have the wrong person," I said. I shrugged my shoulders, maintaining my poker face.

"I hate liars, Bianca," he said.

He reached into his coat pocket get his phone and call someone. A male's voice projected from the other end. "Put 'em on," said Pascal. He handed me his cell phone, and my heart sank into the gorge of my stomach.

"Mom?"

"Michael? Oh, my God, Michael where are you, honey?"

"I'm at school."

"Who are you with? Are you alright?"

"Yeah, I'm with a policeman. He's so cool! He's showed me his gun and—"

The line died, and I feared the worst. Whether the police officer was real or not, I worried about my son's life. I was helpless and unable to think straight while I cried, staring at the floor. "*You son of a b**ch,*" I said.

Rage filled my heart. My emotions grew rampant in an instant before I reached for my gun, yet I experienced a difference—a transitioning into a different state of mind. The ringing in my ears grew louder before I became deaf. It lasted a few moments before I could hear again—and I shut my eyes before a 'darkness' inched its way to the surface of my heart. My tears fell to the floor before I opened my eyes, and my gun was drawn, pointing at his face. "How *dare* you bring Michael into this?"

"I wouldn't do that if I were you, but seeing you have an unloaded Glock in my face, shows me what you're willing to do. Go ahead and pull the trigger," he said. I wanted to but realized he wouldn't jeopardize his own life.

"Your son is safe and in good hands, I assure you. There's no need for violence."

"Maybe... but you're no longer speaking to Bianca."

"What are you, *crazy*?"

I made a display of the power I possessed, grabbing his throat without warning. His eyes widened, and he tried prying my hand away, but I was too strong.

"*Elizabeth* is here, now," I said. I relished the sound of him choking. It was a joy to revel in his pain—to analyze his pathetic face as he clung to life. I experienced pleasure in watching him fall to his knees, but his tactical maneuvering removed my hand from his neck. I yelled in pain before his fist hit my face.

***

The next thing I knew, I was sitting in a chair with my hands tied behind my back. My eye and cheek throbbed, and I could only wonder how I got into that position.

"You'll live... and that'll bruise a little. *Goddammit*, you have one hell of a grip on you, *Bianca... Elizabeth* or whoever the *hell* you are."

"What... what are you talking about? Why am I tied to this chair?"

"You almost ripped my goddamn throat out of my neck like a sadistic assassin."

"I'm confused. Why'd you call me Elizabeth? Where's my son? Where's Michael?"

"He's fine. He'll go home and be happy doing whatever children do these days. 'Elizabeth' is who you claimed to be right before you attacked me. I'm guessing you had some sort of... *episode*. Wait, you *really* don't remember what happened, do you? Wow, I've seen some crazy people in my time, but you... you're like a walking apocalypse." He untied me and allowed me to drink a glass of water. I applied ice to my face.

"I'm not sorry for f**kin' up your face. You had it comin'–
–got some issues you need to iron out. So here's the deal, my long,
lost niece. Return my painting to me. I know it may take you some
time to get it back to me but—"

"Fine. I'll give it back." He stooped down and stared into
my eyes while I sat on the wooden, upholstered chair.

"I can make your life and your children's lives a living hell
if you don't do what I want. I'm glad you chose to tell me the truth.
Wise choice, Bianca," he said.

He handed me a flip phone, walked away, and headed
toward the door. "I'll be in touch—and oh, I almost forgot. You
might want to do more homework on that new girl you hired.
Also, take a deeper look into that angel-of-a-husband of yours,
too." The door slammed shut, and he left without saying another
word. *Oh, God, what have I done?*

I left the hotel sometime after and Pascal was nowhere in
sight. My concern was my kids. School was almost over, and I
hustled there in a cab where I grew uneasy, trying to get in touch
with Claire. As I arrived, I dashed out, heading inside the building.
I wore my sunglasses to conceal my bruised eye before arriving
at the administration desk. The receptionist took her sweet time as
if I didn't exist. Sloths moved faster. My impatience got the best
of me.

"*Hello!* I need to get my kids! It's an emergency. Can you
hurry up, please?" She gave me 'a look,' called their teacher, and
said, "they'll arrive momentarily, Ms. Gallucci."

***

They came running toward me after waiting five minutes,
and I kissed and hugged them as though we'd been separated for
months. They didn't go to school the next day. I wanted them by
my side while I figured everything out. I needed to talk to Claire
and come up with a plan. I was able to get hold of her after some
time passed.

"Claire, where were you? I thought you were going to the
hotel?"

"You hung up on me! And I was on the other side of town. I tried calling you back, but your phone was off. I waited in the lobby!"

"I'm so sorry. I really am, but I need your help, now. Can you get my car out of the parking garage near the gallery and come over?"

"Yeah, sure. What happened at the hotel? Are you okay?"

"I'm fine. I'll explain to you when you get here."

I hung up the phone and stared at it, thinking every aspect of my life was under surveillance. I removed the sim card and placed it into a compartment of my bag I seldom used. Perhaps I displayed an exaggeration of my paranoia. However, my heightened awareness kept me on guard, as I made sure to lock my doors. Claire approached my building, made her way upstairs, and knocked on the door.

"Bianca, I'm here."

She walked in to find me pacing back and forth in the kitchen.

"What the heck is going on?"

She froze in her movements, craning her neck while approaching. "*What the hell happened to your eye?* Who did this you?" I applied makeup to my eye the best I could before we saw each other. I didn't want her to see me bruised and battered, but I couldn't avoid it. She would've seen it sooner or later. I told her about my indiscretion.

"I went. I saw him."

"You could've gotten yourself killed, Bea!"

"I know, but—"

"—But now you have a bruised eye."

"Everything happened so fast."

"And now you have more than you can handle. Okay, we can work this out."

"We? No. There is *no way* I'm getting you involved in this, Claire."

"You are my best friend, Bea. I'll do whatever is necessary to keep you and the kids safe. You can't tell me everything and expect me to sit back and watch. Does Lucas know?"

"No, I haven't told him anything. He *can't* know."

"Why not?"

"Because Pascal, the man I met, hinted that I should look into him."

"And you believe this Pascal guy, even after he threatened you and the kids? Why would he even tell you something like that?"

"I don't know. His behavior is strange—like, he wants to gain my trust, but he's willing to do whatever is necessary to get what belongs to him. He proved to be my uncle. And when he hinted about Lucas, I thought back to the night he and I argued. He dismissed my concern. *Something's* going on with him. Pascal knows about me, Claire. He knows things about my family!" She scoffed, exhaling before bowing her head.

"So now what?"

"So now I wait for him to contact me, but in the meantime, I'm gonna find out everything I can about Lucas and Makaela.

9

Digging

I PONDERED PASCAL'S WORDS. THEY haunted me and kept me awake that night. A black eye was a small price to pay for something I did years ago, but it was better than my kids getting hurt. I'll admit, I was greedy at one point in my life. I was careless and stupid. This, of course, was before I had my children, and now it's come back to haunt me. I never wanted any trouble, and I hoped God would make it go away. I can't remember the last time I asked Him for forgiveness, and I guess it was a good time to do so while I endured a sleepless night. It was a good time to put everything out on the table.

It started with an individual I hired. His name was Allen Shepard, and I wanted him to steal one of Rembrandt's paintings called, The Sea of Galilee. Allen's a ghost when it comes to stealing. Yes, he was exceptional, and his skill-set is a work of art. He taught me an array of skills—from picking locks to using a scalpel. But as his handler, he and I had a great working relationship, and of course, I kept him a secret from my husband. As close as we'd been, nothing romantic ever came of our association. I never told Lucas or anyone else what I had done. Shepard and I—and now Claire were the only ones on this planet who knew about my dealings. You *had to* lay eyes on that painting. The Sea of Galilee was so beautiful and rare, and I had my eyes on it for a long time. Rare, expensive art was my weakness. I didn't dare leave it hanging on the wall of my gallery, and you couldn't hide it in plain sight, as it's was originally stolen from the Isabella Stewart Gardner Museum. I needed to call Shepard, given the circumstances. He answered upon the first ring.

"I was starting to think you were forgetting about me," he said.

"How can I ever forget about the most talented thief in the world? So, hey, listen. You need to watch your back," I said.

"*Come on.* You know me. I'm *always* on watching my back, Bea."

"Shepard, I'm serious. You need to be *really* careful this time. He found me."

"What are you talking about? Who found you?"

"A man named Pascal, and he wants his painting back. The Sea of Galilee," I said.

"Wait, hold on. You said "Pascal?" You mean the International Arms Dealer, Pascal?"

"Yes! He confronted and held me against my will earlier yesterday. He's been looking for his painting all these years."

"So, Bea, you're telling me that you got your intel wrong, and we're now a target to one of the most dangerous men in the U.K.? Sh*t!"

"He used an air-tight alias, I guess. You even cross-checked the name and photo, too! Everything checked out at the time!"

"F**k. Okay, listen to me. You *have to* return that painting."

"You don't think I know that? My children's lives are in danger! Please be careful. He's been watching me and my family for weeks, it seems. It's only a matter of time he finds you, too. He's probably even listening to this call!"

"You're using the encrypted sim I gave you, so you've got nothing to worry about. We're fine. You and your family will be fine. By the way, how did he find out he had the fake you made?"

"I—I don't know, Shep. I have no idea. How soon can I get the painting from your vault?"

"Um...one or two days. That's the best I can do. I'll give you a call the moment I land, okay?"

"Okay, that'll work. Thank you."

I ended the call. Makaela knocked on my office door and entered after I acknowledged her.

"Come in."

"Sorry to disrupt you. It's just that the annual Gala is in a few months, and I've been on the phone with MoMA, (Museum of Modern Art) trying to finalize the event with their personnel. I've also compiled a list of everyone you invited last year. Will there be any new attendees?"

"As a matter of fact, there is. I'll send you an email."

I searched my computer for the list, found it, and sent it in seconds.

"There. Sent!"

"Thank you. Is there anything else you'd like me to take care of?"

"No, That's all. I appreciate the work you're doing here."

She smiled and walked away. I wondered how much of my conversation she heard before knocking on the door. I didn't know who the real Makaela was—what she did during her free time, or if she had hobbies, but she seemed to be normal. She appeared to be the type of person who could never hurt a fly. Looks can be deceiving. I couldn't ignore what Pascal told me. His words birthed seeds of doubt. Makaela was precise with her movements whenever in my presence like she walked on eggshells. *I'll ask Shepard to do an extensive background check on her.* I sent him a text that read, "Need a favor. Do a full scan on my employee—name is Makaela Cooper." *I'm sure he'll get back to me as soon as possible.*

***

Two days passed. Pascal 'rattled my cage' by sending me a surprise package. I had no choice, but to vomit into the wastebasket next to me. Two severed human fingers weren't something I was expecting. I had no idea who they belonged to, but it was as if Christmas had come early that year—gift-wrapped with Michael and Isabelle's name written on a piece of paper.

Shepard was back in the U.S.—the only other person I trusted one hundred percent besides Claire. I couldn't confide in Lucas—the man who kept deep secrets from me. I always knew he did but saw things in a different light when Pascal piqued my curiosity. I thought about asking Shepard to conduct some research on him, too, but to be transparent, I wasn't ready to face the truth. He and I planned on meeting at his warehouse in Brooklyn. My paranoia got the best of me, as I circled the neighborhood three times before parking my car. He welcomed me in, and I followed him into his office upstairs. Every valuable possession sat securely within a seamless, secret wall behind his desk. I stood in awe of all the rare artifacts and treasures before me. My eyes gazed upon Rembrandt's 'Sea of Galilee.' I considered it to be *my* painting, and it warmed my heart to see it. However, it also broke me in half to let it go, but I helped him take it downstairs and packaged it in a small crate designed for transporting art. With my Audi backed up into the warehouse, Shepard placed it in the trunk.

"Be careful with it," he said.

"Yeah, uh, thanks for your help, by the way. Oh, um, what did you find out on Makaela?"

"Come with me. I'll show you. Based on what I found, she's somewhat clean."

"What do you mean?"

"Well, I have everything on her, but a large part of her life doesn't exist. It's like she fell off the grid at some point. There's a huge gap in her history. However, I did find a court case she got involved in a couple years back. It has something to do with theft in England—go figure—and...it doesn't say much more about her. Everything's been pretty much redacted. Also, it looks like her family was murdered, but in light of this scarce information, I do find it a little strange that she would show up on your doorstep looking for a job. Think about it. She's been convicted of theft, and not just any kind, Bea. Whoever she is, she went through a lot to have it expunged. She must know some important people. Makaela may not even be her real name, so I advise you to be careful around her. Observe her. Get to know who she is on a personal level. Don't pry, though. Treat her like a friend instead of an employee. She's bound to slip. In the meantime, I can do some more digging, but it'll take longer than a couple of hours."

I let Shepard do what he did best, and continued with the rest of my day like normal.

***

The next day was a little more nerve-wracking than usual. Pascal had been like the wind—invisible and unpredictable. I had what he wanted in my possession, but Makaela became my pivotal focus. I walked into work focused, ready to begin my day.

"Makaela, hi. How are you this morning?"

"Good morning, Bea. I'm doing well."

"Hey, I was wondering if you'd like to join me for lunch today. You've been here for a reasonable amount of time, and you've done such a fantastic job taking care of this place during my many absences. I couldn't keep this place running without you, and I want to display my gratitude to you for your dedication and hard work. It means a lot to me. My treat."

"Aw, thank you. I'd love to join you, today."

"Great! It's settled, then."

***

Lunchtime came around, and Makaela and I chose a local restaurant two blocks away. We removed our jackets, placed our bags on the seats, and ordered our food.

"Choose *anything* you like, my dear."

"I heard the food here is good! Do you eat here often?"

"I do. Alone, sometimes. The truth is I'm tired of eating by myself. My husband is never around because he works insane hours and my best friend is always away. I have other friends I could have lunch with, but most of them are clear-cross town," I said. The pedestrian foot traffic from outside caught my attention before I refocused.

"Aw, I understand. My boyfriend is always missing in action, too. I don't know what I'd do if I didn't have the gallery to keep me busy," she said.

"What does he do?" I asked.

"He's an architect. It's hard being by myself when he works crazy hours. I spend a few nights alone. Yeah, I do get lonely, but I'll be alright. I mean—I *chose* to be with him."

"When I married Lucas, I never thought I'd be who I am, today. People change over time—especially when children are involved. You start to want different things in life, and those desires take you in a direction you never see coming. If you're strong-minded and willing to fight, you'll be fine. Things will work out. I promise."

"Thanks. I've been a little discouraged lately, so thank you for the encouragement...and for lunch. Much-appreciated."

We continued eating. She was perceived as innocent, but I didn't let my guard down. We sat in silence, and I admired her Oscar-winning performance. I couldn't tell if she was telling me the whole truth, but something didn't resonate with me. *Did she really have a boyfriend? Did she spend her nights alone?* My mind wandered, thinking I hired a thief, like Shepard told me. There was so much I didn't know about her, yet so much I wanted to learn. Why she chose to work for me was elusive to my knowledge. But perhaps she was in pursuit of my stolen art collection—my Monet, Michelangelo, Picasso, and da Vinci.

Maybe she knew all about me—fishing for clues, poking around for a revelation. I didn't confront her about her past. We soon walked back to the gallery. My intuition—the unnerved sensation in the pit of my stomach bothered me till I couldn't ignore it anymore. I sat in front of my computer to view my security recordings. My cameras remained hidden in plain sight——one disguised as an electrical box in the corner of my office, and the other, a simple desktop camera with the internal built-in microphone. Scrubbing through the footage lasted forty-five minutes.

***

It appeared that Makaela had walked into my office many times for various work-related reasons without my knowledge, but the particular recording I was viewing was different. She entered, sat in front of the computer, and began typing before making a call. The worst possible outcome kept me on the edge of my seat. I waited for her actions to unveil. She was speaking to someone on the other end of the line, but I could only hear her part of the conversation.

"Agent Clarke, here. Oh, hi. Yes, I'm sitting at her desk, sir."

"..."

"Yes, I'm copying it to the hard drive, now."

"..."

"It's only a matter of time before I find everything regarding the stolen art. I have no doubts she's working with Pascal. I'm almost done here, and will report back to you."

Agent Clarke? What is she, FBI? And Pascal? Why would they think I'm associated with him? What the hell? I just met him! Stunned by this new information, I continued watching as she discovered one of my hidden cameras, erased the footage, and walked out. They somehow found out I might've held Rembrandt's 'Sea of Galilee' in my possession—the same one Pascal wanted me to hand over.

I watched it all until she left. A sudden knock on my office door startled me, and I logged out as fast as possible. "Come in," I said. My phone buzzed at that exact moment. It was Shepard. I answered his phone call. Negative emotions encircled me when she walked in. "I'm sorry, Makaela. One moment, please. I've gotta answer this call, but have a seat. I'll only be a minute." She sat in front of me with her paperwork in hand. I avoided eye contact with her while I answered Shepard's questions.

"Hello?"

"You're not going to believe what I have for you, Bea. Are you alone?"

"No. Not at the moment."

"Is she there with you, now?"

"Yes. That's right, hon."

"I can call you back when she's gone."

"No. It's not a problem. You can deliver the info."

"Her real name is Kate Clarke. She's an FBI agent working for their Art Theft division, but she wasn't always one of them. It looks like she'd been given a deal. God, her file is fortified! She lived in London for quite some time. Uh—looks like her mother and father were...murdered—bound and shot in the head when she was sixteen. She bounced around from home to home till she was eighteen. Then she became friends with the wrong people and got arrested for art and jewelry theft a few years later. She got sloppy."

Makaela, well, *Kate* wasn't looking in my direction, so I glanced at her while she got distracted by her phone. I redirected my gaze, continuing my coded conversation with Shepard.

"Thank you for informing me, hon. I appreciate it. Mm-hmm, yes. I'll call you later and let you know how everything goes with the kids. Mwah. Ciao." I hung up the phone.

"I'm so sorry. How rude of me."

"Oh, no. It's not a problem. I wanted to say thank you again for lunch, and everything is set for the Gala. It's going to be stunning."

"I'm sure it will be...as it is every year. I appreciate your hard work."

"It's a quality I inherited from my mom—being a hard worker," she said. She folded her hands.

"What about your father? I'm sure he had some positive qualities passed on to you."

"Uh, no, not really—never knew him. It's always been me and my mom."

"I guess I can say the same about mine when I was a child. She worked so hard. My dad, on the other hand, hardly ever worked. He never cared a great deal for my sister and me. You know, I remember one time when he was in a fight with another man—drunk, no doubt. I didn't know what he did to get him so angry. I remember him yelling, "*You dare stick your nose in my business? You dare steal from me?*" He was furious, and as a child, you don't forget moments like those, you know? He beat him to a pulp right in front of me. You can imagine how petrified I was. That man went missing—never to be seen again. Not only was I terrified, I learned a *valuable* lesson about stealing, that day. Our past no matter how well we try to hide from it comes back to haunt us."

I stared at her with intent and witnessed the change in her breathing pattern. She sprang up off her chair without uttering a word, fixating her gaze.

"Well, it's getting late, Makaela. I'm sure you have some evening plans. I still have some work to do, so I'll be here a while."

I stood, smiled, and extended my hand, holding a folded sheet of paper. She stared without moving her head, contemplating taking the note from me.

"So, maybe I'll see you tomorrow," I said.

My eyes lingered into hers, waiting for a confession. She viewed the note, smirked, and walked out. *I guess I touched a nerve.*

10

Alias

ANOTHER DAY COMMENCED and I neglected to take my medication. I had been so caught up in my world, I hadn't been thinking about my health at all. My concern didn't involve my diagnosis. It was for the safety of my family. The folded sheet of paper I handed Makaela said, 'Kate Clarke.' Nothing else. After having some time to reflect, I understood I made a bold, impulsive move. And as for my hard drive, since employees had access to my office, I didn't store important information in it. Shepard installed heavily-encrypted spyware and enabled all recordings to be transferred to a secure hard drive at his home. The FBI can go to town on it. They won't find anything useful—only legal transactions made within my gallery. *I imagine Makae—Kate might send someone to snoop around for The Sea of Galilee soon.*

My primary objective was to hand the painting over to Pascal without the Feds on my tail. I wanted nothing to do with him after the delivery. I desired to get my life back, selling art and enjoying life with my family. After I learned of Kate's alias, I made it a habit of looking over my shoulder wherever I went—including the gallery. I used reflective surfaces to my advantage to avoid looking like a crazy person in public.

Shepard decided to visit me early one morning. He accompanied me to work, and we bought a cup of coffee one block away from the gallery. I assumed Kate's last day was yesterday—and I was right. She never showed up. Two hours passed, and she was nowhere to be found. The FBI might have taken a step back since I revealed her identity, but I failed to be one hundred percent sure. Shepard sat in my chair and evaluated all the information she copied.

"Wow. She's *damn* good. She got past your firewall in no time at all and downloaded every last file. I wouldn't be surprised if she was in the government vehicle sitting outside this place right now."

"What? Where?"

I sprung out of my chair and sprinted toward my office door to peek.

"No, wait! Don't go out, yet. They're in a black sedan across the street, adjacent to us—tinted windows. License plate: J49828. I saw it on our way in."

"Wha—why didn't you say something?"

"Because I knew how you'd react."

A profound idea dawned on me, as I stood in the doorway. I thought to use the opportunity to my advantage—to lead them to Pascal without being considered an accomplice. *Yeah, this can work.* I needed to pivot the situation in my favor, allowing them to discover his location. I awaited his phone call.

"Shepard, I can spin this—lead them to Pascal. You think it can work?"

"As long as you're discreet, I don't see why not."

He liked my idea, and we headed out, closing the gallery for the day. I spotted the car idling across the street. It was as Shepard described. I did my best to act nonchalant, as we made our way to the end of the road before departing, going our separate ways. I was on my way to visit Lucas at his office to confess everything, but I grew apprehensive. The mere thought of telling him about Pascal altered my steady breathing. I made my decision solely on his aid to protect our children.

Access to the truth was easy because of Pascal, but I was in denial. I considered how my indiscretions as a public figure would've affected Lucas. I also imagined the New York Times front-page headline with my face below, stating, "International Art Thief Apprehended." As a doctor, Lucas associated with a lot of various lawyers—and made a ton of friends over the years. I hoped to sweep everything under the rug without making a scene.

Apart from the cold, brisk air, I was also numbed with fear, as I contemplated the ripple effect of the decisions that needed to be made. I took a deep breath, placing one foot in front of the other, and walked into Lucas' workplace. Security officers and reception allowed me to walk past the front desk. They greeted me with a smile, as I made my way toward the elevators. My destination was the top floor. I got off the elevator after a couple of stops, walking toward Lucas's office. His receptionist, Jana, smiled.

"Hi, Mrs. Gallucci. How are you?"

"I'm doing well, Jana. Thanks."

"Would you like me to tell your husband you're here?"

"No, thank you. That won't be necessary."

I strolled past her toward my destination, knocking on his office door upon arrival. No one answered. I turned around to discover an employee walking by.

"Excuse me. Have you seen Mr. Lucas Pope? I'm his wife. Know where I can find him?"

"Oh, hi, Mrs. Pope—"

"Gallucci. Pope is my husband's last name."

"I'm so sorry, Mrs. Gallucci, I just assumed that—"

"It's fine."

"Umm, the last time I saw him he *was*—oh, check the conference room. He said something about resolving an issue with one of the interns before his meeting or something like that. It's down the hall—first door on you left."

"Thank you."

I walked toward the conference room. The lights were off, and the room appeared unoccupied. However, I knocked to be sure. No one answered, so I tried turning the handle. No luck. Locked. I sighed, turned around, and texted him before hearing a noise come from inside the room. I knocked on the door once again. "Lucas I know you're in there. We need to talk about something. It's important," I said.

He opened the door, looking somewhat disheveled.

"Uh...Bea? Honey, what are you doing here? Is everything alright?"

"Why are you in the dark all by yourself?"

"I was... uh... just closing my eyes for a couple of minutes before my meeting. I have an awful headache." His erratic behavior, undone button, and undecided stance didn't convince me. "Um, why are you here, hon? Did something happen to the kids or something?"

"No...uh...the kids are fine."

"Okay, then, what's the matter? Spit it the hell out."

"Spit it the hell out? Is that how you talk to me, now?"

"No, I'm sorry. I don't feel well. This is a bad time."

"That might be true, but it doesn't explain why you're acting so... nervous."

"Nervous? Why would I be nervous?"

"I'm not sure. You tell me, Lucas!"

"Look, I have a meeting to attend. Can we talk about this later, please?"

Someone was walking toward me from around the corner. A woman. I didn't have a reason to peek, but the clacking of heels echoed in the hallway. She got closer, slowing down as she approached the door before turning the corner.

"Oh, my! I had no idea anyone was standing in front of the door, here! I'm so sorry," said the unidentified person in heels. Lucas scratched his neck and cleared his throat before I turned around to address the woman.

"Honey... uh... this is Amanda Blake. Amanda, this is my wife, Bianca. Amanda's one of our interns here."

I turned around to face her. She presented herself as Amanda but wasn't at all who she claimed to be. It was Kate Clarke! She extended her hand to shake mine, acting as though she didn't know me. I folded my arms, refusing to touch her. My body temperature accelerated, escalating to a boiling point. Lucas cleared his throat. That's when his affair with her dawned on me. *Do I make a scene? How do I react to this?* I never imagined her to be so ruthless, yet she stood indifferent, gazing into my eyes, as if for the first time.

"Oh, Bianca. I heard so much about you. Nice to meet you."

"I wish I could say the same, *Amanda.*" I turned my head to Lucas. Well, time for me to get out of here. I'm sure I'll see you tonight. I *will* see you tonight, *right* Lucas—at home, in bed? Or will you be in *hers*?"

Kate watched while I stormed away. Lucas sprinted toward me.

"Honey, wait. It's not what you think," he said. My tricep experienced a gentle squeeze of his grip.

"Don't you f**king touch me!" I said. Everyone's attention diverted to us. His eyes wandered, unable to look me in the eye.

"How long, Lucas? How *long* have you been sleeping with her? Months? A year? Two?" He couldn't deny it and expelled a heavy exhale before trying to remain in control of the situation, downplaying his wrongdoing.

"Look, I'm sorry you had to find out like this. I really am, but I ended it. She doesn't matter to me. It didn't mean anything."

"F**king great! I feel *so* much better, already!"

"Can we not do this… *here,* right now?"

"Oh, you've got some nerve. How long have you been sleeping with that slut? Spit it the hell out!"

"… A few months," he said. "Bea, I'm so sorry."

I stormed off, crying, as I headed to the elevator. His patients, colleagues, and staff stared, but I didn't care. I had bigger problems to deal with. The elevator took forever to arrive, and I pressed the call button numerous times as if I possessed the power to speed it up. It soon arrived… and so did an overwhelming rush of emotions—the weight of the world perched on my chest. My mind catapulted into overdrive.

I was foolish, ignoring all the signs of Lucas's unfaithfulness. *I should've known.* I grabbed the railing and tried inhaling and exhaling to catch my breath to regain my composure. I wiped the tears from my eyes the best I could, but they kept running down my cheeks despite my efforts. Claire was the only one I thought to contact. The heartbreak and betrayal continued to settle in. My voice broke while I left her a voicemail.

"Claire, please call me back. I've made such a mess of things. I'm scared, and don't know what to do! Please call me!"

My mind wandered into space while I thought of the profound reality of my situation. My legs became weak again—nausea consuming me. I almost passed out the moment I exited the building. I slid to the ground—upright against the wall—closed my eyes, and hoped everything was only a bad dream. A passerby asked if I was alright.

"No. I'm not. I'm having a *horrible* day. Do you mind hailing a cab for me?

"Sure. Not a problem. You'll be okay, though? Should I call you an ambulance instead?"

"Oh, no, a cab is all I need. I'll be fine. Thank you."

Kindness is rare, but I got lucky. It happened to be the only good occurrence that day. He extended his arms, offering to help me up.

"Thank you so much. I appreciate this."

"No problem. You take care of yourself, okay?"

"Yes. Thanks, again." Claire called me the moment I got into the cab.

"Bianca, what is going on?"

"Can the kids and I stay at your place tonight? Everything's gone from bad to worse. I need to tell you more of what's happened."

"Come over whenever you want. Are you alright? Are you in danger?"

"No, I'm not. We might need to stay a couple of days. Is that alright with you?"

"Yes, whatever you need, hon."

"Okay, I'm heading home. I'll pack some things, get the kids, and we'll be over in a few hours. Wait, do you mind coming over first before we head over to your place? I need to speak to Lucas alone when he gets home."

"I'll be there, Bea. I'll be there."

11

The Call

I DIDN'T KNOW HOW TO HANDLE the curveball thrown at me, so I poured two shots of Jameson Irish Whiskey from Lucas's stash, and gulped them down within seconds of each other. I followed through with my plans to collect the kids from school, pack our bags, and waited for Lucas to arrive. Claire agreed to come at eight o'clock in the evening and he showed up around nine o'clock as usual. A text from Claire came through, saying, "Almost there." I called her right away with detailed instructions for our pickup.

"Hey, circle around the block three times to be sure you're not being followed. Park your car across the street from my building and text me. I'll be down with the kids, afterward. If you notice anything strange or out of the ordinary, send me a message."

"Got it, Bea," she said.

She did as I instructed, remaining in her car with the engine idling. I receive another text from her saying, "All clear," and soon made my way downstairs with the kids. We approached her car.

"I'll be right back. He should be here any minute. Give me about ten minutes or so," I said.

I made my way back upstairs and sat at the kitchen table with my unsettled thoughts. Lucas arrived a few minutes later. You can imagine how unhappy I was to see his face—to be in his presence. Our inevitable fight commenced.

"*All these years*, Lucas! Was she the first or are there others?"

His head hung low, avoiding eye contact for as long as possible.

"Look at me, damn it!" I said.

I figured his answer would be 'yes,' but I needed to hear it for myself.

"I'm sorry, Bea," he said.

"Sorry? That's not *close* to enough for me." I clenched my fist, wanting to beat him to a pulp. He ran his fingers through his hair, leaning against the kitchen sink. "No! I don't think you're as sorry as you say. You're only sorry because I figured it out!"

Our fight, filled with rage, persisted, and he said I was partial to blame for my acute PTSD years ago. I couldn't *believe* he was trying to justify his actions.

"*Goodbye*, Lucas."

"Where are you going? Where are the kids?"

"They'll be with me, but the house belongs to you. Oh, and don't forget to take your little blue pills when you're ready to f**k 'Amanda' again. You'll need them."

I grabbed my coat and slammed the front door as I exited my home. At that point, I had no more tears to cry. A callousness lingered, forming around the walls of my heart. I entered Claire's car to discover the twins asleep in the back seat. Claire witnessed the anger blanketing my face but didn't utter a word until after I buckled my seat belt.

"We're not being followed. No need to worry, Bea. You're gonna be fine."

Her tone held such confidence. I clung to those words of hope as she extended her hand to mine, reassuring me she'd be there for us every step of the way. At that moment, I wondered what I could've done in my life to deserve an amazing friend like her.

"What are your plans tomorrow morning?" she asked.

"I have to take the twins to school before work."

"I can take them while you do what you need to."

"Really? Oh, thank you so much. I need to catch up on a couple of things. Today was hell, to say the least."

***

I kissed the kids goodbye the next morning, sending them off to school with Claire. She navigated uptown, and I traveled downtown. My commute to work was challenging—not because I was taking a cab during rush hour, but because I lacked concentration. A dark cloud of anxiety hovered over me. It was easy to let the weight of my circumstances drag me down, but I continued pushing forward. I stood in front of the gallery and scanned my surroundings for the FBI, but they were nowhere to be found. It appeared as though they were backing off, but I sensed it was only for a short while. As the morning carried through, I found myself buried in a mountain of tasks I neglected—and without an assistant, I had *double* the work.

Early morning visitors were rare—which made it impossible to complete anything. A particular man caught my attention. He stood in front of a painting longer than most, admiring its beauty. I approached him, as I would anyone else.

"This one is *beautiful*. I find it speaks to me on a personal level," I said.

"Yes. I agree! Original... and *so* full of life. It kind of reminds me of one I stood in front of in England when I was a boy," he said. His smirk lingered.

"You have an eye for great art."

"I used to spend the summers touring Europe with my mother. Those were some good times. It's a shame I won't ever see it again—or her."

"Oh, I'm sorry for your loss, but you can *always* honor her memory by visiting the painting again one day, you know?"

"I'm afraid that won't be possible. Rembrandt's 'Sea of Galilee' is what this reminds me of, and word on the street is the FBI is looking for it—that amongst some others."

Only two types of people would've been looking for the painting. Pascal's men weren't one of them. He turned, reaching into his suit jacket to display his credentials. His badge read, 'Special Agent Gerard Hall.'

He peered into my eyes with judgment and desperation, fishing for a single clue. A breadcrumb of guilt, perhaps. I gave him a blank stare as if I had no idea what he was talking about—nonreactive to his insinuations. He mentioned Pascal's name, and while he made no accusations, his tone seethed with belief that I knew where Pascal and the paintings resided. The more I lied, the better a liar I became.

"I have no idea who this... Pascal character is... and I'm sorry you think I have something to do with The Sea of Galilee. That's quite an accusation."

He smirked, staring with speculation. He couldn't touch me.

"You're free to look around for any evidence—oh and by all means, I grant you access to my office, too!"

"That won't be necessary."

My phone buzzed. *Sh*t, Pascal couldn't contact me at a worse time!* I stood wondering whether or not to answer. Agent Hall smirked and raised his eyebrows.

"You gonna get that?" he asked.

"No, my husband can wait. I'll call him back later," I said.

"The truth doesn't stay hidden forever. You'll slip soon enough," he said.

He turned away from me, strolling toward the front door.

"You can stop following me—you and your men. I've done nothing wrong," I said.

"I'll be the judge of that, Mrs. Gallucci. You have yourself a nice day, now."

A heavy exhale rushed out of me the instant he exited. He was no longer in sight, so I scurried to my office with a relentless pounding in my chest. *Breathe, Bianca. Breathe. He doesn't know anything. You're in the clear.* Pacing back and forth helped ease my nervousness. It took me a minute to calm down before returning Pascal's call. My hand trembled the instant I rang him. He instructed me to answer when he called, and an apology was all I had to offer. I was unsure of how he would've reacted.

"I'm sorry, I—"

"I did not ask to hear excused. You do as I instruct. Understand?" he said. The subtlety of his voice screeched fear into me.

"...I understand," I said.

"You're going to bring me my art tonight at 145 East 135th Street at eight o'clock. If anyone comes with you, I'll see to it that you suffer. Be sure no one follows you to this location. Do I make myself clear?"

"Yes, I'll do whatever you need me to."

"That's good to know because I need you to do something else for me. I need you to retrieve a... *particular* recording in Kate Clarke's possession. Find it and then "*take care*" of her. I don't care how you do it. Just do it, but first, I want what you stole."

"Are you crazy? You want me to do *what*? No, the agreement was to deliver the Rembrandt. I never signed up to kill anyone! I'm *not* a murderer!"

"Oh, but you *are*. You just haven't realized it yet. The day we met you had your hand gripped tight around my throat, and all I could think about was death. I recall you not being yourself, as if you became a different person—*Elizabeth* is the name you gave me. And as I struggled to breathe, I looked into your eyes and saw something I'm familiar with. The eyes of a murderer aren't like anyone else's. When you've done the things I have, you begin to recognize that look. It's in your genes. It's in your blood."

"No, I *can't*. I *won't!*"

"I have no doubts Elizabeth will. Your children's lives depend on it."

I hated being leveraged. My kids had nothing to do with my theft—and yes, Kate deceived me on many accounts, but she didn't deserve to die.

"Do as I ask, and I won't be a threat to your family."

"She's an *FBI* agent, Pascal. I'll go to prison for life! Why can't you do it yourself? What evidence does she have on you?"

"She was in the wrong place at the wrong time. Goodbye, Bianca."

The phone line died, and it was time for me to gather my kids from school. *I have to tell Claire and Lucas what's going on.* An unplanned decision to leave New York was imminent. I would've done anything for my children. Disregarding Pascal's demand and skipping town was a possibility.

I got my car out of the garage and sped off onto the West Side highway toward my kids' school in a panic. I tried calling Claire, but her phone went straight to voicemail. I soon received a call from Shepard, instead.

"You're not going to believe this. Pascal wants me to kill Kate," I said.

"*What*? Why?" he said.

"He says she was in the wrong place at the wrong time. I don't know what that means, but he said I have to get a recording from her before I kill her. If I don't, he'll hurt my kids. *I'm not a murderer!*"

"This a goddamn mess."

"I'm on my way to get the twins out of school, now, before heading to the Poconos to our vacation home. An FBI agent came snooping around earlier, too. Shepard, I need your help, please!"

"Try to calm down. Of course, I'll help you. We'll fix this. Listen, I'll call you back as *soon* as I can, *okay*?"

"Yeah. Okay, bye."

I hung up and tried calling Claire, again. Relief draped my heart the instant she answered the phone.

"Thank God you picked up! I'm getting the kids out of school, now, and leaving town!" I debriefed her of my situation while running a few red lights.

"Be careful, Bea. Call me when you arrive," she said.

The closer I got to my destination, the heavier my foot was on the pedal. My display of recklessness was unbecoming of me, but I couldn't help it. I *had* to be there as fast as possible. *Errk!* The tires screeched, as I slammed on the brakes. Time was of the essence. I placed the car in park before sprinting out, leaving the keys in the ignition. The few steps from my car to the school's front door took forever to reach. I hustled inside, making no hesitation of my request at the desk.

"Excuse me, Susan. I'm here for my kids. It's an emergency, and I need to pull them out of class."

"Is everything alright, Mrs. Gallucci?"

"Yes, everything's fine. I'm late for an appointment, and I need them with me. I'm also double-parked so if you can hurry up, please."

"I'll see what I can do," she said.

"Can you tell me what room they're in, so I can just get them myself?"

"Ma'am, we don't want to disturb the entire class. Let me check my computer, call the teacher, and have them come out, okay?"

I possessed no interest in waiting. Getting the kids out of New York as soon as possible deem to be my primary objective. *This is unbelievable. Hurry up!*

"Look, I know what class they're in. I need them *now*, so let me in," I said. I stormed toward the door, pulling and rattling the handle to the door that partitioned it.

"Ma'am. Would you please wait a moment?" she asked.

"You're taking *forever!* I *need* my kids... now!" A scruffy-looking security guard approached.

"Whoa! Hold on, now. Is there a problem, here?"

"I need my kids. We need to leave. I'm their mother, and I have a right to remove them from school grounds if I want without an explanation. I pay a lot of money for them to attend, here."

"Susan, do you know this woman? Is she clear to get them?" he asked.

"She's here to pick them up every day. They're in room A114."

I left the area and scurried down the hallway to find the correct room. By the time I arrived and approach the door, I was out of breath. They stood at their classroom door with their backpacks on. I was *so* excited to see their faces. We exited the school, and I got bombard with questions. Isabelle grew the most curious.

"Are we going home, mom," she asked.

"We have somewhere important to be today, and we're taking a *special* vacation. We have to hurry, okay?"

Exhilarated, they got into the car. It was crucial to keep a smile for them—especially while I kept thinking of Pascal's demand. I knew he was serious—as serious as the severed human fingers he delivered to my office. No way was I taking Kate's life. Elizabeth would probably do it, but not me—not in my conscious state. *That reminds me. I should take my medication.* I needed some aspirin to soothe my headache but didn't place either in my purse. *Damn it. I left them on my desk at work.*

I wanted to retrieve it. However, I was on my way out of the city. Isabelle and Michael behaved themselves in the back seat while the radio played, and I planned on leaving to the Poconos within the hour. I sped, headed down the West Side Highway, traveling south. My phone rang. It was Shepard on the other line. I answered, using my Bluetooth headset.

"Do you have the kids with you?" he asked.

"Yes."

"You're all safe?"

"We're okay. No harm done."

The light in front of me was turning yellow right before the Pier 89 dock, and I slowed down, ready to stop. A police officer pointed at me, demanding I pull over to the shoulder of the road. *Why? What did I do?*

"Shepard, the police are telling me to pull over. It's weird. I think I'm being singled out."

"Be careful. It might be one of Pascal's men. Where are you?"

"I'm on the West Side Highway at a light right in front of Pier 89. He's standing right in front of me." I rolled down my window while the radio played at a low volume.

"Is there a problem, officer?" I asked.

"There's been a report of a vehicle matching this description to be stolen. License and registration, please," he said.

"What? This is *my* car. Cars like mine are all over this city. Are you stopping all of them, too? Is this necessary?"

He ignored my question, glaring into the back window at the kids.

"Ma'am, I'm gonna need you to step out of the vehicle."

"*What*? What for? I didn't do anything wrong. What did I do?"

"Ma'am, don't make me ask you again. Now, step out of the vehicle!"

"...He sent you, didn't he?"

He placed his hand on his gun. My heart sank into my stomach. Cars slowed down, rubbernecking. He opened my door from the outside. The air grew thin. My car's engine remained idle, and a familiar song played on the radio while I somehow transition into a different state of mind. My headache worsened, the more I rubbed my temples. The kids grew more afraid as the officer raised his voice, commanding me to step out. His malicious tone became too much to handle, and thus... I crossed the threshold of rationale. I looked into the rearview mirror at the children's faces, and as I processed my next move, a man wearing a black mask approached from behind in his car.

He didn't move. He sat while the officer continued yelling, and I realized he, too, *had to* be one of Pascal's men. They both were. Shepard remained on the line, listening to everything. He yelled my name, trying to get my attention, but it was too late.

"I'm Elizabeth. Bianca will call you back, later," I said.

I ended the phone call from my Bluetooth earpiece, dropping it into the cup holder. The cop drew his gun, pointing it at my face. Nothing angered me more. I ignored his relentless command—white-knuckling the steering wheel while contemplating an alternative. He crept closer with caution like her was afraid of my unresponsive and unpredictable behavior. His approach to grab my arm didn't go unnoticed. I witnessed his every move from the corner of my eye, and grabbed his wrist, along with the gun, pulling him toward me. He fired twice, shattering the passenger window. The kids screamed. I struggled to place my finger on the trigger over his, and my attempt was successful, forcing him to fire the gun until the magazine emptied. I caught a glimpse of the masked man behind me. Pedestrians screeched, shrieked, and shouted, running and peeling away in all directions. The cop tried releasing himself from my grip with his other hand—and from my perspective, his life remained in the balance. But with both of his arms restrained, he was unable to budge. I extended my leg, pressing my foot against his jaw. His face grew red. His eyes, bloodshot, and he grunted while resisting the force of my limb. The harder I pushed, the more he resisted. I could tell by the way he looked at me, he knew he was going to die. Letting him live would've been a mistake. *Push a little more.*

Snap! His lifeless body fell to the ground. Bystanders remained stationary with their mouths open while I closed my door and hit the gas pedal as hard as possible. My tires screeched, and the masked man ran back toward his car to pursue me. The children witnessed my first killing. They never should've seen that side of Bianca. I wish they hadn't.

"Keep your seat belts on, kids. It's gonna be a little bumpy," I said.

Traffic proved to be difficult, but I didn't give a damn about anyone else. I wanted to get the hell out of there. Weaving in and out of lanes was the real challenge. I ran a few red lights, leaving a trail of accidents. *Argh! He's still on my ass!* There was gridlock traffic ahead, and I had no choice but to drive on the sidewalk parallel to the road.

The masked driver was tenacious, pursuing me without relent—his determination reflective of his actions. He sped up and hit me from behind. The kids yelled in fright, and I swerved back onto the street.

I did all I could to throw him off course, but he continued to follow. *Slam!* He hit me from behind and made me fishtail, spinning us around one hundred eighty degrees. He came to a stand-still after hitting another vehicle. I drove in reverse, making my way in between two vehicles before I fishtailed myself back into drive. He pursued, and I witnessed his rage, as he hit his steering wheel with an open palm.

Bang! A loud crash commenced behind me. He was t-boned by a jeep in the middle of an intersection. I slowed down, and stopped in the middle of the street, staring into my rearview mirror, hoping the crash killed him. No sign of movement. *There's no way he survived.*

I diverted my attention toward the kids and witnessed him getting out of the car in the distance. *Impossible!* He sprinted toward us like a fearless, unstoppable machine. It was my chance to end him—to put the car in reverse. I accelerated ten... twenty... thirty miles per hour with a smile—satisfied in knowing I'd kill him. He showed no signs of stopping.

Whack! A black van collided with the front of my car, spinning us around multiple times before we came to a halt.

***

Smoke rose from the engine. Disorientation encapsulated me. Blood streamed down my face, and somehow, I had no idea how I ended up in an accident. The last I remembered was asking the police why he pulled me over. *How did I get here? What's going on?* Distant echoed male voices approached. My vision blurred. My children screamed for me as they were being kidnapped—two men pulling them out of the vehicle against their will. *What's going on?*

"No! What are you doing? Stay away from my kids! *Don't* touch them!"

I used every bit of strength I possessed, but they were still taken. It wasn't enough ... *I* wasn't enough. My head started spinning. I closed my eyes and watched it all fade to black.

12

Ransom

"MY KIDS. WHERE ARE MY KIDS?" I faded in and out of consciousness. No one responded, but I discovered my wrists handcuffed to a gurney. *What's going on? Why am I in the back of an ambulance?* An EMT shined a small light into my eyes.

"Ma'am you were in an accident," he said.

"Where are my kids? I have to get my kids!"

He glanced at his colleague, saying, "Laceration to the head might be worse than we thought." They're stared before diverting their gaze.

"My kids were in the car with me. Where are they?"

"Ma'am, no one else was in the vehicle with you."

"Ge—Get me out of here!"

I struggled to break free, but my attempt proved unsuccessful. I was terrified Pascal kidnapped Isabelle and Michael. *Oh God, please! Let them be safe.*

"I need to call my husband and tell him where I'm going. What hospital are you taking me to?"

They remained silent. My intention wasn't to contact Lucas. I intend to call Shepard, but the more I pleaded, the more the EMT ignored my request. The police followed the ambulance, and whatever I did—well, it was serious. My first instinct was to flee—to free myself of the straps fastening my body to the gurney. The lights and sirens continued blaring before coming to an abrupt halt. I couldn't see much but was able to lift my head for a better look outside. We were somewhere in Brooklyn—judging by the appearance of the neighborhood's architectural design.

"What's happening to me? Where are you taking me? Someone tell me what's going on."

No response. Without warning, the EMT approached me with a syringe, injecting me with something that lulled me to sleep.

***

I opened my eyes a while later to pure darkness, unable to see a damn thing. Some sort of soft fabric draped my head. Indistinct chatter of maybe two or three men resonated in the distance. Their voices ceased the instant I began fidgeted. Not only was I fearful for my life, but I was freezing—sitting on what felt like a metal chair with my hands bound behind my back.

"Hello?" Who's there? Where am I?"

A sterile, desolate sensation encompassed the atmosphere. My questions, still unanswered. The room remained dead silent while I anticipated *anything* to happen. I sensed my abductors didn't leave the room yet.

"Hello! I know somebody's there. I can hear you! What's going on?"

A metal door creaked open, and the unidentified strangers shuffled through, allowing it to slam shut behind them. My attempt to untie my hands failed—although my struggle to break free lasted a few seconds. My restraints caused my fingertips to tingle. Tears ran down my face, as guilt strangulated my existence. I put my children's lives in danger and didn't know if I was ever going to see them again.

"You killed one of the men I hired," said a recognizable voice.

"Pascal. *N-n-no*. It wasn't me. I don't remember anything. I swear!"

"I recall you telling me you weren't a murderer. My employee tells me you were 'more than he expected.' He's talking about Elizabeth, isn't he? I'm now positive you are capable of meeting my demand." He pulled the black fabric bag off my head, standing in front of me. A metal folding chair stood behind him.

"Please don't hurt my kids! Let them go. I'll do whatever you want!"

"You should visit the *dark side* of yourself a little more often," he said. He dragged the chair closer and sat down.

"Please, let them go!"

"You're wasting your talents on that ridiculous gallery when you could be working for me—together *with* me."

"Let them go!"

"You know, I've never seen a woman kill an officer of the law, before."

"*Let them go!*"

"Ahh, *there it is—right there* in your eyes. *That* look is the look of love from a mother who will do *anything* for her own flesh and blood." He pulled his phone out of his breast pocket to call someone.

"Bring 'em in," he said.

A squeaky, rusty door opened in the distance behind me, followed by a draft waltzing in—pressing against my body with the force of an arctic wind. Apart from the cold air nibbling at my fingers, nothing hurt me more than the uncertainty of my children's welfare.

"So, here's the deal... again. Do as I tell you, and your children live. It's as simple as that," he said.

"Mommy?" they said... My eyes widen, as I heard their distressing voices.

"Isabelle? Michael?"

I craned my neck left and right, trying to catch a glimpse of their faces. Pascal stood behind me, calling them to stand by his side. Their footsteps grow louder before they stopped, standing a foot or two away from me. I tried catching a glimpse of them but was only able to see their feet. They cried, pleading to return home to be with me and their father.

"It's gonna be okay, my babies. Everything will be okay, soon. I promise, oka—"

"Yes, everything will be fine as long as your mother does what I want," said Pascal.

"I'll do it. I'll do whatever you want—just don't hurt them. I'm begging you," I said. My face was saturated with a mixture of tears and blood while I continued pleading for their well-being.

"Okay, okay. We have a deal. I swear on their lives. I'll do it."

He walked away with the kids by his side, allowing them to exit through the door in which they entered. They screamed for me, but I could do nothing.

"I love you! Everything will be okay. Mommy will see you soon!" Pascal strolled back my way, standing before me with a malicious smirk.

"I knew you'd see things my way. Oh, by the way, thank you so much for my painting. The crate in which it is enclosed served its purpose quite well. Not a *scratch* on it. Your children's lives are contingent on your ability to follow my orders. They will be well taken care of—food, showers, a place to sleep in the meantime. You hold up your end of the deal. No police. No FBI."

I nodded and allowed him to place the bag back over my head. After everything I endured, I didn't put up a fight, nor did I bother asking any questions. He made it clear he controlled my life—that I was at his mercy. He owned me, leveraging with the 'checkmate' maneuver. I was certain that wherever I was being taken, it wasn't going to be a random dumpster or the East River. Again, I couldn't see a damn thing but heard him walking toward the back door. The draft nibbled at my ankles, but that was the least of my problems. Two unidentified men approached me— each one grabbing my arms, guiding me outside into a vehicle— possibly an SUV, due to the roominess of its interior. The vehicle stopped, not too long after leaving the warehouse, and I was dropped off somewhere in the projects of Brooklyn. My hands were untied and belongings returned to me—wallet, I.D, and phones were present. I discovered an unfamiliar item—a small, black handgun with a full round—the same one from my first encounter with Pascal.

I needed to find Shepard and could've called him, but I was afraid of a possible tracker installation on my phone by my adversary. *I could trash it—wait, he could've planted something inside the lining of my bag as well.* Leading him straight to Shepard would've been an enormous mistake.

***

It didn't take me too long to arrive at his house, but I discarded my bag after removing the memory card from my phone a block away. Everything fit in a greasy, brown paper bag I found in the garbage, inconspicuous to anyone. I made sure I wasn't being watched, and the gun remained concealed within my coat. I banged on his door, hoping he'd let me in before I was spotted by anyone suspicious-looking.

"Open up! It's me, Bianca!" He opened the door with haste.

"Bea, oh my God. Where've you been? I've been looking everywhere for you! What happened to you?" he asked. I hurried inside, and he closed the door behind me, peeking out the window.

"Did you—"

"Yeah, I made sure I wasn't followed," I said.

"Here, sit down," he said.

I stumbled onto his sofa, claiming it as my own to rest my aching head. He ran to my side with an ice pack and first aid kit. I had a lot of explaining to do, so I exhaled, ready to 'get him up to speed.'

"What happened out there? You're all over the news! One minute we're on the phone, the next I'm talking to *Elizabeth*? What the hell is going on? Wait, *where* are your kids?" he said.

"I have to tell you something about me. Elizabeth is my twin—my other personality, and I think whenever I'm in trouble, experiencing trauma, I turn *into* her. The next thing I knew I was tied to a chair in a warehouse somewhere. Pascal took my kids."

My eyes filled with tears, as I reflected upon their voices, imagining the terror and uncertainty they faced. I considered myself a failure—a mother who couldn't protect her children. I know Pascal said he'd take care of them, but there was no telling what he was capable of doing. I couldn't bear those ill-conceived thoughts. Only God knew if I was ever going to see them alive again.

"I couldn't save them, Shepard. I failed them. I can't do anything for them until I kill Kate. He's holding them ransom, and he also has his painting. There's only one way out of this. She has to die."

He tapped his fingers against his thigh while pacing back and forth, furrowing his eyebrows with an intense, taut stare into space.

"Okay, think. What can we do to get them back? There must be another way."

"The only way is to shed innocent blood."

"Bea, you're a lot of things, but not a killer."

"You're right, but when I'm Elizabeth *I am* one. *God*, I can't imagine."

"Maybe we can ambush Kate and find out why he wants her dead. We've got to stay positive. *You...* must stay positive. Try not to worry about them too much, Bea. They'll be okay. Wait, I have an idea. I can hack the FBI again, and find out where she lives. We'll go together and have a talk—you know, find out everything we can."

"We? No, I don't want you involved, Shepard."

"It's too late for that. I'm with you all the way, Bea, whether you like it or not. We're gonna get your kids back. What about Lucas? Does he know they're gone?"

"He knows nothing, and I plan on keeping it that way. He's been calling and leaving messages. If I tell him, he'll get his lawyer friends and the media involved. 'Missing children—a wanted wife?' I can't have him entangled in this, jeopardizing my kids' lives."

"I understand," he said.

He tapped on his laptop keys before pulling out a small electronic-looking chip from the kit lying next to him on the table.

"What's that?" I asked.

"A tracker. Give me your watch," he said. I looked at my wrist realizing I didn't have it.

"I threw it away along with my phones, and sim. Everything's inside my purse. Didn't know if Pascal put a tracker in them," I said.

"This is why I love you, Bea. Don't worry. I'll get them. Oh, by the way, there are some clean clothes for you in the bottom drawer upstairs. Shower, eat if you can, and get some sleep. I'm gonna make you a fake I.D. in the meantime—just in case you need it. We have a busy day tomorrow. I'll take the couch."

***

Shepard retrieved my belongings from the trash, cleared my phones, and handed them back to me. As some time passed, I found my way to the second-floor bathroom, showering the day's blood away—watching it disappear into the drain. I wished my problems could've slithered away with ease. It wasn't long before Claire and I spoke while I sat on Shepard's bed. I asked her for a favor, needing to see Dr. Summers again the following day. I had to visit him before I did something that would have haunted me for the rest of my life.

13

Reminiscence

SHEPARD AND I RETURNED TO Manhattan the next day, where I wore his baseball cap as part of my disguise. We made our way to 5th Avenue, squeezing through the dense, crowded sidewalk near Rockefeller Center's tree lighting staging area. I admired it from afar, remembering the first time I brought my kids to experience its splendor. However, I caught a glimpse of a woman who bore a strong resemblance of Claire holding the hands of two young children—one on each side, standing in the distance. I was certain it wasn't her after I obtained a better view of her face. Catching a glimpse of that woman made me think of our conversation. I asked her to set up a 'get-together' with Francis. Neither the police nor the FBI asked her any questions concerning me, but it was a possibility they contacted him. I didn't want to risk being seen at his office. To my understanding, he was going to be at Claire's around ten o'clock in the morning, and I needed his assistance. I called Pascal to talk to my kids and was able to speak to them for a brief moment without a hassle.

***

Shepard and I went our separate ways—soon to reconvene. I walked toward the door of Claire's building where the doorman greeted me from afar. A new employee stood behind the desk, upon entering, asking if she could help. I took a quick look around, analyzing the area for anyone who displayed odd behavior. My foot tapped the marble floor while I stood in front of the receptionist, having an intermittent rhythm of its own.

"Claire Benoit would've called, saying she was expecting a visitor," I said. I couldn't help but twirl the gold band around my finger. She searched her computer after I gave her my fake I.D.

"Ah, yes. I see a message here in the notes, Ms. Romano," she said.

I questioned everything and almost anyone around me who appeared suspicious and made my way upstairs to Claire's apartment. She hugged me before I removed my coat and baseball cap.

"Oh my God! I'm so glad you're alright, Bianca! Any word from the kids, yet?"

"Yeah, I spoke to them earlier this morning on my way here. Pascal says he'll keep them safe as long as I keep my end of the deal."

"You must be a complete wreck. Here, let me take your coat. Make yourself comfortable. I'm making tea. You want?"

"Yeah, I'd like that," I said. She hung my items on the coat rack before entering the kitchen.

"Can you trust him to keep his word?"

"I had to learn the hard way, but yes. As long as I do what he asks, he won't hurt them."

"Francis should be here any minute. Um, I meant to ask you this last night, but why the urgency in seeing him?"

Her doorbell chimed and she scurried to the door. It was Francis. He removed his coat and scarf before greeting Claire with a kiss on the cheek. I traded places with her, leaning against the counter next to the stove.

"Brr. So cold out, but great seeing you again, Claire," he said. "It's been far too long that we've gotten together like this. Been quite busy at the office the past few weeks."

"Nice to see you as well! How would you like your tea, Francis? Same as always, I suppose?"

"Yes, that would be gr— "

"Hi, Francis," I said. I ambled into the living room with my hands sitting in my back pockets.

"Bianca? What in the bloody hell are you doing here? What's the meaning of this?"

"I'm so sorry to ambush you like this, but I need your help."

"*My* help? Bea, the FBI came to my office asking all sorts of crazy questions about you. They even came with a warrant for your medical history; our sessions—everything. They've been looking for you everywhere. Where have you been?"

"Francis, listen to me. Something bad happened to my kids, and I need your help right now. I understand you had to give the FBI my file under court order. It's okay. I'm not worried about that. Do you remember the huge, multi-car accident all along the West Side Highway yesterday?"

"*...That was you?*"

"Unfortunately."

"Did you *really* kill that officer?"

I glanced at Claire. My eyes welled with tears. Hers did, too.

"*Oh dear God.* I know you, Bea. You're not capab— "

"Elizabeth did this, Francis. Not me. I don't remember doing any of those things. That's why you're here—because I need to remember my past—from when I was a child. I needed to remember every detail as it happened the night my family died, Elizabeth as she once was, and why I adopted her personality. Look, if I can't get rid of her, then I need to control her. I can't let her have the best of me, and destroy my life—my children's lives."

"Bea, we have drugs for suppressing your condition. Have you been taking the medication I prescribed?"

"I have two scared children out there. The last thing I'm thinking about is meds, and the man who took my kids sees *me* as a killer. He *knows* what Elizabeth's capable of. Pascal doesn't care about my episodes. He wants results, but I don't have the stomach to do what he asks. I need to remember my past. That's my *best* option. My *only* option, now."

"What do you suggest I do?"

"Hypnosis. Right here. Right now."

"No. No way. I can't do that. I haven't done that in almost a decade."

"But you *can* still do it, right?"

"There are possible side effects, Bi—.

"Such *as*...?"

"Such as psychotic episodes and suicidal depression! I stopped doing hypnosis because a patient died in my care. He killed himself, and I felt responsible ever since. That was on *me*. I don't want to do this. I don't appreciate the ambush either." He glared at Claire.

"Don't do it for me. Do it for my children. They *need* their mother. They need me. *Not* Elizabeth. You've seen her for yourself. *Please*, Francis."

He knew how much I loved my kids. He also knew my life would've been ruined if I didn't find the root of my problem. Francis took a deep breath, paced back and forth, and exhaled.

"Bianca, you're a fugitive. I'm aiding and abetting by not calling the police. I can lose everything I worked so hard for," he said.

"You would've called them by now if you didn't believe in me. I'm asking you to trust me. As far as Claire and I are concerned, we never had this conversation, and you were never here. You *know* me and my family. You also know that I don't have the capacity to kill a man all by myself—and if later on in the future you need to prove to a jury that I was unstable, then do what you have to when the time comes. But now, I need to at least *try* to control Elizabeth before anyone else gets hurt."

He exhibited reluctance and compassion through his eyes, as he held his gaze before turning away. He pondered my desperate request, knowing he was the only person capable of helping me. A deep exhale followed.

"... Lie on the couch as you would in my office," he said.

I was unsure of what to expect while I took deep breaths, hoping that everything would turn out alright. I had faith in myself, but more faith in him. He removed his phone from his pocket, downloaded a metronome application while I got comfortable, and set it on the coffee table.

"Bianca, once you're under hypnosis, you'll be helpless."

"What about Elizabeth? What if she emerges?"

"She can't. Your mind will be submissive to my voice. It's like being sedated without drugs."

"Okay. Got it. Let's do this, then."

I closed my eyes and focused on the constant ticking. It helped me relax like I was listening to a melody without music.

"Alright, I'll need you to relax every muscle in your body. Think only of Elizabeth as you remember her. Think of the last time you saw her. I'm going to count backward from the number five, and when I say number one, you're going to fall into a deep sleep. And before I bring you back to consciousness, I'll count down to one again before snapping my finger. Are you ready?"

"Yes."

"Five... four... three... two... one."

I experienced my body sinking in through the couch, like a magnetic force pulling through from the other end. The fear of being submerged didn't come to mind. I allowed the unknown force to take me wherever it wanted. It placed me in a pitch-black room—one where I couldn't see any farther than three feet in front of me in all directions.

"Hello?" I said.

I waited for a response to my echoed voice. My surroundings sustained some haziness. I took a few steps forward, pausing before looking up. It seemed like an instinctive thing to do—look up, that is. I didn't know how the phenomenon worked, but I viewed myself from afar, lying on the couch across from Francis. It was as if I watched everything on a projector. Claire sat in the love seat adjacent to us. I called out to Francis, hoping he could hear me. He couldn't, but I witnessed everything he told me in real-time during my 'out-of-mind' experience.

"Francis. I'm down here!" My lips moved, above the same time I spoke.

"What do you see, Bianca?"

"I don't see anything, except a dark, empty room. Wait, I see something. A tiny flame is in front of me. It's growing bigger."

The projection above me dissolved like fire melting plastic. However, the flame hovered mid-air—standing before a scaled-down, three-foot-high red door. The fire dissipated, but the door's visibility grew as I approached. It was far too small for any adult to fit through. A child could, though. I advanced with caution, and stood in front of it, uneasy about its size. *What do I do with this?* It got larger—big enough for me to walk through. I placed my hand on the handle, turned the knob, and entered. The moment I swung it open and stepped inside, I somehow exited the closet of my childhood home, ending up in my old bedroom. To my surprise, I was no longer an adult, but the little girl I once was, reliving the day that changed my life. Elizabeth stood in the distance.

"Lizzy!" I said.

"Bianca, come on! Let's hide!"

She expected me to follow her back inside the closet—almost as dark as it was outside. The moon illuminated and stars shined bright. That part of the night was peaceful, but the arguing we soon heard resonated throughout the house. Neither one of us wanted to be a victim of drunken, senseless squabble. My father's vexatious tone escalated, elevating to a pitch that almost drowned out "What a Wonderful World," playing on the radio from the living room. An unfamiliar male voice—a third party jarred into the conversation.

"Shh! Someone's here, fighting with mamma and papà. Stay here," said Lizzy.

She tiptoed from the closet toward the bedroom door, cracking it open to observe the disturbance. *Bang!* I never heard a noise like that before. Nothing about it felt comfortable. Something fell soon after, like a large sack of potatoes impacting the floor. My mother's scream thereafter sent chills up my spine. The commotion was enough to lure me out of the closet. I finagled around the somewhat loose, worn-out wooden floorboards to avoid being detected. Elizabeth didn't move a muscle—and I witnessed mamma kneeling next to papà, crying a river of tears. The stranger stood in front of papà's body with his back toward us and didn't hesitate to point the gun at her either. *Bang!* Like papà, a single bullet to the head ended her life. My heart slammed against my rib cage, making it almost impossible to move, and more difficult to breathe. Lizzy reacted, grabbing a knife she kept hidden under her bed. She sprinted out of the room toward the stranger from behind, slicing his forearm.

I cried, hoping she would injure him enough for our escape. He grabbed her arm, pushed her to the floor, and shot her in the chest. I dashed into the kitchen toward the loose section of flooring. That area was a common hiding place for Elizabeth and me. I lifted the boards, descending into the dark, musty crevice underneath, and eased them back in place. His heavy, evenly-paced footsteps grew louder with each step—right up until he stood motionless above me. His blood trickled down off his fingers and onto the floorboards, seeping through the cracks to my face. A drop fell into my mouth, which tasted like some sort of metal. He'd kill me if I made the slightest noise, and I tried my best to refrain from crying. My heartbeat was the loudest sound in the room—louder than the creaking boards and his shuffling feet. He pivoted, revealing his face, and I laid eyes on the man who killed my family. He carried the spitting image of my father—except for a more stylish wardrobe. The kitchen towel nearby served as an immediate bandage for his wound, and a small gas can next to the stove facilitated the decimation of my reality. He ambled toward the living room while I trembled, lifting the floorboard to witness his next move. My parents were the first to have gasoline dumped on them. Elizabeth was next before he set the couch and curtain ablaze.

The fire consumed the house with a dull, droning roar that grew louder by the second. The smell of brittle aged wood and tar claimed my nostrils. I had to escape. I needed removed the floorboards with ease. One chance was all I had to run away. I sprinted toward the back door, inhaling the descending smoke. He laid eyes on me. "Hey!" he said. I thought I was going to die while I ran toward the rear door. *Bang!'* He fired his gun, having a clear shot. I screamed and pushed the back door open, sprinting into the surrounding darkness whence I came. Francis' voice grew louder, echoing around me.

"Five... four... three... two... one!"

He snapped his finger. I gasped, opened my eyes, and sat upright, trying to catch my breath. An epiphany dawned on me.

"I opened my eyes when he was standing above me! I never remembered seeing his face! Why didn't I remember that? How could I forget something like that?"

"Trauma is tricky, Bianca. Our minds tend to filter traumatic events to protect us. Are you alright?"

I busted into tears, having to relive that moment again. Claire cradled me in her arms.

"It was Pascal. He killed my family and set the place on fire. I remember seeing the scar on his right arm at the St. Regis Hotel. That bastard lied to me, pretending he cared when we met. Elizabeth was trying to protect me. She loved me, Francis. Now I know I don't have to try to control her. She protects me when I'm in danger. She was always the stronger one and could do what I was always afraid to do. It's time I embrace her and get my children back. I gotta go."

Francis raised his eyebrows and sprung out of his chair. I gathered my belongings.

"Bianca, you should take it easy," he said.

"I'm fine. I'll be okay. Gotta get my babies back."

"Bea, let us help you in some way!" he said.

"I appreciate the offer, but I don't want you two getting into any trouble. Plausible deniability would work in your favor. This is *my* fight. *My* mess. Thank you for everything," I said. I hugged Claire and walked out the door, adjusting my baseball cap.

***

I experienced a sense of bravery after my revelation while walking in the cold. Seeing my past gave me some strength and hope. Shepard kept himself busy inside a Starbucks on Lexington Avenue across the busy street from Kate's home. I walked by, making my presence known as subtle as possible. He nodded, sat tight, and waited to join me until after I accessed her building's front door. No doorman—only a dozen buttons to choose from. I pressed all of them and hoped someone would buzz me in. A gruff-sounding resident responded through the intercom while I stood in the cold.

"Yeah?"

"Uber Eats for apartment 3-D," I said.

'Bzzzt.' Well, that was easy! Shepard scurried across the street, making his way over to me as fast as possible. I held the door open for him, and we walked toward the elevator.

"She's on the sixth floor, right?" I asked.

"Yeah, apartment 6-F."

We advanced to her place without delay. Her residence was down the hall—second to last on the right. We stood on either side of the door.

"You ready to do this?" he said. His eyebrows raised. I took multiple deep breaths. He knocked. No one answered. He tried again, and still, no answer.

"Okay, so what do we do now? Wait around, right? We can go back to the Starbucks until we see... Shep, what is *that*?" I asked.

He removed a few small tools from the inside lining of his coat pocket.

"We're not *actually* breaking into an FBI agent's home, are we?"

"Of course we are. I'm a professional thief. We're doing what needs to be done like we always have," he said. He smirked while picking the lock. I expected Kate to be a little hostile if she were home, but she wasn't.

"Shepard, let's get out of here and wait!"

The door unlocked, and he took his time pushing it open. I made sure no one saw us, and we scurried inside, remaining unseen by any neighbors. Kate's apartment was quiet, and we were ninety-nine percent sure she wasn't home. Shepard searched every room validating her absence. He came back into the living room, placing three guns on the wooden coffee table.

"Where'd you find those?"

"Everywhere—one hidden in each room. I bet one's secured under the coffee table." He knelt before craning his arm. "Found it. Not the most trusting girl," he said.

I dragged my finger along the surface of the table.

"And a bit of a neat freak. Everything in its place—and a place for everything in here," I said.

"Neat freaks are all about control. Look at this place. Notice anything wrong with it?"

"No, it looks immaculate."

"*Too* clean. A girl with her history has lots of secrets. Hiding things in plain sight is the best way to conceal anything. Start looking for anything that may appear 'odd' to you. Anything at all."

We searched every room, but didn't find anything out of the ordinary.

"Bea, come here!" said Shepard. He stood in the doorway of her bedroom. I scurried over to him.

"There... on the wall," he said.

"What, the painting?" I asked.

"Yes... and no. Look at the edges of the frame. You see those scratches close to the edge, there?"

"Yeah,"

"Give me a hand with it."

We stood on each side of her bed, lifting it away from the wall—our gaze fixated on the back of the painting at the same time.

Whoa. Is this for real? It was remarkable. We laid it face-down, viewing her detail-obsessed collage. She collected files, pictures, and documented events of Lucas, the twins, Pascal, and myself.

"What the—"

"She's been all over the world looking for Pascal. Shep, look at these pictures and documents. I've been followed for quite some time. She made sure to be well-qualified to work for me...but *why me?*"

"She must've somehow linked you two. Can't say for sure."

Shepard searched under the bed to find a folder containing files strapped to the underside of the box spring.

"Hey, look at this. These documents say she'd been assigned to work for you—to find Pascal. It looks like she's been using her case assignment to leverage the opportunity to find him. This is personal, Bea."

"Remember when you told me her parents were killed? Well, that's why. Pascal killed them the same way he killed mine! She's after him for revenge and used me to be close to him. But wait, why would she think I had anything to do with him?"

"My guess is—the only thing that makes sense is—she seized the opportunity when the Feds targeted you. You showed up on their radar, and they suspected you of theft. They knew you two were related even before *you* did."

"He's an international arms dealer with an insatiable taste for expensive art. I own a well-known gallery. Makes sense."

Nothing could prepare me for the deliberate, unexpected *'Click'* sound traveling to my ears from behind me, followed by a profound, spine-chilling silence. That *'Click'* seemed familiar. Kate stood at the door of her bedroom. No exhibit of anger, contempt, or disgust—only a gun pointed at me. I froze but sensed a change happening—a sort of 'inner transition'—a reverberate wave of energy coupled with a slight pounding headache. I turned around and stood face-to-face with her.

"Congratulations. You figured it out, and you're gonna tell me what I need to know."

"Kate, please put the gun down."

"Shut up! I don't take orders from you anymore. I don't know what you're doing here or how you found me, but you have two seconds to get on your knees and place your hands behind your heads."

"Kate, please... if you would listen to—"

"I said, shut up! Now, tell me. Where's Pascal?"

"I don't know. I swear," I said.

"You're lying! Tell me where he is or I swear I'll lodge a bullet into your friend—then you," she said. Shepard held a stack of files in hand, unmoved.

"Kate, please. I'm begging you. Put the gun down. Let's talk about this!"

"Shut the *hell up,* and get your *hands behind your head!*"

"Oka—"

"Get on your knees!"

Elizabeth was emerging from within. My heart's rhythm slowed down. A part of me wanted to suppress her. Another part of me wanted her to take charge. We got on our knees, placing our hands behind our heads. I had no gun, no weapon to defend myself, and no idea what she intended to do with us. Kill us? A possibility. I had to act fast.

The room spun. I closed my eyes, and covered my ears, as a high-pitched noise subdued my being. I crouched in pain, becoming dizzy in the process, tumbling over her dresser.

"What is this? What's happening to her?" she asked Shepard.

The ringing dissipated. She lowered her weapon a bit. My distraction served as a window of opportunity to overpower her. *You can do this. Here goes nothing.* I advanced, lunging toward her. The timing couldn't be more perfect, and it was my only chance to pry the gun from her hands. I wrapped my hand around her Glock 21. Thirteen intermittent shots were fired in our struggle. Shepard took cover behind the bed.

Her magazine was empty, and it was 'do or die,' for me. She clutched her weapon, but I slammed her wrist against the spine of the door as hard as possible. With luck, it fell to the floor, but I proved ill-prepared for the head-butt that knocked me off my feet. I was vulnerable. Kate bent down and picked up her gun. Shepard got up on one knee, pointing his Glock 19 at her.

"Eh! Drop it, or I'll shoot," he said.

"I doubt it," she said.

She bolted out of the apartment with her gun in hand. Shepard scurrying to my aid.

"Bea, are you alright? What the hell were you *thinking* charging at her like that?" he asked.

"Yeah, it's *you* again. 'Shepard,' right? Bea couldn't do it, so here I am."

"*What?*"

He examined me with a stale, somewhat frightened look in his eyes before they widened.

"*Tah-dah!* Well, don't just stand there, staring at me. *Let's* get her!" I sprung to my feet and grabbed one of the many guns--a Glock 45 Shepard found. We sprinted out of her apartment after her.

My lip had been split open—just a superficial wound—nothing to cry over. I *enjoyed* an adrenaline-pumping, blood-thirsty fight. Tasting the blood on my lips made me feel devilish. He and I ran down the stairwell as fast as possible, hoping to catch up with her. She swung the second-floor door open, dashing into the hallway.

"She's mine!" I said.

"I'll get a car!" said Shepard.

He ran down the stairs to the lobby while I pursued Kate. I enjoyed the game of cat n' mouse. She fired her gun at me in the hallway, and I took cover, hiding around the corner wall. The bullet impacted the drywall about six inches above my head, dispersing a cloud of dust onto my face. *Close one.* *'Bang!'* She fired another shot before pushing through the metal door at the end of the hallway, making her way to the lobby.

***

My steady pursuit continued across two avenues and into a large crowd on 5th Avenue's Rockefeller Center. *You've got to be kidding me!* The swarm of people was so thick, rubbing shoulders with strangers was inevitable. Somehow, she made it through without knocking anyone over. Sirens traveled my way, and as I looked behind me, two federal agents were tailing me on foot with their guns drawn. Agent Gerald Hall was one of them. "FBI! Freeze!"

I ignored their demand. *They wouldn't dare risk shooting an innocent bystander.* I turned back around, spotting Kate making her way through the horde about fifteen yards away. "Kate! Stop!" I said.

She paused, breathing heavily before taking off through the crowd, again. The two agents continued pursuing, desperate to apprehend me. *'Bang!'* A single shot forced me to remain still.

"Bianca! Stop! That was a warning!" said an agent.

People screamed and scattered like ants, knocking each other over. I stood still with my back facing the agents while the swarm of people continued scrambling in front of me. Kate slowed down at the corner of the street, turned around, and took a few deep breaths. She crouched over, breathing ragged, leaning on her knees. The thickened crowd made visibility unforgiving, but I kept her locked in my sight. Her long, deliberate glare stirred resentment within me, yet I could do nothing. Agent Hall and his colleague maintained their focus on me. Shepard approached Kate from behind—subdued by his attack during the commotion. I turned around, as the agents inched toward me with weapons drawn.

"What a beautiful day, today! Isn't it, gentlemen?"

"Bianca don't make this difficult. Put your hands behind your head and lie face down on the ground, now!"

"There must be some mistake. You have the wrong person. I'm not who you think I am."

I didn't have the luxury of options at my disposal. Reaching for my weapon tucked into the rear of my pants, would've gotten me killed. Lucky for me, a random, innocent bystander ran in between me and 'the pigs' dressed in suits. I seized that opportunity to grab him, using him as a shield. The barrel of my gun pressed against his temple.

"Oh, God! Please, please don't kill me, I beg you!" said the hostage.

"Shut up! Your life depends on their cooperation. What's your name?"

"Gilbert," he said.

"Gilbert, tell these men to drop their weapons and back away."

"Bianca, it doesn't have to be like this. There's no escape. Let him go. He has nothing to do with this," said Agent Hall.

"He has *everything* to do with my escape. Now, do as Gil says... or he dies."

"Drop your guns and back away, or she'll kill me!" he said. He cried. His voice quivered. "Please do as she says!"

They stopped advancing, honoring Gilbert's request. He trembled, shaking like he'd been submerged in a vat of cold water. A puddle of urine formed around his feet, inching toward mine. *Ugh.*

"One wrong move, Gil, and you're a dead man. Do as I say. Do you understand me? Okay, I'm going to release my hand from your collar for a moment. Take my phone and dial the first number you see," I said.

My eyes were glued on to the FBI. The line rang. Shepard answered.

"There's more headed this way soon. We don't have much time, Liz," he said.

"Do you have her?" I asked.

"She's right here with me on the northwest corner from where you're standing. You're in a tight spot."

"All under control."

"I'm in a red Audi about fifteen yards (0.01 km) behind you."

"Gil, end the call," I said. "Gentlemen, if you will remain where you are, this man won't die for nothing." They didn't move an inch. "Gilbert, I'm gonna release you, now. If you turn around, I will put a bullet in your f**king skull. Do we have an understanding?"

He nodded and remained stationary. I minced backward with my gun drawn—eyes fixated on the agents. One rushed to his aid the moment I entered the car. I, however, sped off with Shepard, staring into the side mirror. Agent Hall stood in the middle of the street, staring at us, and an unconscious Kate Clarke remained in the back seat. She was *all* mine—one whom I looked forward to interrogating.

14

Common Enemy

LOSING THE FBI WAS EASY but getting rid of the police proved to be more of a challenge. A pain in my ass. To be crystal clear, I viewed them as the cockroaches of the justice system. The moment you extinguish one, you find more somewhere else—and the instant you shed light on the truth, they scatter. They follow orders like trained dogs on a leash. Kate wasn't like them. Yes, she wasn't a cop, but possessed a mind of her own, and did what she believed to be right. I was anxious—eager to interrogate her inside Shepard's home. I waited hours before the chloroform she inhaled wore off, and my patience wore thin. She remained knocked out for a long while, and I had a million-and-one questions to ask. I paced back and forth behind the couch she occupied, deciding whether or not to wake her. Kate groaned— the moment I'd been waiting for. Shepard and I took a seat in front of her. She sat up, taking her time, rubbing her eyes with one hand, and used the other to balance herself upright. Neither one of us said a word but stared at her until she regained her composure. Her instinct compelled her to rush for the gun on the coffee table.

She wasn't going to shoot us, though. We wanted her to feel like she had some control—like she had a choice.

"I know how you're feeling, Kate—this moment of vulnerability," I said.

"You don't know anything."

"Here's what we know. You're an only child, and Pascal killed your family when you were young. Years later, you found yourself a hobby... stealing high-end goods. You were very skillful, no doubt, but sloppy. You got caught. However, someone wiped your slate clean and you joined the Feds. They saw you as an asset, and you agreed to work for them—for time shaved off your sentence. Perhaps you didn't even serve *any* time. Am I right? So, you took that opportunity to avenge your parents and got yourself into the Art Theft Division knowing Pascal was an avid art collector. He stripped you of everything, robbing you the chance of having a normal life. So my questions for you are... Why does he want you dead, and why do you think Bea had anything to do with him?"

"What? Whoa... hold on a sec. Why are you talking about yourself in the third person?"

"This is Elizabeth, Kate. Bea's... sister," Shepard said.

"Okay, so how do you know all those things about me?"

"Shepard wields a unique talent, and apart from some of those files in your apartment, we don't know everything. However, you and I have a common enemy. Pascal. He kidnapped Bea's kids, and I need them back, but he demands a recording you hold in your possession. Oh, and I'm supposed to kill you after you hand it over. His words. Not mine."

"So, I'm being forced to give you something... and then you kill me? That's why I'm here?"

"Wow, you're an FBI agent and yet, not that attentive. How does that happen?" I asked. She pointed the gun at my face.

"You know what? I don't like your tone, and I don't have what you're looking for, so I'll be leaving," she said.

"Oh, stop with the lies. It's written all over your face. And if I wanted you dead and delivered, you'd be dead and delivered by now, okay? But it's not up to me, so sit your ass down. Oh, and I'm not angry about the blistered lip you gave me, nor am I pissed about the marathon you made me run. I just want Bianca's kids back, and to show that a**hole my idea of a good time. We can either work together or make this a messier situation."

"What if I don't like your offer? What if I find him on my own?"

"I'm your best chance of finding Pascal and you're gonna... walk away? Look, I know you won't kill us. You had your opportunity at your apartment and chose not to. You need me, and my priority is to save Bianca's kids, so—"

"Yeah, I didn't know she had a twin," she said.

"... It's complicated," said Shepard.

"So, you're Elizabeth?"

"Shepard, are we playing '21 Questions,' here?" I asked.

"Look, Kate, do you still have that recording?" Shepard asked.

"Fine. Yeah, it's hidden. If he ever came after me, it would go public, both the murders and molestation. His dealings would plummet. No one would want to work with a man who has an appetite for little boys. "

"Wait, what? Are you saying Pascal is..."

"I was fifteen. He was a friend to my dad. Patrick, my thirteen-year-old brother complained that Pascal was "too friendly." When my dad confronted him about it, he flipped out, denying the accusation, but my dad had proof. He took security very seriously—paranoid, even. He installed hidden cameras everywhere, including the pool house. My dad worked for MI5— pretty much the same as the FBI. I came home early from tutoring one day to find them all dead. Pascal lingered in the house. Long story short, I grabbed the hard drive from my dad's computer and kept it a secret before calling the police. Pascal's been after me ever since."

"Kate, I'm very sorry for your loss," said Shepard.

"Okay, so what about Bea? Why'd the Feds target her for stolen art?" I said.

"You two figured it out at my apartment—their relation to one another. Not many Galluccis left in the world. Pascal remains on the 'most wanted' list. However, the odds were you two might've been related. The bureau went to great lengths to confirm that, and I volunteered to work on the case. It was my only chance to nail him—to find him before my unit did."

"Hmm. I understand," said Shepard.

"So, if that's all the questions you have for me, then I have one burning question for the two of you. Where's Bianca? Everyone's looking for her."

"You're looking at her," I said.

"What? I thought you said you were Eliz—"

"I am, but Bea's in here," I said.

I pressed my fingers against my temple. Shepard explained everything to her. She reacted as I imagined—eyes widened and mouth opened big enough to shove two sticks of dynamite in. It wasn't easy for me, but I was inclined to believe her story. It made sense. However, I still kept a watchful eye—unable to trust anyone one-hundred percent. Shepard reassured me she wasn't going to be a problem anymore and convinced me that it was more of an advantage to have her on our side. True, but allowing her to stay the night didn't vibe well with me. I believed she felt the same way—not trusting people.

Kate wasn't a problem, as long as she stayed in her lane ––and I'll admit, she helped devise a plan to corner Pascal without the kids getting hurt. She knew a lot about him—his security, the places he visited, and his illegal dealings. Her Intel was the breadcrumbs we yearned. As for me, I had to stay out of sight. The cops and feds were on the hunt for me... well, for Bianca.

"Shepard, I'm going to bed. I had enough action for one day," I said. I headed up the stairs. "I'm taking your bed tonight, by the way."

I imagined they both fell asleep downstairs. I yawned multiple times and tossed about with a persistent, nagging headache. Waking up every thirty minutes wasn't ideal, but unavoidable. I scanned the room each time, hoping Kate wasn't standing over me at any point in the middle of the night with a gun pointed at my face. The most I could've done was lock the bedroom door. *What if she turns on us?* Bianca lived inside me, wanting to trust Kate, but I struggled to give way to her naïve and benevolent nature.

***

I woke up the next morning to the smell of coffee, eggs, bacon, and toast. My nagging headache wore off, but I was still a bit disoriented, making my way downstairs.

"Shepard, what am I doing here? Why is my lip bruised?"

"You don't remember?"

"Uh, I remember Kate at her apartment. I also remember the name "Gilbert" for some reason. Does that mean anything to you?"

"Not at all, but I'm glad you're back, Bea."

"Wait, I remember fragments of Kate being here, and us planning Pascal's capture. Oh, my God. 'It' happened again, didn't it?"

"You were fierce."

"Well, where is she? Where's Kate?"

"She left."

"What? Why?"

"She vanished before I woke up. I'm guessing she had to show up to work, today."

"What if she reveals our location?"

"Relax, Bea. She won't. She's on our side. Besides, I put a button tracker on her coat while she slept. I doubt she'd notice it. I also placed a replica onto her cuff as a backup. Please sit, drink a cup of coffee, and try to relax. Trust me, she won't turn on us."

I couldn't relax. His advice fell to deaf ears, but I applauded his genius for thinking ahead. He was right, though. She would've returned because of her obsession with finding Pascal. However, flashbacks of the last twenty-four hours occurred where I started piecing everything together.

"You were pretty bad-ass yesterday. Remember anything else?" he asked.

"It's kinda hazy, but coming back to me. Did I hold a man hostage or something?" I asked.

"It was kinda sexy."

"Oh, stop it."

"Quite daunting, seeing you change personalities like that. One minute you're a normal woman—the next, you're thirsty for blood."

He couldn't have been more correct. As strange as it was, Elizabeth stirred inside me—like a restless ball of energy, waiting to explode—ready to take another life. It was as if her bravery masked my fears. In that instant, I wasn't afraid of anyone, including the authorities. I only longed to have my kids back. A cup of black coffee and toast was all I needed before heading out, ready to face the world head-on.

"Do you remember our plan?" he asked. Shepard tied his boots.

"Some of it," I said.

He gave me the rundown before we got ready to leave, and I needed a better disguise before leaving his home. A blond wig, pair of non-prescribed glasses, and a Yankees ball cap helped change my appearance.

"Are you sure Kate won't turn her back on us?"

"Positive. She needs us. Trust me, she wants Pascal just as bad as we do. You've been closer to him than anyone else."

"Yeah, you're right."

It had been a while since I checked my phone. I was ignorant of maintaining contact with everyone except Pascal. Lucas had been calling me, leaving texts and voicemails. I didn't bother reading them but called him right away.

"Bianca, hon, what the hell's going on? Your face is everywhere! I've been calling you and leaving messages. The FBI came to my office asking all kinds of questions about you. Where the hell are you?"

"I can't tell you that, but I'll explain everything. Drop what you're doing and meet me on 42nd and 6th in one hour. Come alone. There will be problems if the FBI strings along. Do you understand?"

"Yeah, I got it. I'll be there."

I hung up before entering the subway with Shepard—confident we blended in on the C train to Manhattan. It stopped on Jay Street in Brooklyn where two police officers walked in. *Act... normal. Just keep calm.* He and I remained seated while they stood beside us, alongside the bench near the doors. I couldn't resist the urge to steal a glance at the officer's gun, nor could I explain the reason for my impulsive, irresistible action if I wanted. I experienced a morsel of satisfaction, and grew nervous, hoping they wouldn't recognize me. Shepard interlaced our fingers and whispered into my ear, "They aren't looking for a couple. Giggle and follow my lead." I never gave much thought to myself as an actress, but I needed to played the part of a woman in love. Fright and undiscovered affection saturated my being at the same time. Shepard tucked my hair behind my ear, whispering into the nape of my neck with a light, breathy tone. His lips grazed the surface––enough to trigger arousal. He gazed into my eyes, and I reciprocated before caressing his jawline with my fingertips. Our display of fondness appeared... well, it felt natural. Authentic. *Is this happening?* Rebound feelings? Maybe. Perhaps vulnerability got the better of me. *We're just putting on a show, right?*

Shepard didn't let me go until they appeared to be out of sight. It was comfortable, having his hand in mine—until reality kicked in. *That was close. Just a few more stops, and we'll be in Manhattan.* Shepard and I got off the train and walked up the subway stairs.

"Okay, this is where we split up. Remember, I put a tracker in your watch. If anything goes wrong, I'll know where to find you, okay? Chin up. You can do this," he said.

"I can do this."

We went our separate ways—Shepard tracking Kate. I managed to hail a cab that took me to my destination. New York wasn't glitz and glamour in the grand scheme of things. I was in a city of 8.5 million people, feeling like the only one with a target on my back. It took a while to arrive, but I spotted Lucas, standing alone on the corner. I rolled the window down.

"Get in."

Confused, he looked around, opened the door, and sat down. I couldn't tell who was or wasn't watching us, due to the multitude of people. The driver accelerated.

"What the hell are you wearing? You died your hair!" he said.

"No, Lucas. It's a wig."

We moved away from the corner, continuing our drive uptown. I divulged a few vague details of my story before getting to the point.

"Look, you slept with another woman and it hurts, but what I want more than anything is the kids."

"How could you let this happen to them?" he said.

Although the situation grew tense, he and I remained civil. An all-too-familiar moment of silence fell between us soon after, before he expressed his anger. He exhaled, reaching for the door handle the second we came to a halt.

"Lucas, wait.... you didn't ask about the kids when I called you earlier."

"Of course I did. I asked you where they were."

"And my response was?"

"Okay, fine, I didn't ask because I figured they were in good hands!"

"Good hands?"

"Whose hands are you referring to, Lucas?"

"I assumed they'd been with Claire."

"What father doesn't ask about his children after what they've been through?"

Something didn't sit right with me. I grew uncomfortable. He appeared a little too calm, and his cavalier attitude ignited an inclination of disdain within me. He babbled a few words while removing his wallet to pay the driver, and I caught a glimpse of something I never noticed before.

"Wh—where did you get that?"

"Get what?"

"That gold card in your wallet. Where is it from, Lucas?"

"Oh, uh, it's my new AmEx card."

"Lucas…why are you lying?"

I snatched his wallet, fixated on the card. He turned his head away, dropping his shoulders. His shallow, uneven breathing and somewhat slouched posture exposed his secret.

"Oh, my God, you already knew, didn't you? You didn't ask about the kids because you know where they are! Pascal gave you this, right? You piece of sh*t. Where are the kids, Lucas? Where are they? Tell me! Tell me, right now! What did he promise you? You had the balls to sit here with me and act like you didn't know a damn thing! *Tell me!* Tell me where they are, goddammit!"

His association with my enemy alternately dismantled my psyche. Most women would have—at the least—slapped him if they were in my shoes. Not me. I threw my fist into his face without the slightest hesitation before grabbing his throat. He gagged, bleeding all over my hand. A tear trickled down my cheek. Whatever trust we had left constituted a severance. I'm sure it was a small price to pay—broken nose n' all, but the hospital was right down the block. Easy fix.

"Tell me where they are, you son of a bi— "

"Out! Get out!" yelled the cab driver. Lucas freed himself from my grip.

I knew him too well. Maintaining a poker face wasn't his strong suit. Not only did I experience emotional pain, but a wild rage began to take form. Within a few short moments, my heart no longer bled—and like the flip of a light switch, my emotions altered. Elizabeth was channeling her strength, both emotional and physical. He rushed to open the door before falling onto the street, gasping. He stared at me as if he'd seen a ghost—surprised I was unlike my normal self. I threw money at the driver, exited on the other side, and approached Lucas. The cab sped away.

Car horns blared, wanting me to move from the middle of the road. A random police officer walked toward us, shouting in our direction. I tossed his wallet at his feet and shuffled across the street. No more tears. No more sorrow—only a phone call to Shepard while making my way around the corner.

"Shep, where are you?"

"I'm sitting across the way from the FBI building on West 36th."

"What? Are you crazy?"

"I *know*, I know. They aren't looking for me. I'm a ghost, remember? Don't worry, I have eyes on our little helper. Meet me at the Starbucks on 7th and 36th in twenty minutes."

***

I arrived at Starbucks to find Kate and Shepard sitting together in a corner.

"The FBI building is right across the street and this place could be crawling with them. We need to leave," I said. I kept my back toward the crowd.

"How'd you two find me, anyway? You've been following me the whole time, haven't you?" asked Kate.

"Something like that," said Shepard.

"Here I am in a coffee shop colluding with a thief and a killer. Wait, are you Bea or Liz?"

"Not Liz," said Shepard.

"You two need to disappear from this city. You're not safe here in Manhattan. Bianca, there's no doubt in my mind they'll find you if you stay. *Everyone's* looking for you. Lucky for you, I own a small house in Lake George—bought it from a retired doctor and his wife years ago. We'll be there for a couple of days. No one will suspect it. I'll have to drive you, though. There's no way you'd slither past the search parties by yourselves."

"This delays our plans. Is there any other option for us right now? Can't we just hide out at my place?" said Shepard.

"I have eyes on me at work, but came up with a believable story as to how I got away yesterday. Not sure they're buying it. Stay cool, but they're watching me now, cross-checking everyone I talk to. Shepard, you don't look concerned."

"Feds don't scare me. Besides, I'm not who they're looking for. So, I guess we'll just have to roll with your plan, then," he said. "Let's get you out of here in one piece, Bea."

"I'll meet you guys at Canarsie Piers tonight at eight o'clock. Bring what you need. You're going to be up there for about two, maybe three days," said Kate.

"What about you? How do you leave work when you're supposed to be looking for us?" I said.

"I'll swallow Ipecac—an over-the-counter, vomit-inducing pill, before throwing up in front of them. I'll feel sick for a few minutes, but my superiors will give me some time off."

"Okay, then. Let's do this," said Shepard.

I didn't want to be so far from my kids. I wanted to be wherever Pascal wanted me at the drop of a hat, but it wasn't wise to stay. He sent me pictures of them when I asked, assuring their well-being, and gave me time to fulfill his demand. I used that to my advantage. Despite my many occurrences, I appreciated the help from Shepard and Kate. I also kept Claire in the loop. Elizabeth was of great assistance, too, helping me persevere. Everything that would occur within the next couple of days made me stronger than I ever anticipated.

15

The Answer is "No"

I SAT IN THE PASSENGER SEAT of an old, stolen black Toyota Corolla while Shepard sat behind the wheel with his laptop, encrypting and reprogramming my phone. "I put a new sim in for you. Now, it's just like a burner," he said. Kate arrived, parking next to us under the low-lit dismal area of an abandoned lot. She placed her car in park and pressed a button near her dashboard which resulted in the ascension of the trunk door. She exited, scuttling toward the rear for us to place our belongings.

"You guys ready?" she asked.

"Yeah, I guess so," I said. A burst of air rushed out my nostrils.

"There's an exit before JFK Airport where officers are conducting a checkpoint. Bianca, you'll have to get in the trunk a mile prior."

"You're kidding, right?"

"It's the only way. I'll flash my badge, and they'll let us through in no time."

We headed eastbound on the Belt Parkway. I sat up front––Shepard, in the back. It wasn't long before we arrived at the tail end of a long line of cars. Flashing red and blue lights trailed up ahead. The search was in progress as Kate foretold.

"Time to make the switch," she said.

She pulled over under an antiquated, well-fortified bridge. I made my way into the trunk before taking a few deep breaths.

"Shut your phone off, and whatever you do, don't make a sound," said Shepard. "Don't worry. Everything will be fine," said Kate.

It closed with a muffled thud. *This is really happening. I'm really doing this.* The pungent, heat-enhanced odor of mechanical oil and auto-grade rubber made me hold my breath. I powered my phone down. It was so dark inside, and I couldn't see my hand in front of my face. I froze my ass off, lying in the fetal position.

Kate accelerated, driving back on the highway where I endured the effects of every little bump and divot in the road. The intermittent braking and accelerating within the long line of cars bothered me the most. She soon brought the vehicle to a complete stop.

The low-whirring screech of her window descending, generated a spark of nervous anticipation. Heavy-plodded footsteps grew louder. Someone was approaching—most likely a police officer. A short silence reigned before he spoke. I listened to every muffled word, hoping he wouldn't suggest opening the trunk.

"How's it going tonight?" he said.

"Could be better, I suppose," said Kate.

"Ah, the FBI! I'm sure you're aware of the 10-75."

"Affirmative, officer... Jacobson, I'm one of the agents spearheading that Wanted Persons case. Let's hope you catch her before we do?"

"Our boys will. New York's finest." Shepard opened his door, vomiting on the asphalt.

"Uh... he okay?"

"Flu season. We're headed to the emergency room."

"Well, you can rule out Covid. Thank goodness for the vaccine. Good luck to you both."

"You, too."

"Alright, let 'em through!" he said.

You have no idea how relieved I was to hear those words. Kate pressed the gas pedal and moved through the checkpoint without raising suspicion. Being in the trunk wasn't easy. I felt like a pinball being launched, thrown, and jolted around. This continued for about a mile down the road until the coast was clear. The car came to a complete stop. Shepard opened his door, scurrying to help me out. We got back inside the car.

"Shepard saved our asses," said Kate.

"How'd you manage to do that?" I asked.

"I can't take all the credit. Kate gave me one of her pills."

"Well, I'm just glad you threw up outside, and *not* in my car."

The further we drove from the city, the more uneasy I grew. However, sporadic pulses of bravery engulfed me. *Strange.* It existed one minute, and soon left, but I didn't feel like myself in its duration. A veil of unearthed consciousness cloaked my mind. And the past couple of days replayed with flashbacks of my arduous events—the kid's abduction, being held against my will in the warehouse, and Lucas' betrayal. Random images of Pascal's face and the scar on his forearm surfaced while I laid down on the back seat. I didn't verbalize my experience to either of them nor did I start a conversation. No one said a word on our way to Lake George until we got close to our destination. A sort of... inevitability—a dampened calm of uncertainty filled the car's interior. None of us could've predicted my future outcome, but I held on to a thin thread of hope for a positive conclusion.

We stopped at the local convenience store for milk, bread, and other household necessities before arriving at the house. Shepard and Kate walked into the store and returned fifteen minutes later before driving off again. Her cabin wasn't too far away.

***

It was quaint—nothing fancy, but possessed a quiet, creepy aura next to the frozen lake. The brown shingles on the house were intact—somewhat faded, though, and the windows exhibited a mixture of frost and dirt clinging to their edges. I imagined the interior to be immaculate compared to the exterior––due to Kate's incessant need for cleanliness.

"This is it—our home for now," she said.

"Eerie," said Shepard.

"Keeps strangers away."

The place hadn't been occupied in a while from the looks of it. Some of Fall's dead leaves resided on the porch, pinned underneath the weight of the leftover snow. We gathered our things and headed up the stairs to the front door before walking in. The inside was as cold as the outside, and I shivered in anticipation of some heat. A large, instant fire would've been nice. Shepard read my mind, taking the initiative to gather some wood.

"I'll go get some firewood. Kate, where—"

"Out back under the tarp. Thanks."

She walked about the cabin, making sure everything was tidy and guest-worthy. I started putting the groceries away a few minutes later, finally alone with my thoughts. As she headed upstairs, I took a moment to admire her wall of memories. She came back downstairs, headed toward the stove.

"Bianca, would you like something to drink? We have water, coffee, hot cocoa, bourbon, and tea."

"Tea would be great, thanks."

Kate and I didn't talk much. Sure, the awkwardness between us prevailed, but I didn't mind if it meant avoiding an awkward conversation. I *was* thankful she didn't betray us earlier. However, I still harbored some resentment. She handed me my tea before I had a chance to sit down. Shepard stoked the fire. The flames increased, and I needed more warmth, so I stood in front of it as close as possible.

"Kate, I'm sleeping here, tonight. Shepard, too," I said.

"Your beds are upstairs, but, uh... suit yourselves. I'll get your pillows and blankets."

I wasn't sure how much rest I was going to get—being in unfamiliar territory, but Shepard's presence gave me a strong sense of security.

"I'll take the love seat. You take the couch," he said.

"Shep, I wanna say, "Thank you."

"Oh, no big deal, Bea. What kind of man would I be if I let you sleep on that tiny thing?"

"No, I mean, thanks for being with me every step of the way. This hasn't been easy for me. Look at me, sleeping under the same roof as the woman who slept with Lucas. It doesn't get any more uncomfortable than this, does it?"

He chuckled and placed his hands around mine, warming them with his breath while we sat in front of the fire. We shared the flames—each flicker mirrored from his dark, brown eyes. I admired his display of kindness—amorous at the moment. I wanted to be close to him—to feel his bare skin against my inner thighs. A primal need for an overflow of dopamine to distance me from my anchoring stress dominated my soul. I almost forgot what it felt like to be desired by a man the instant he moved his coarse hand down my thigh. Kate traveled back downstairs with an abundance of pillows and blankets, which somewhat blocked her view. *What if she fell and broke her neck? That would work in my favor, but I need her recording.* I left Shepard's side to help.

"Thanks. Get comfortable. There are two bathrooms—the one upstairs has a shower. The one down here is the half-bath."

"Thanks, yeah, I'm gonna shower. Be back in a bit," I said.

"Shepard, I peg you for a hard liquor kind of guy," said Kate.

"Never turned down a free drink before. No reason to start now."

"Make it two... for when I come back. I won't be long" I said.

***

I returned to the living room twenty minutes later, wearing a clean beige sweater, black sweatpants, and a pair of thick woolen socks. I wanted my drink and sat on the couch closest to the fireplace. Two glasses of Bourbon took the edge off.

"So, are you guys gonna stare at me the whole night, or am I not allowed to have another drink?" I said. Shepard smiled. Kate got up and returned with an unopened bottle. "Thanks. So, let's get rid of the elephant in the room, Kate, shall we?"

She paused and sat down after pouring me a third glass.

"Look, Bea, I know what you're referring to. I was just doing my—"

"What... your job? Sleeping with Lucas was *your job*?"

"No, I misspoke. My jo—my assignment was to get as much information out of you as possible, but I started with him first. I found nothing. You two were *too* clean, so I had to get "creative." It went on longer than it should've... and I'm sorry I ruined your marriage.

"At first, I was furious. I wanted to rip you apart, but the more I thought about what *he* allowed, the more I realized... he had the power to resist. That's what it came down to. So no, you didn't ruin my marriage. It was over a long time ago, but I chose to ignore the signs. I couldn't face my reality at the time. He's been hiding things from me. I know he's been involved with Pascal somehow. I found an identical gold card in his wallet earlier today like the one given to me, and I have no idea what its true purpose is."

***

The night grew colder as time passed, and the abundance of firewood Shepard gathered was enough to keep us warm until morning. I worried about my kids but reminded myself they'd be okay from time to time. 'My hands were tied,' so to speak—and although I appeared to wait around like a sitting duck, a plan was in place. I decided to relax my mind and recline my thoughts with the help of another glass of Bourbon.

"I'm calling it a night. See you two in the morning," said Kate.

She walked upstairs to her room. I stared into the crackling fire, daydreaming of the worry-free life I lived before my world turned upside down. Shepard stood with his drink in hand, walking in front of me as I reclined on the couch. I extended my arm, diverting his attention. He grasped his hand, and we gazed into each other's eyes knowing, without words, the uprooted affection we shared.

"Kneel," I said.

He didn't hesitate to comply. I sat up, fixated on his lips. I wanted him—no, I *needed* him. He leaned in, as I anticipating the touch of his soft, supple lips. One justifiable kiss transitioned into another—soon to be entangled in a cyclone of desire. I crossed the line with him but didn't care anymore. I craved affection, hoping it would either ease or nullify the burden I carried—even for a little while.

He pulled my sweater off, ravishing my body with his hands and lips before I laid down on the carpet. He removed his shirt before placing his hand around my throat, applying a small amount of pressure. I inhaled and then exhaled, thrilled by his strength. The contour of his arms and chest enhanced my desire to unbuckle his belt, ready to enjoy a morsel of bliss.

"*Bianca,*" said someone.

A compelling, unfamiliar whisper coming from somewhere in the room caught me off guard.

"Shep, wait—stop. Did you hear that?"

He met my gaze with furrowed eyebrows.

"I didn't hear anything—just you and me."

I looked around the room, thinking Kate may have called out to me. Although it didn't sound like her, it couldn't have been anyone else. I regarded it as a figment of my imagination and diverted my attention back to Shepard's company underneath the blankets. His kisses were all too distracting and much too enjoyable to resist.

***

He satisfied my craving after some time. My eyes grew heavy as we laid together under the comforters. The crackling fire and his warm embrace lulled me to sleep before hearing my name whispered once again.

"*Bianca...*"

I awoke to the faint, eerie sound of my name, thinking it was Kate. Shepard remained asleep. My alcohol consumption made my head feel like it weighed a ton. I scanned the room again, hoping I wasn't experiencing an auditory hallucination. As expected, no one was in sight, so I rested my head on the pillow and closed my eyes.

"*Bianca...*"

Another whisper jolted me out of my sleep while the fire continued burning. My heart raced, as I looked around, wondering where the eerie voice came from.

"The answer is no."

"What? Who are you? Where are you?" I asked.

"It's me, Bianca. Lizzy."

"Lizzy? I can't see you."

"The answer is 'no' to the question you've been asking yourself."

Her voice carried through the air, reverberating. I stood confused in the middle of the living room.

"What do you mean? What question have I been asking? Lizzy, where are you?"

"Over here, Bianca."

Her voice came from the bathroom, so I followed—afraid the floorboards would creak. Shepard remained in a deep sleep, uninterrupted by the noise.

"I'm over here, Bea," she said.

I hesitated to move forward. The fire provided some light—enough for me to see my surroundings. Her whispering voice overlapped like an echo. I entered and flipped the light switch on. A small, isolated *'POP'* coupled with a diffused cast of light shrouded the room. I turned around and caught my faint, low-lit reflection in the mirror. Somehow, the overhead bulb dispersed a slight amount of luminosity, getting brighter. My intuition compelled me to stare, waiting for Elizabeth to appear, but she didn't reveal herself as I expected. My reflection dissolved, transitioning into a visual memory of my childhood home.

I viewed us playing together, and my eyes filled with tears as I whispered her name. I couldn't rationalize the phenomenon before me. It was as if I watched my life on a television screen. *I miss you, Lizzy.* A cluster of emotions invaded me. My father charged into the room. The door swung open before it collided with the wall. He swayed, pointing his finger at me.

"You. You're coming with me!" he said.

Elizabeth ran toward him, yelling and pounding her fists as hard as she could while I was drug by my hair out of the room, clinging to an immovable object.

"Let her go! Leave her!" she said. "It's not her turn!"

I remembered the pungent stench of alcohol on his breath as well as his putrid, pit-stained wife-beater. The odor alone was like acid burning the lining of my nostrils with each inhale. Small patches of hair separated from my scalp as a result of my resistance to his clutched grip. The pain. The horror. A day I won't ever forget. *'Wap!'* He swung the back of his hand into Lizzy's jaw in anger, immobilizing her.

"I can never tell you two apart," he said.

He released my hair, and walked over to Liz, grappling her arm. She didn't fight. She left with him, and turned around, looking back at me through the mirror.

"The answer to the question you've been asking yourself is 'no.' You can't trust everyone, especially the ones closest to you," she said.

Her voice dissipated into the silence, like a fog floating along the surface of the earth. I was left with the nagging realization I asked myself in secret from the start. *Can I really trust anyone?* However, my visual memory faded, transitioning into my faint, low-lit reflection. I stood motionless, overwhelmed with grief and stricken by a recollection I thought would never haunt me again. My consciousness waned and my legs gave way before I fell onto the cold, tiled floor.

16

Nightmares

I OPENED MY EYES TO THE MORNING light as Shepard repeated my name. He sat on the bathroom floor with the upper half of my body in his arms, stroking my head and cheek. His eyes widened, followed by a deep exhale before a smile. Kate was present, too, staring and kneeling in front of me with a white washcloth in hand.

"Bianca, can you hear me?" he asked. "Are you alright?"

"Yeah, I'm okay," I said.

Confused, I tried gathering my bearings, failing to recognize my whereabouts. *I must've slept here half the night.* My legs, stiffened and cramped regained full mobility in time. He helped me up off the floor and toward the couch before I sat down, checking for any more bumps, cuts, or bruising around my head.

"My head hurts. A little headache is all. Coffee and two aspirins will do the trick, please, if you don't mind."

"Yeah, sure. No problem," said Kate.

"Some water, too."

"Do you remember how you got yourself on the floor?" asked Shepard. Flashbacks of my vivid hallucination struck me as I stared into his eyes, but I didn't feel like talking about it.

"No. I don't remember anything—no clue why or how I got there."

"Are you a sleepwalker?"

"No, but I'll be fine."

I endured grogginess and soreness, trying to settle into the right position, as I sat up on the couch. Kate scurried back into the living room from the kitchen, holding the items I needed. She held my cup of coffee in one hand and two tablets of aspirin in the other. Her dark, downcast eyes spoke volumes as she approached me.

"I don't need your pity," I said.

"It's not pity. I'm concerned, Bianca," she said.

"Oh, yeah? Well, I recognize it when I see it. Since when do you care about me, huh? The only reason I'm here is because of Isabelle and Michael."

"Listen, I'm sorry he took your kids from you, and I'm sorry I slept with Lucas, but I was doing whatever necessary to acquire the Intel I needed. Let's not also forget you're here because you're the most wanted woman in New York, and *I'm* the one helping you. I'm risking my *career*, and *my life* aiding and abetting. Some appreciation would be nice."

Her rebuttal cascaded a light of truth onto me. I swallowed my pills and my pride with the understanding and acknowledgment that she was right. My predicament was my own doing, stealing from Pascal in the first place. Although I took responsibility for my wrongdoing, apologizing didn't occur to me until she walked away, disgruntled. I sat with my eyes closed, trying to ease my headache.

"Shepard, get ready. I need you to come into town with me for some additional things if you don't mind?" said Kate.

"Sure. Give me a couple of minutes."

He glanced my way before nodding, gesturing everything would be okay. He didn't ask me to go, nor did he seek my input. I didn't want to accompany them, regardless.

"We'll be back before you know it. Need anything while we're out?" he said.

He smiled, nodded, and grasped my hand before tying his boots.

"Are you sure you're okay?"

"Go. I'll be fine. Just my head that's bothering me."

He walked toward the bathroom, washed his face, and grabbed his coat to head out with Kate. I sat awhile, motionless, as I allowed my headache to dissipate. My thoughts of Elizabeth ran rampant, rendering me unable to forget her message. My paranoia compelled me to scavenge the house, hoping to find some proof of foul play. I found a black taser in one of Kate's drawers surrounded by folded pairs of socks. I decided to hold on to it and place it in my pocket before continuing my search. It was the only item that served as my security while I was alone.

We all have our skeletons hidden deep, somewhere in our closets. I had mine. Shepard, too. Containing Elizabeth was difficult, although, a part of me didn't want to let her go. We as people hold on to our secrets tight, because deep down inside, well, sometimes we're terrified of being judged. Kate had secrets under lock and key and had yet to tell us where the recording remained. *If I were her, I wouldn't keep it close to me. I'd hide it far away, like in this house, perhaps. Maybe I'm wrong.* I continued in her room for a thorough search, replacing every item as it were. Nothing found. I also explored the other bedroom. Still, nothing suspicious. Nothing worthy of a 'red flag.' I checked each squeaky floorboard in the living room. Still, nothing incriminating. *Wait, I didn't check the basement.* I headed in that direction, cutting the corner sharp from the bottom of the first-floor stairs.

Someone's hand appeared in front of my face from behind, clasping my mouth and nose. It was the strength of a man, no doubt. He managed to grip my left wrist, forcing my arm behind my back. My muffled scream served no purpose. Resisting was my only option, and the more I tried to fight back, the more he twisted my arm. I grew terrified of the possible scenarios. *Will he break my neck, stab me in the back, or worse, force me against my will?"*

"Don't move... and don't scream, Bianca," he said.

The airy tone of his voice crawled into my ear, like a centipede making its way into my eardrum. I closed my eyes, thinking of the inevitable the second he kissed it. *No! This can't be happening again!* The strength and bravery I needed, sprouted. He released his grip from my face and fumbled for my breasts. His hand advanced toward my navel, moving below it at his leisure.

"Wa—wait. You don't have to do this. Take anything you want in here and leave, *please*. I beg you." He whispered into my ear, "I like it when they beg."

His voice made me cringe before my disgust transitioned into anger. I swung the back of my head into his face and jolted my elbow into his nose. He released his grip from my arm, yelling and grunting, and I scurried back upstairs to the second floor. He managed to grab my ankle, yanking it from the third stair before I lost my footing. I placed my hands on the stairs to break my fall, yet tumbling down toward the floorboards was inevitable. The ultimate fight for my life began when he turned me over, slapping me across the face. He wore a black ski mask to hide his identity, but I stared into his malicious, blue eyes, hoping he'd release his grip from my throat. My attempt to free myself failed. I was running out of options, and couldn't find anything within my reach to use against him. He had 'the look' in his eyes—the distinct look of a man who'd killed before—the same look Pascal described to me. I didn't know who the assailant was, but forcing himself on me was *not* an option. *Enough of people treating me like I have no value.*

My ears rang without fail. I reached for my thigh, remembering I placed the taser in my pocket. The chance of electrocution during physical contact posed a possibility, but I was more than willing to take the risk. *'Dzzzttt.'* The crackling surge of electricity immobilized us, stiffening our bodies. He fell over onto the floor, and I tried regaining full consciousness before him. I coughed and gasped, struggling to recover. My ears rang louder, and I knew whatever was to happen next wasn't of my own volition.

Elizabeth's coming. For the first time, I didn't resist. I allowed her to consume me—to take over. I zapped him again with every ounce of energy I possessed—but longer than the first time. The ringing subsided, I stood up, and searched him, confiscating any weapons he might've concealed.

"Hmm... a phone, cash, wallet, knife, and a gun! You came well-prepared, sweetheart. These might come in handy," I said. I focused on my thoughts. He groaned and gnashed his teeth before the surge of electricity wore off. A vacancy for pity didn't exist within me.

"I hate introducing myself, so I won't. The only thing you need to know is you made the biggest mistake of your life," I said.

I kicked him in the stomach three times, breaking a few ribs, and stomped on his hands for touching Bianca against her will. He yelled, coughed and groaned, and remained incoherent after zapping him again. Bianca's travel bag sat nearby. A pair of jeans appeared to be more suitable than the sweatpants I wore. He laid on the hardwood floor in agony, mumbling some words minutes later.

"What? Speak up!" I said.

Well, the difficult part came—dragging him. He didn't respond. "You know what, I think the basement is the best place for you! Don't you agree?"

I had some fun taunting him until I noticed he pissed his pants. *What is it with you men and the peeing?*

"Okay, you piece of sh*t. Time to make some changes— oh, I'm not talking about your clothes. We're gonna go downstairs and figure out what fate has installed for you."

I zapped him once again before dragging him to the basement—and, of course, it was like no other basement. I mean, it was unfinished, dusty and damp, but well-organized. An old pool table, covered under an old white sheet, sat in the middle of the room. A row of dated oak cabinets hung on the wall across from the table. Next to that lie a white pegboard multi-purpose organizer which hung on the wall as well. Every item, labeled. She had nails, a nail gun, glue, an ax, gardening tools, and much more. A tall, square piece of furniture, covered with a white sheet, sat on the other side of the room next to the freezer. An old medical table sat in the corner nearby. My curiosity got the best of me, but I needed to focus on my assailant first.

"Wow! I am appreciative of Kate's organizational skills down here, mister. Oh, look! Duct tape... and rope, too!" I said. He laid motionless on the basement floor. I was eager to remove his urine-soaked clothes and move him onto the pool table. Deadweight—maybe two-hundred pounds (ca. 91 kg), and difficult—not impossible to lift. I removed his clothing, sat him up, and stooped down behind him, wrapping my arms around his torso. I used all my strength, lifting the upper half of his body onto the table. The rest was easy. "There. Done! Naked as the day you came into this world."

He regained some consciousness as the seconds passed, slurring a word I was familiar with.

"... You... witch," he said.

"Oh, honey. I know what you're trying to say. Save your voice and energy for when you're screaming."

I positioned him on the table, binding one limb at a time to each leg before I removed his mask. I didn't recognize him. His only distinct markings were a scar on his cheek parallel to the length of his eye, and a Semper Fi tattoo on his bicep.

"You got some balls, coming in here—touching a woman against her will. It takes nerve and a f**ked up mind to do something like that. I hope bravery is your strong suit today." *Okay, so I have the duct tape—the rope... uh... I also have super glue, and my taser if necessary.* I leaned into him, staring. "So, what's your name?" I asked. He spat in my face, and I reacted, throwing my fist into his eye twice before he yelled.

"Take it like a man," I said.

"You broke my fingers and ribs. You're gonna pay for this." He struggled to release himself from the restraints.

"I'm not impressed. Try again," I said.

"F**k you."

"Bravo! *Now* we're getting somewhere..."

"I had my orders. I do what I'm told."

"You know, I never quite understood the whole, 'following orders' thing, ya know? *You* do whatever you're told. You're brainwashed into believing you need a leader. I guess men *are* dogs, right? It must suck so much to not think for yourself. How does it feel to be spoon-fed every decision of your life?"

He ignored me, but glared into my eyes, as I stood beside him.

"Unlike you, I do whatever I want... and whenever I want––plain and simple. S*o much freedom* in it—being your own boss, don't you think? You should try it sometime... if you get out of here."

He stared at the ceiling emotionless, fostering contempt––ready to accept his brutal interrogation with a clenched jaw and pressed lips.

"I'm ready to die," he said.

"Die? I never said anything about *dying*. You're gonna give me the answers I need, and if you don't, we get to play doctor for the day. Are you ready? Of course, you aren't." I left his side to sift through the items I found earlier.

"Okay, let's take another look at what you have, here. A phone…and a wallet. Maybe it's about time I start calling you by your real name. Oh, no I.D., but some cash. Hmm…I bet Bianca would enjoy this moment as much as me."

I peered into his eyes with an everlasting gaze. He stared back without so much as a twitch, exercising his silence. That's when I realized he knew about me.

"You see, she and I are the same person... and when bad things happen, I come to the rescue. But you thought you could 'handle' me, didn't you?" I asked. His gaze drifted to the ceiling.

"Do what you need to. I won't talk," he said.

"There are ways of getting what I want. I *enjoy* making men like you suffer. You *all* deserve what I have in mind," I said.

I took a deep breath and flipped his phone open to search for any helpful information.

"You're a careful man, but not careful enough. No photos, recent GPS locations—nothing except one international number. Who does it belong to?"

"I won't talk."

"I've got a friend who's gonna get me the answers I'm looking for, regardless, so, you might as well save us both some time," I said. He shivered, refusing to make eye contact, so I taunted him some more.

"It's a bit chilly in here for you, don't you think? I'm sure you'd like—"

"Go to hell," he said.

"Okay, then. Let's do this the fun way."

I headed toward the tall cabinet on the other side of the room. The chance of finding medical utensils—although slim—was worth a search. I removed the sheet and found what I suspected. It was, indeed, an old medical cabinet. The utensils were rusty, and I gathered what I could onto a tray before grabbing the duct tape off the white pegboard. If I was going to muffle his scream, it had to be done right. I didn't want my ears ringing later on. He didn't struggle while I applied the tape. He stood his ground—and although he was 'in between a rock and a hard place,' I applaud his bravery. He thought he could violate Bianca, but I considered her lucky to have someone like me, shielding her from men like him—like our father. We protect the people we love at all costs.

"All men have ever done is take, take, take. They take land, money, people's lives, and everything else they desire. The list goes on, but don't you think it's time *women* take what they want? If a child misbehaves, you take away the thing they love most... for a while, of course. Then, you give it back after they've learned their lesson. So, think for a minute. What do you hold most precious to you that I could take away, but *never* give back?"

His sharp, shallow breaths at the sight of the rusty utensils satisfied a small portion of my desire to see him worry. He clenched his fists and flexed his arms, yanking the restraints until his face turned beet red.

"This basement turned out to be a gold mine—all these *wonderful* things down here. I'm not the type of woman to skin you alive or anything. That's cliché. Basic. I'm willing to bet there's ice in that freezer on the other side of the room, though. Can you guess what I need it for?"

He mumbled a few words under the tape's adhesive before I ripped it from his lips.

"Oh, my apologies," I said.

His eyes widened, but he didn't yell. *Good.* Fracturing his mental psyche shed some light on my progress.

"You're a f**king psycho!" he said.

"So I've been told. You're scared, and you should be. Bad actions and choices lead to consequences."

"You think I'll talk? Never."

"Listen, you're expendable. A 'gun for hire' with an appetite for violating women. You forced yourself on them, stripping them of their dignity—stripping them of their pride. Their souls are crushed and stifled to an irreparable end. You took something they can never get back. Let's take something away from you, Mr... Epstein... Weinstein, maybe? Yeah, I'll call you that."

I lowered my eyes, staring at his crotch.

"No, you *wouldn't,*" he said.

"Give me a name, and I'll consider letting you go. I need to know who sent you here to hurt Bianca. Was it Pascal?"

"Pas–who? Never heard of him."

"You're lying. I *know* he sent you."

I removed a scalpel from the tray, laying it next to him. His face turned pale and sweaty as if he acquired a fever. His breathing pattern increased, and his lips quivered. I stumbled across an unmarked box of miscellaneous items sitting under the table behind me. A few mason jars, cereal bowls, and eating utensils sat inside. I walked to the freezer and collected a small bowl of ice before heading back to the foot-end of the pool table.

"Time's up," I said.

He thrashed about, using every bit of strength he could to set himself free. I let him try. I had time on my hands—enough to begin reading and viewing the basics of the procedure from Bianca's smartphone. A piece of cake—nothing *too* difficult. I thought if I made a mistake, well, it wouldn't have been the end of the world... not *mine* at least, but I wanted him to live a long, unsatisfying life.

***

He appeared exhausted by the time the medical YouTube video was complete.

"You done with your fit yet?" I asked. "It's time for another piece of tape. Hold still."

I propped the bowl of ice under his scrotum before applying another strip.

"I'm a strong believer in doing an infallible job. In other words, I'm 'incapable of failing,' in the removal of your testicles. You *will* live, but you'll have great difficulty having an erection in the future. You see, by performing this make-shift surgery, I'm helping the helpless, victimized women in this world. I'll be *taking* what I want from you—your *most valued* possession. Men like you need to understand what it's like to be violated—to be stripped of everything you know and love. You need to *know* what it's like to have your world destroyed. Men like you rape their daughters *over* and *over* again without batting an eye. Bianca and I endured that abuse for a good length of time. I'm glad my uncle killed my father. In a way, I'm glad he killed every one of us—all except Bianca, the only survivor. From this day on, I'm positive you'll treat women with respect. Today's the last day you'll ever violate another woman. Are you ready?"

He peered into my eyes with pity, mumbling before I removed the tape from his mouth again.

"*Please* don't. Wait... just... wait a second, okay? You don't have to do this. I didn't rape you!"

"You don't get it. I *want* to do this."

"Please, don't. *Please!* I'm begging you!"

He cried in a way I never saw a man cry before. I annihilated his pride, tearing his defenses down.

"Human beings don't always learn until they experience pain and loss. Change comes afterward," I said.

I placed the tape over his mouth for the last time, and sterilized the scalpel, spritzing it with alcohol. A copious amount of his sweat dampened the table's musty felt. I retrieved my phone to reference the YouTube video of the castration procedure once again. I leaned in to flick his scrotum. He didn't flinch. My attention reverted to the screen.

"Okay, it looks like we're in good shape. I think you're ready. Fingers crossed!" His muffled screams grew louder, as the blade inched closer to his scrotum. "Oh, shut up! I didn't touch you, yet. Stop overreacting."

I wanted him to remember my face every time he so much as *glanced* at another woman. I performed the incision with delicacy. He was so numb from the ice, he didn't flinch much, but it was messy and a little disgusting, yet necessary.

"Hey, I'm almost through with the first testicle. Don't pass out, yet. You know, I'm sorry about having to do it this way—without anesthesia n' all. Alright, one down—one to go."

He cried, whimpering. Terrified. His testicle remained inside the mason jar before I made the second incision.

"So, I don't think you'll have much of a dating life after today. No hard feelings, but I'd say 'no' if you were to ask me out. Not my type, anyway. Well, one thing is for sure—we're not meant for each other, but fate *has* brought us together. Okay, now let's cut out the other one."

***

A few minutes passed before I removed the second testicle while following the instructional video.

"Wow... I did it! "Dr. Gallucci..." Kinda like the sound of that. Ugh, I never thought testicles looked like this. Weird—lookin' don't you think?"

They resided in the jar before I placed it near his head within his field of vision. He remained silent—awake, but unmoved—in and out of consciousness before I strolled upstairs to gather more towels. Kate and Shepard returned the moment I got to the top of the stairs, calling out to me after walking through the front door. I ignored them, assuming she would've freaked out, and also assumed Shepard would've been proud of me once he saw my assailant. I had no plans for my prisoner, but I believed fate would have taken its course. My actions, justified. Justice served.

17

Our Next Move

I RETRIEVED MY TOWELS, making my way back into the basement before Kate and Shepard spotted me. He took one look at me, staring longer than most people felt comfortable with. His eyes shifted from me to my assailant, and back to me without uttering a word. Kate gasped, covering her mouth with one hand and her gun in the other. I waited for the much-anticipated multitude of questions with my scalpel in hand.

"The hell is going on, here?" she said.

"Liz, what did you do?" asked Shepard.

"I did what was necessary. He broke in when you two left, threatened and molested Bianca, held her against her will, and tried killing her. I took care of it. Like always, I take care of it."

"Oh... my God you *are* insane. What the... oh, God is that his..." said Kate.

"Mm-hm. Oh, don't worry. He'll live. All done, now."

"We need to move him. He needs a doctor. The snow's building up, and we can't *walk* into an E.R. without being on camera. Damn. How did he find us? The moment this guy wakes up in the hospital, I'm sure he'll find a way to call Pascal or whoever sent him," said Shepard.

"Pascal didn't send him," I said.

"What? What do you mean he didn't send him? He's the only one twisting your arm," he said.

"Listen to me. It *wasn't* him. This *rapist* didn't know who I was talking about when I mentioned Pascal's name. Someone else is involved. Someone wants Bianca dead."

"What's this guy's name? Who else would be after you?" said Kate. She walked over to Shepard's side.

"No idea. He had no I.D.—just a wad of cash, wallet, knife, burner phone, and a gun." Kate stared at my assailant like she experienced a short daydream.

"Alright, well, he *can't* stay here. Gotta take him to the emergency room or something," she said. I took a step forward in her direction with my hands on my hips.

"I was gonna let him live, but I think I've changed my mind based on the circumstances," I said. She re-positioned her stance, pivoting her leg and folding her arms.

"What, are you, crazy? You can't just *kill* someone, Bea... Liz or whoever the f**k you are!" she said.

"Whatever! Take him and drop him off," I said.

"I can't *show up* and drop him off. I'm an FBI agent! Hospitals have surveillance."

"Wear a mask, leave him in front of the E.R., and you'll be fine," I said.

"Kate's right, Liz. She can't do it. Questions will be raised. I'll take him, and I'm sure whoever sent him will want an update. I'll hack his phone and pinpoint the origin of his incoming— outgoing calls."

"I'm coming with you," I said.

"That's a bad idea."

"I'm not staying here with her! Fugitive or not, I'm going with," I said.

Kate grew restless, gesturing with her hands as she spoke.

"Are you *listening* to yourself? What if you're caught, Liz? *Then* what, huh? You gonna *change* personalities and pretend to be someone else while you're in cuffs? Or maybe you'll find a magic wand nearby and disappear when the police spot you. Maybe those kids are better off without Bianca."

I expected a lot of her, but her comment was out of line. She understood how much I cared about Bianca, and how much Bianca cared for her children. I lost control of my temper, pinning her against the wall with my forearm pressed against her chest. The scalpel's blade, clenched in my other hand, rested on her throat, grazing the pores on her neck. She gripped her gun—the one sitting in her hip holster, and her eyes widened, transitioning into a strong, fixed leer. She was either ready to die or die trying.

"Liz, don't do anything stupid," said Shepard.

"I should kill you right here. Right now," I said.

I glared into her eyes. Her nostrils flared, and her breathing intensified. I believe she knew, without a shadow of a doubt that I could've sliced her throat faster than she could've drawn her gun. I didn't break eye contact and delivered an intense, taut stare—one that plunged into her depths, trying to spot a morsel of fear.

"You wanna kill me?" she said.

She lifted her chin, fixating her contemptuous glare. I pressed the blade against her neck, applying more pressure—forcing it deeper into her unblemished skin. I sought pleasure in the display of her pain but denied such enjoyment when she showed no emotion. Not a trace. As much as I wanted to slit her throat, I couldn't disappoint Bianca. We needed her alive. A revelation dawned on me while I scrutinized her character while peering into her eyes. She and I shared a similar trait. Hate and revenge birthed and fueled our motives, cut from the same cloth. Those two ingredients made us who we are, relying on them to survive. It kept us moving forward. I released her from my grasp before she exhaled and walked away, making her way upstairs.

"Liz, why the hell would you do that? You need to get a grip! She's our *partner,* and we all have a common goal. We're not here to fight each other!" said Shepard.

I glanced his way, tossed my scalpel on the table nearby, and plodded toward him, headed for the stairs.

"Shut up," I said.

I took a few steps past him, and he clasped my arm, forcing me to pause. I didn't care for his lecture, but he was going to say his piece, regardless.

"I don't know what happened when we left, and I know you're trying to protect Bea, but, you took it a little too far, in my opinion."

"Oh, is that so?" I asked.

"Yeah, it is. You could've tied him up for an interrogation, but now we have a kink to deal with."

"Look, when you experience being molested by someone you're supposed to trust, say what you want. Otherwise, keep your mouth shut. He was a problem the moment he entered this house, and I dealt with it. *No one* touches me or Bianca without my say-so. No one."

He stared at the floor and nodded before making eye contact again.

"I'm sorry. You're right. Just try playing nice with Kate, please. We *need* her, and can't get to Pascal if we're not all on the same page."

"Noted. Now, let go of my arm before we have another 'kink' to deal with."

I turned away and walked halfway up the stairs before a dizzy spell fell upon me. 'It' was happening again—the debilitating ringing. I held on to the rail with one hand to stabilize myself, and with the other, rubbed my temple. Shepard rushed over to me after I lost my footing. My first thought was to resist and fight through it, but I had no control. I needed to take a seat. Shepard's voice, while calling my name, carried through the air in distortion. My eyes grew heavy, and I covered my ears with hopes to somehow stop or ease the intense, high-pitched noise. It ceased seconds later.

"Wha—what happened? Shepard, what's going on?" I said.

He exhaled a sigh of relief, and I gasped, looking over to discover the man who attacked me restrained to the table. The sight of his testicles caused me to gag.

"Did I... Did she... ? I asked.

"Yeah... Liz's doing. This is how she left him. He's alive and unconscious, but we gotta get him to a hospital quick," he said.

"Where's Kate?"

"Upstairs somewhere. You two just had a fight, and she made her way past you a moment ago. We'll talk about that later. Right now we need to leave for the emergency room. Come with me, but you'll have to remain out of the camera's view, though. Promise me you'll stay in the car."

I understood why she removed his testicles. I would've been dead had she not intervened. Fragmented flashbacks of the attack, conversation, and dissection occurred.

"*Bea*—hello. Are you with me?" asked Shepard.

"Yeah... sorry. I'm starting to remember," I said.

"You'll be okay?"

"I'll be fine."

"Good. Wash up, change your clothes, and start the car. Here are the keys. I'll take care of this down here. Go. We don't have much time."

I did as he instructed, and headed upstairs, but not before receiving a nasty glare from Kate who paced back and forth in the kitchen while a pot of coffee brewed.

"It's me, Kate. Bianca. Shepard told me what happened. I'm so sorry."

"Your 'switch' is a lot to process right now, but...it's fine," she said.

I left her presence and made my way outside, turning the car's ignition. Shepard struggled to haul my assailant on his shoulder. We placed him in the back seat and swapped the license plate with an old one found in the basement.

"We'll be back soon," Shepard said to Kate. I turned my attention toward him. "You know where the hospital is?" I asked. He sped off. "Yeah—saw a sign on our way to the store earlier."

He went into depth, telling me about Elizabeth's conflict. I couldn't remember much—only fragments of the happening. My assailant uttered intermittent groans.

"How much longer?" I asked.

"About five miles up this way."

"You think he'll make it?"

Shepard peeked back at him. "Yeah, he'll live." It took us about fifteen minutes to arrive. We pulled into the emergency room parking lot. Security cameras were mounted everywhere, so he took no chances of being identified. He carried the assailant out of the car, plopping him onto the ground in between two cars. I handed him the jar and hopped into the driver's seat.

"C'mon. Let's go before someone sees you!" I said. He scurried back in.

"Do you think someone will find him?"

"Yeah. Step on it," he said.

"Think he'll rat us out when he wakes up?" I asked.

"To his boss, and only if he makes it. His pulse was faint––lots of blood loss. I took his wallet and phone. Gonna be a long while before he wakes, and even longer before the police can identify him."

"Okay, can you hack his phone?

"I think so—shouldn't be too hard. You know, I think we may need some help in the near future. I don't know how this guy found us, but I'm not taking any chances. You remember my friend, Ace—the one you met a few years back?"

"Yeah, I sold him that Renaissance painting he really liked. He lives in Harlem—uh, he had a missing thumb, right?" I said.

"He owes me a favor. I'm gonna contact him—tell him to meet us in the city. We can't stay here, anymore," he said.

I received a phone call from Pascal, and answered on the first ring, forcing Shepard to be quiet.

"Please let me talk to my kids."

"No. Pictures only. You do it, yet?" he asked.

A part of me wanted to peel the skin off his face and force-feed it to him. He was being difficult.

"I'm trying, and it isn't easy, but I'm getting close. I need to know something, though. What deal did you make with Lucas?"

"You have twenty-four hours, Bianca. Digging two four-foot graves, six feet deep is tough this time of year."

Our call ended. "*Hello? Hello?*" Frustration got the best of me, as I cried, thinking about my kids. I worried about their health and current living conditions. I pulled the car over to the side of the road to unleash my anger on the steering wheel, punching it before screaming as loud as possible. Tears ran down my cheeks.

"Talk to me. Bea, what happened?" asked Shepard. I couldn't control myself. My emotions, all-consuming.

"We have *twenty-four hours* to do what Pascal wants, or he's going to hurt my kids if I don't kill her. I'm gonna have to do it, Shep. I'm gonna do it!"

"Bea, look at me. *Look* at me! We're *going* to get them back, but we need that recording as leverage. We'll get it. It's the only way to buy us more time and make a trade. But first, let's get back to the cabin to hack this guy's phone. Look, who's to say Pascal won't hurt them if Kate's dead, anyway?"

Shepard had everything under control, and I trusted him with my life. I also trusted him with my children's lives. Pascal's threat, although eminent, punched a hole right through me, as their pictures appeared on my phone. I was joyous they were alive and unscathed, but their existence carried an expiration date.

"Bea, take deep breaths. Inhale through your nose and exhale out your mouth, okay?"

I followed his lead, mimicking a breathing exercise. My tears ceased, and my heart returned to its normal rhythm.

"Lucas won't let anything happen to them, right?" I said.

He reached for my hand, holding it tight.

"We'll give Pascal what he deserves. Everything will work out. I promise you. C'mon, let's switch seats."

He drove, and I received a call from Claire. She asked about my well-being and if I got wind of anything new concerning the kids. I found comfort in the sound of her voice.

"They're alive and well, thank God. Listen, if Lucas calls you, don't answer. If he or anyone else you didn't invite comes knocking at your door, don't let them in, okay?

"Bea, you're scaring me. What's this all about? What does Lucas have to do with Michael and Isabelle being kidnapped?" she said.

"He's involved somehow. I don't have the proof yet, but I can't trust him," I said.

"Where are you?"

"I'm near Lake George."

Shepard's eyes widened. He snatched my phone from me and shut it off.

"What the hell are you doing?" he said.

"What's your problem? Why would you do that?"

"You can't tell *anyone* where we are!"

"It's *only* Claire... my *best* friend."

"Doesn't matter! We can't trust *anyone* except me and Kate."

"Look, *I* trust Claire. She's always helped me when I needed her. We know everything about each other."

He remained silent and didn't care that he was angry with me, judging by his posture and demeanor. I struggled with processing his reaction to my conversation with her.

"Give it back."

"*Do not* call her again."

"Fine. *Alright*! I won't."

He handed it to me, and as we continued driving, neither one of us had much to say. The car keys jingled every time we hit a pothole, and the coarse friction of fresh snow and rubber carried on until we got back to the cabin. We hurried inside.

"Are we in the clear? What's wrong?" asked Kate.

"Pack your things," said Shepard.

"What happened?"

"We gotta leave, like, now. It's no secret someone knew our location and waited until we left to attack Bea. We're sitting ducks, here, and another threat was made by Pascal, wanting you dead in a day's time. We're gonna have to take our chances back in the city. I'll hack that guy's phone as fast as I can. The both of you should start packing. We need to hurry."

"Bianca, you're still all over the news," said Kate. She turned toward the television. Almost every major network displayed my photo.

"Turn it off. I can't deal—never imagined this. I wanna get out of this mess. My sincerest apologies to you for what Elizabeth did to you earlier, by the way. I'll do everything in my power to control her. She can be quite unpredictable and aggressive."

"No kidding... and thanks," she said.

"I just want my kids," I said. "Truce?"

"Truce. Now, come on, I'll take you guys back."

Shepard was on his computer doing what he did best while Kate and I gathered our belongings. She lent a helping hand, and for the first time, she and I got along without any lingering animosity.

"Got it! I *got* 'em!" said Shepard.

"You got the address?" I said.

"Not quite. Triangulation isn't enough—it doesn't give exact locations, but I can piggyback Internet router frequencies within the triangle to pinpoint its current location. Finding the owner is impossible—most likely a burner phone."

"Okay, so where is it coming from?" I asked.

"The city. Looks like Midtown... on the northeast corner of 42nd and 3rd. I'll be able to pin its exact location the closer we get. Let's leave."

A sudden revelation illuminated my thinking, as I connected the dots. I couldn't move my feet, and yes, I wanted to but they wouldn't budge. That street corner was all-to familiar. I didn't want it to be true. An avalanche of despair rendered me motionless. Shepard and Kate headed toward the door, ready to leave with their belongings in hand.

"Bea, what's the matter? We gotta go," he said.

"I know that corner—42nd and 3rd. Francis works in that building."

18

Betrayal

KATE DROVE. I SAT ON THE BACK SEAT in a daze, displaced from the rest of the world. My eyes took an inadvertent glance into the rearview mirror, catching Kate's as well. She winked, reassuring me everything would be okay before cracking the silence.

"We're gonna get Pascal, Bea. Thank you—the both of you—for helping me track him down."

"I should be the one thanking *you*. We escaped the city, thanks to you. You know, when I first hired you, I never pegged you to be the tough-girl type. Well-played."

"For what it's worth—again, I'm sorry," she said.

Moments later, our attention shifted, looking straight ahead at the long line of cars a tenth of a mile away.

"Wait, what's going on? I can't see anything around the corner. Someone check it out," said Kate. Shepard checked his phone.

"Google maps says it's a major accident. No one's moving anytime soon. The road's shut down. We can't sit here. It's one o'clock, and we need to be in that building before five pm. Kate, how far is the train station from here?" he asked.

"Seven to ten minutes—give or take," she said.

"Even if we *do* drive through, the snow is only gonna delay our trip the closer we get to the city. Take the next exit up ahead, and we'll catch the next train. It's our best bet."

"He's right. We can't risk it," I said.

The diverted, off-ramp traffic jam took about ten minutes to travel through before we found a clear path to the station. I asked Shepard, within the time, to do a background check on Grace Willow, Francis' assistant.

"What's it for," he asked.

"Just a precaution. We might need it."

***

We arrived soon enough, driving up to the entrance. Kate waited in the car while we stood in a short line, inside. We got lucky, getting tickets without a guarantee of buying them. Perhaps the universe was on our side. Shepard gave her a call, wishing her safe travels driving back into the city. She held on to our luggage until later that night during our scheduled rendezvous.

We soon boarded the train, and it departed to Grand Central. Being in unfamiliar territory made me nervous, but I kept my wits and followed Shepard's lead. Luck was in our favor, and I hoped it remained that way. I wore half of my disguise, forgetting my wig in my duffel bag. My ball cap obstructed the view of my face. Our seats happen to be in the last train car, and I avoided eye contact with everyone, keeping my head down as much as possible.

"I gotta take a leak. Be back in a flash, okay?" said Shepard.

"Don't worry about me," I said.

He walked away. The periodic glance from a stranger with a tablet in hand two seats in front of me made me restless. Average height, husky, and breathing with his mouth open, he continued asserting his gaze. His eyeglasses resided in the breast pocket of his untucked dress shirt. He removed them, placing them on the bridge of his nose, eyeballing me. I turned my head to avoid making eye contact, hoping and praying he wouldn't recognize me. A descending clamor of anxiety bounded me so tight, I couldn't sit still. *Please come back! Oh, God, I hope this guy stops staring!* I got up and left, walking toward the creepy stranger and into Shepard's direction. He peered while adjusting his glasses, examining my every move. Shepard exited the bathroom. His expression, fixed. I scurried to his side, ready to expose the creep before Shepard cupped my elbow, guiding me inside with him.

"We have to get off this train. The man across from me recognizes me."

"Are you sure?"

"I'm positive. He kept staring and scrolling on his tablet! We have to get off this train, Shep. We *have* to do something!"

"The short-nosed, white guy with the ugly shirt—glasses in his pocket?"

"Yeah, him!"

"We can't get off, yet. There isn't another stop until we get to Grand Central. Let's head back. Follow my lead, okay? I got this."

"What do you plan on doing?"

"We'll be fine. Just do as I tell you."

We opened the door and peeked out to discover "Glasses" heading our way with his phone in hand. Shepard reached behind his back and removed his Glock from his waist, pointing it at the man as he walked by.

"Psst," said Shepard.

'Glasses' looked up and froze, unable to move a muscle. Shepard pressed his finger against his own lips, gesturing to stay quiet. He also motioned with his hand, 'come here' to enter the bathroom. The stranger complied, mincing toward us before being grabbed by his collar.

"Don't make a sound. Close the door behind you," said Shepard.

He pinned him against the wall with an open palm, using brute force. "Open your mouth," he said. He followed his orders, crying and shaking while Shepard placed the barrel in his mouth. "Give her your phone." His hand trembled while extending his arm.

"Why were you staring at me, earlier?" I said. Shepard removed the gun from his mouth. His short, shallow breaths made it difficult for him to respond. "You know who I am, don't you?" He nodded, exhaling with a subtle wheeze. "I *knew* it. So, what are we going to do with him?"

"What's your name?" Shepard asked him.

"Ma—Marty."

"Marty, you seem to be a law-abiding citizen, and I know you think you're doing the right thing by trying to alert the authorities—which is why you headed this way—to inform the car attendant, right? That would be a mistake. Wouldn't it?" He nodded, staring at Shepard while the Glock pressed against his ribcage. "So, here's what's gonna happen. My lady friend, here, is going back to her seat, and *we* are going to chat. Any other electronic devices on you?"

"No, sir, only my iPad in my overhead compartment. That's all. I swear." I checked his pockets and found nothing.

"Bea, start heading back. He and I are going to get acquainted."

He whimpered before I could exit the bathroom. I took my time, making my way back before I watched them both—Marty walking down the aisle with Shepard behind him. He sat next to Marty in silence with his gun concealed under his coat. Shepard turned his attention to me—jerking his head, motioning that I join them. As instructed, Marty reached for his iPad in his overhead storage and handed it to me. I was curious to find out what he viewed, examining his search history log. *Bingo*! My intuition didn't fail me. He was reading my article in the New York Times.

"So what do we do with you, Marty? We don't *wanna* hurt you, but things will get unpleasant if we feel threatened in any way. All we want is to get off this train and get to the people who kidnapped my kids. We won't have any reason to be unreasonable, as long as you cooperate."

"I won't cause any problems. I swear," said Marty.

"Good. We understand each other."

"Give me your I.D.," said Shepard.

***

He became our priority—compliant for the remainder of the ride with nothing to say until we arrived at Grand Central Station. We were the last people to off-board the train. Shepard returned Marty's electronics the moment we stepped onto the platform. I thanked him for not causing a scene.

"I'm curious. Is it true what the news is saying?" he asked.

"You got any kids, Marty?" I said.

"A sixteen-year-old son."

"Is there anything you wouldn't do for him?"

"I'll do *anything* to keep him safe."

I displayed a curt smile before walking away with Shepard.

"I don't think he'll call the police, Shep." He removed his phone from his pocket to viewed the screen.

"I think you're right. Let's hurry. The signal is still active," he said.

People aren't aware of all the facts, yet quick to judge. The media painted a picture that depicted me as a monster. Sure some truth resided in that, but my actions rendered justified in my eyes. I'm sure Marty felt as though he was exercising his civic duty, protecting himself and others around him. I was glad Elizabeth let me handle that situation.

***

Shepard and I walked a few blocks toward the corner of 42nd and 3rd avenue. I stood in front of the building like I had many times before, but that time felt different. I experienced a moment of surrealism, being in search of the truth under such circumstances. He checked his phone again, tracing and confirming the signal he found earlier.

"Still active," he said. I contemplated the possible outcomes, standing on the southwest corner.

"Bea, hell or high water, are you ready for this?" asked Shepard.

"Yeah... I am. Look, there's a chance we can just waltz in, but I left my wig in my duffel bag."

He removed his phone from his pocket to search a wig store nearby.

"I found one a few blocks north of here. Let's get you a pair of glasses, too. We can make it back in time if we hurry."

***

We found what we needed and returned to the building minutes later. I wore a blonde wig, and black, retro-looking eyeglasses. Amble security occupied the lobby. A steady, confident walk was as important as the friendly nod he gave a guard while holding my hand. The real challenge was getting through the security doors upstairs. I kept my head down, and he took another look at his phone. We boarded the elevator with a bunch of strangers. He and I stood in the back.

"Which floor?" I said.

"According to this, it's somewhere on the 31st." My fears, confirmed, yet, still I hoped to be mistaken.

"Are you sure?"

"Take a look for yourself, he said. He handed me his phone. A tear fell from my eyes, running down my cheek. "What's wrong?"

"... Nothing," I said.

"Bea, what's wrong?"

" ... "

I didn't want to say, but he deserved to hear my thoughts. I caved, telling him what was on my mind.

"Bea, what's wro—"

"Francis' office is on the 31st floor."

"Your *shrink?*" A succinct nod sufficed. "You think *he* has something to do with—"

"I don't know. I *hope* not."

As I handed the phone back to him, a sense of unrelenting dread encompassed me—almost too much to handle. I did the best I could to remain calm—to act inconspicuous.

Shepard and I didn't speak any more until our destination. My muscles tensed and my heart raced faster. *Ding!* The doors parted, and my adrenaline rush began to dissipate the second I stepped off. Bravery filled the gap in my dread. Shepard checked his phone again, re-confirming the location.

"The signal's there to our left," he said.

"This is Francis' office."

We stood in front of two large glass doors. I removed my glasses, placing them in my pocket, wanting him to recognize me. Grace Willow, the receptionist arose from behind the desk, greeting us with a smile about forty feet away.

"There's no doubt the signal is coming from the space behind her," said Shepard.

"Okay, so what do we do?"

"Hi, can I help you two with something?" said Grace. Her voice carried over the small intercom box. She didn't recognize me, so I pressed the intercom button to communicate.

"Grace, it's me, Bianca Gallucci. I need to talk to Francis," I said.

"Oh... Bianca? Um... hold on a sec. I'll get him on the line."

She sat down. Her smile transitioned into a frown—her eyebrows furrowed, eyes widened and moved with rigidity before reaching for the phone. Shepard removed his gun from the inside of his coat, pointing it at her through the glass. She trembled at the sight of it.

"Don't touch the phone, Grace. I know you're scared, and we don't want to hurt you, but he *will* shoot right through this glass if you touch it. I'm sure you want to see your daughter, Emily, and your husband, Sam, tonight for dinner, right? Do as I say, and there won't be any trouble. I need you to let us in, okay?" Her breathing labored and her hand shook.

"Just buzz me in," I said. "Open the door, Grace. We're not going to ask again." She hesitated, but buzzed us in, granting access. Shepard bustled toward her, pointing his gun.

"Hands. Let me see your hands," he said. I entered after him, and he scurried toward Francis' office door behind her.

"Open it," he said. She quivered in her chair.

"I can't. He locks it from the inside when he doesn't want to be disturbed," she said.

"Bea, keep an eye on her. Don't move a muscle, Grace. Do you hear me? Do you understand?" said Shepard. He stared into her eyes, firing rounds of fear into her soul. She nodded and swallowed so loud we both heard it. "Take her phone. Unplug the landline, too."

I did as he asked, unapologetic to her. Shepard stepped back and lunged his foot forward into the door, forcing it open. It slammed against the office wall. Francis stood from behind his desk.

"What in the bloody hell is going on? Who are you?" he asked.

"Shut up and sit down," said Shepard. His gun pointed at him.

"What do you want? I'll give you whatever you want— just don't kill me, please!"

"We don't wanna kill you. We want answers."

"We? Answers to what? I don't know what you're talking about."

I strolled into his office, making myself visible with Grace by my side—my hand gripping her tricep.

"*Bianca?* What's going on? What are you doing here?"

"Hi, there, Francis."

The truth, resulting in that manner uploaded a great deal of disappointment for me. I *had* to confront him—he of all people. He was someone I trusted—someone I never thought ill of. *"Trust no one,"* came to mind, like a phantom whisper into my ear.

"Shepard, check the exact location of that signal again... and give me your gun." He reached into the inside lining of his coat pocket and removed one.

"Here. Take it. I knew you'd forget about it at some point," he said.

He sauntered about the office, trying to pinpoint the location of the signal. I was holding the Glock Pascal gave me a few days ago—the one he wanted me to use on Kate—the one I threw in the garbage along with my phones and purse. I wielded dominance, having such power without Elizabeth.

"Grace. Francis. Stand in front of the couch. Move. *Now*," I said.

They scurried into the middle of the office, standing next to the small marble statue sitting on the end table. I stood a few feet from them. Shepard slowed down, taking small steps. The signal beeped, pointing to the sofa where I used to sit during my sessions. I turned my attention to Francis.

"I *trusted* you! Why did you try having me killed?"

"What? I don't know what *you're talking about!* Why would I do that?"

"*Don't you* lie to me, Francis! I *swear to God* I will shoot you!"

"Why would I want to hurt you? It doesn't make any sense, Bianca!"

"You sent someone to kill me this morning, and we traced the correspondence back to this location—this office. *Why* Francis?"

"How could you even entertain such a question? We've known each other a *long* time, Bianca. This doesn't make any sense to me!"

Shepard removed the cushions and found a phone lodged in between the upholstered frame. Francis raised his eyebrows. His lips, parted.

"Bingo," said Shepard.

"No, no, no. That's not mine. I swear."

"Whose is it, Francis?" I asked.

"I don't know, Bea. Never seen it before in my life. I swear it!"

"Then explain how this burner got here," said Shepard.

I was sick of the lies, and sick of the secrets that left a gaping hole within. I was fed up with the games. Dejected. Despondent. *Everyone* was in the loop except me.

"Give me your wallet, Francis, " I said.

"What? Why?"

"Do it!" I said.

I raised my gun, pointing it at his head. He scrambled to remove it from his pocket before extending his trembling arm.

"Toss it over to Shepard."

He caught it, asking, "What am I looking for?" Francis' breathing pattern changed. He also avoided eye contact. *I'm not leaving until I get what I need.*

"You're looking for a gold card, Shep. No imprinting or inscriptions anywhere. It looks like an ordinary hotel key, but I'm willing to bet it's more significant than that."

He continued looking through Francis' thick wallet and discovered a few cards, but nothing matching the description I gave. Grace kept her mouth shut, never uttering a word. She stared at the floor without lifting an eyelid. It took Shepard a few moments to sort through everything, but he found the exact item I described. "I got it," he said. I couldn't handle Francis being a bastard like Lucas. The debilitating sting of betrayal lodged its way into my back, like a knife forced into my spine. My impulse was to blow his head clean off. I cocked the gun and took a few deep breaths before pressing the barrel against his forehead. He shook, having no control over his body.

"I don't want to, but if you don't tell me what you know, I *will* pull this trigger, and I'll kill Grace afterward. Don't make me a monster, Francis."

"Bianca, if there's anything I can do to make this right..."

"*Make this right*? Start talking!" I said.

He frowned, and his eyes welled up before shaking his head. That's when I learned he did something he couldn't take back. A tear fell down my face, not that I felt remorse for him, but because I arrived at the end of myself. The thought of ending his life—*actually* erasing his life crossed my mind under such duress. His betrayal thrashed around my chest like a violent storm at sea. I waited for the ringing in my ears to commence, but nothing happened. I needed Elizabeth, but she didn't surface while I anticipated my transition. No blackout to embarked upon—no headache, but I soon experienced an inner strength—a heavy mutation of Elizabeth morphing over me. My identity dwindled. Empathy slipped away. I was ready to pull the trigger, glowering at him with my heart slamming against my rib cage. I wanted to *so* much, the desire overflowed. *This is what I'm becoming. This inner strength—this calloused heart I now have.*

'It' happened. Elizabeth transitioned so seamlessly. So subtle. If killing him would've somehow brought my children back into my arms, I wouldn't have hesitated. The transition commenced in full, but not as before. I was aware of my identity, yet, in some way aware of Elizabeth's, too. I took charge and released the gun's safety. Shepard stepped forward.

"Now, wait, think about this. I know it's hard," said Shepard. He approached me. "You don't need to kill him. Look, I know he betrayed your trust, but he's not who we want. Besides, he *knows something*. We need him alive, Bea. We both know Elizabeth wouldn't hesitate to shoot him, so you *have to* fight her. Dead men don't talk."

"I *am* Elizabeth, Shepard—just not the way you're used to me showing up. It's only a matter of time before she and I become one."

"*Bea*, if you're still in there, I need you to give me the gun... please. We don't go around killing people because we get emotional. It's *not* what we do."

Shepard advanced toward me with his palm facing the gun. I ignored him.

"Francis! Tell me, why are you working with Pascal?"

"I'm not!"

"You're still lying!" I yanked his collar, and shoved him against the wall, pressing the barrel against his jaw. "Open your mouth."

"Okay! Okay! I'll tell you what I know." He wept, displaying a waterfall of tears. "Oh, God... I didn't get it from him! I got it fr—"

Without warning, Shepard fell to the floor before I could make sense of the dull, muffled sound coming from behind me. Grace dropped the marble statue, scuttling out of the office. Francis took advantage of the distraction and pushed me so hard, I stumbled, hitting my head on the coffee table.

***

I struggled to stand, staggering toward Shepard, waking up with clarity seconds later as myself again.

"You okay?" I asked.

"I'll be fine. Let's go," he said.

We staggered toward the reception desk where I was able to catch a glimpse of the closing elevator. Francis and Grace, from my angle, disappeared. Shepard leaned against the desk, gathering his bearings.

"Are you alright? Can you stand?" I said.

"Yeah, gimme a sec. Where'd they go?"

"They took the elevator. Come on!"

We hoped to capture them as soon as possible before they left the building. Traveling down the staircase toward the lobby was our only option. As luck would have it, I happened to see the elevator opening on the 20th floor. People walked in. No one walked off. I had a hunch—a nagging intuitive nudge he was on that *exact* one. Shepard followed my lead out of the stairwell and toward the elevator.

"There he is," I said.

Grace wasn't with him, and it was safe to assume she got off on an unknown floor. We entered, drawing zero attention to ourselves—and kept our eyes on him like hawks watching its prey. We made our way toward the back. His face draped with disappointment before his heavy exhale. Shepard and I stood on either side of him.

We watched his every move—every twitch and nervous tic. He was *not* getting away again, and I, judging by his tensed posture, believed he knew that too. No way of him escaping until we got to the lobby. *Ding!* The elevator door opened, and I whispered into his ear, "Don't try anything stupid."

We were the last to walk off. He complied and made his way through the lobby with one of us on either side. Emergency sirens wailed, bouncing off the marble-tiled walls. We figured Grace notified the authorities. Security officers dispersed, and again, he took advantage of the distraction, pushing us out of the way. He sprinted through the entrance doors, and into the occupied street, disregarding traffic. It was difficult, chasing him on foot during rush hour. Francis was the only person who could provide me with a clue. Car tires screeched while he dashed through the busy intersection of 42nd and 3rd avenue. Such commotion alerted the attention of the nearby crossing guards. He made his way into Bryant Park, unscathed, where the thick, unforgiving crowd of people elevated my frustration. I *had* to catch him.

"Francis! Stop!" He ignored us, frantic and glancing back.

"Francis! Please stop! It's me. Bea!"

He kept running until he paused to catch his breath on the southeast corner of 42nd and 6th. I stood in front of him, trying to calm him down on the busy sidewalk.

"Stop! Stay away from me... the both of you! I'll yell 'gun' if I have to!" he said.

"Tell me what you know. Who gave you the gold card, and why did you have that phone?" I said.

"*No*. You don't understand! They'll kill my family if I talk!"

"*Who*, Francis? Pascal?"

"I can't... I can't say, but I swear on my children's lives that phone isn't mine."

"Then whose is it? If it isn't yours, then it's gotta be one of your patients. Did you see any patients today?" asked Shepard.

"Only an eighteen-year-old boy I've been seeing for the last six months, and he's in a wheelchair."

"Think! Has anyone—*anyone* else visited you *at all*, today?" asked Shepard.

Francis' eyes widened and his mouth opened like he experienced some kind of epiphany.

"What is it, Francis? You can tell me," I said.

"Oh my God. Why would she... No, it can't be her..."

A child walked in-between us. I moved to the side, trying to guide her out of my way.

"It can't be who, Francis?"

His head lurched backward in a fraction of a second. His eyes, nor eyelids moved. A dark hole appeared in the middle of his forehead. Brain matter and blood jolted out the other side before his body became limp, falling to the cement. I couldn't believe what I was seeing. My instincts compelled me to run for cover, yet I wanted to scurry to his aid. I couldn't do anything for him, but I thought either Shepard or I would've been the next immediate target. Oh, my God. *This can't be happening. Francis!*

19

Reflection

I REMAINED IN A DIMINISHED, foggy frame of mind. Witnessing Francis' death cascaded a light on my mortality. My bewildered brain couldn't handle such a thing, seeing a friend massacred. I cried on the inside, yet identified the lingered devilish smirk Elizabeth loved displaying. She reveled in the presence of danger and death to those whom she believed deserved it. I wished to un-see Francis' face, and couldn't stop the constant loop of his demise, which functioned like a movie excerpt in my mind. Every frame and fraction of a second fragmented, as if his murder occurred in slow motion. I tried recalling the sound of a gunshot. No distinctive sounds stood out to me—only Francis' last words, "*No, it can't be her.*"

"Bea, let's go!" said Shepard. He held my hand, continuing down the block. I struggled to move my legs, tottering along the sidewalk. I would've stood in place, staring if he didn't pull me away.

"Bea! *Let's go!*"

He pulled my wrist, forcing me to run. I staggered along, looking back at Francis multiple times in a state of shock. We had no choice but to take a cab, leaving his body on the frigid, unforgiving cement. Shepard closed the door.

"We're in a hurry," he said.

"Where do you want to go?" asked the cab driver.

"I'll give you a hundred bucks to drive six blocks north of here as fast as you can."

I sat traumatized at the crowd of people swarming Francis's body, as we drove past the crime scene. The distance between us grew at an exponential rate. My gaze out the window lasted as long as possible until my visibility of him diminished. I turned my head, facing forward, glancing at the driver through the rearview mirror, but our eyes didn't meet. Elizabeth's eyes appeared, instead, smiling. The likelihood of any eyes meeting from my angle proved to be impossible. "Turn the radio off," I said to the driver. He honored my request before adjusting his rearview. Shepard was on the phone with Kate, asking her if we could stay at her apartment. Claire called me, but I didn't answer––and my eyes welled up, reluctant to deliver the bad news.

"Kate, hold on—you know what, we're on our way there. Thanks," he said. He hung up, diverting his attention to me.

"I'm so sorry about Francis."

I showed him the missed call and text from Claire which read, "I'm worried about you. Where are you, Bea? You hear from the kids, yet?" How was I going to tell her, her cousin died because of me—because of the choices I made? *Or maybe it was the choices he made?* Regardless, she had no clue of his death, and I couldn't stop thinking of his last words.

"Shep, Francis never finished what he was saying. He said, "No, it can't be her," I said. "It can't be who?"

"Do you remember the look on his face right before he said that?" he asked.

"Every detail."

"He knew who 'she' was. Trust me. I saw that look *many* times before. Whomever she is, he knew her well."

Shepard bit his lip, exhaling before turning his head away from me. Something bothered him—like, there was something he wanted to say but held back.

"What? What's on your mind?" I asked.

"Nothing. It's nothing. Just a theory."

"What is it?"

"I don't wanna upset you any more than you are."

"Just tell me!"

"Okay, look. In my experience, the people closest to us are the ones most likely to stab us in the back, right? What if... hear me out... but what if it was someone he trusted with his life who planted the phone? Who does he trust the most besides his wife and kids?"

"Clai—no. Forget I said that. It can't be her. It's gotta be his wife or something." I lifted my eyebrows.

"And her motive would be?" asked Shepard.

"Money? I dunno. Claire wouldn't do something like that to me *or* to him. She has no motive!"

"Alright! Like I said, only a hunch, but the only way for us to be sure is if I hack the security footage from Francis' office and building. If she was there, she's the one," he said.

I had nothing else to divulge. She had no reason for wanting to hurt me. I understood his theory, but Claire and I would die for each other.

"Drive around the block, please," he said aloud while texting. My mind floated upon a sea of worry. Emotions flowed free, thinking of Francis and the future impact on Claire. My short-lived, asphyxiated grave of guilt and anxiety lasted until we arrived at Kate's place—which was about fifteen minutes away. However, something strange happened minutes before arrival. Elizabeth integrated more of herself in me, making my mind her habitat. It was like she packed a suitcase, abandoned her home, and strolled into mine, *telling* me she was moving in. Or more like she glued a puzzle piece of her soul into a compartment of my core. The more she merged and consumed my identity, the more seamless my transformation. Her presence, viral. The pain of Francis' death subsided in seconds, and I grew stronger in mind and heart in the minutes followed. His passing, surreal, yet I could only imagine Pascal was the one responsible.

***

We got out of the cab, arriving at Kate's place, and made our way upstairs. Shepard picked the lock again, but of course, with her permission. We entered, seeing our luggage Kate dropped off, sitting next to the couch. My body and mind drained themselves of energy by that time of day. I laid down on her couch—the most comfortable place in the world, and closed my eyes. Francis' face appeared in an instant. I sat up in a panic, expelling a heavy exhale. Shepard searched the cabinets, bringing me a glass of Vodka.

"You alright? Here, drink this. It'll take the edge off," he said. I gulped it without batting an eye.

"Thanks," I said.

"You should change your clothes, shower, and figure out our next move. The phone we found was a burner. Untraceable. I'll hack the building security footage recordings from earlier. There's still hope, Bea." I stood near the window, exhaled, and stared out. "Again, my condolences about Francis. Not easy seeing him gunned down like a dog. It must've been a sniper."

"How do you do it, Shep? How are you so calm after everything? Doesn't all this scare you?"

"My world doesn't involve seeing murdered people on a daily basis, but I have come to a crossroads before when I *had* to pull the trigger. We *do* what we must to survive, Bea. Don't feel guilty for pointing the gun at him in his office. You did what you *had to* for your kids—and in that alone is *all* the justification you need."

"You should shower first. I'm gonna lie here a little," I said.

He kissed my forehead before heading into the bathroom to shower. I continued staring out the living room window, pondering my loss. My phone buzzed, and it was about the one-millionth time Lucas called me. I refused to respond to his earlier texts and voicemails unless by some miracle he stated he had the kids. I chose to reply to Claire's text first. "I'm alright, and the kids are okay, but still out of my reach." The guilt weighed me down, standing there in front of the window. I was alone with my thoughts, walking back to the couch, but paused a moment, staring at the large mirror hanging on the wall. A time of reflection embarked, analyzing the woman I evolved into. Returning to the 'old me' wasn't an option. *My greed got me here.* I screwed up, and I couldn't live with myself if anything worse happened to the kids. They were suffering because of me. I missed them dearly and was willing to fight to my death, if necessary. I stared at my reflection and beheld a woman morphing into someone she never thought imaginable. *Everything will be alright.*

I turned my body away from the mirror with the intention of heading back to the couch. I paused, freezing in motion— noticing something strange about my mirrored image. It didn't follow me, catching it from the corner of my eye. It stood still, behaving like its own individual. *What? Lizzy? This is a dream, right? I've gotta be dreaming.* She read my mind, responding to my thoughts.

"That's always been the problem, Bea. You were always the dreamer, growing up. I was always the doer."

"Liz, how is this happening? How are you... here?"

"I'm here because you want me to be. Deep down inside, you need me."

"But, I don't understand. I haven't seen you *all* these years since you died. Where have you been?"

"I awoke within you when you saw our uncle, and I'm here to warn you. Your journey is gonna get more difficult."

"It always gets worse before it gets better." She smiled from ear to ear without showing any teeth.

"It *was* you in the rear-view mirror, smiling while we drove away from Francis' body, wasn't it?"

"I was trying to give you the strength you needed."

I was still in shock, talking to my sister, but the more we talked, the more I was willing to accept such a strange hallucination... if one at all.

"Lizzy, I can't do this without you. I need you."

"Don't worry. I always got your back, and we'll *always* be together."

"So, can I trust Shepard one-hundred percent?"

"He has your best interest at heart."

"Liz, I want my kids back. Pascal is making my life a living hell, but we *can't* kill him, alright? I won't ever see them again if you do."

"I won't. You have my word. We'll get them back, Bea. I'm with you every step of the way."

Her promise delivered comfort, safety, and strength, knowing she was with me all the way. I extended my hand, touching the mirror's surface in anticipation of her energy. She did the same, and I experienced a solid, internal transformation commencing—a 'shedding of old skin'. A slow-moving metamorphosis. Transitioning *into* Elizabeth over time—a beautiful monster, rendered me helpless to acknowledge the person I once was would disappear forever. A whirlwind sweep through my soul, lasting only a few seconds before Shepard entered the room, startling me.

"Hey, where's Kate?" he asked.

"Um... I dunno. It's just me."

"I thought I... who were you talking to, then?"

"No one."

"I could've sworn... never mind."

He walked away. I glanced back at the mirror, and Liz disappeared as quickly as she appeared. I stood in awe of the phenomenon, invigorated and more powerful.

***

Shepard and I sat down a half-hour later to talk about our plan for getting the kids back while eating some Chinese takeout.

"Someone didn't want Francis talking. You didn't see the shooter or hear a gunshot earlier, right?"

"No. Nothing—no one," I said.

"The only conclusion we can draw is our mystery shooter didn't want us dead. Our only option is to contact Pascal and tell him we have what he wants."

"Are you saying we should betray Kate?"

"No. Let's present a counter-offer. We deliver Kate, telling him she refuses to cooperate, and *then* ambush him. *Or...* after we get the recording, we leverage him, putting him in a position where he'll *have to* back down when we threaten to publicize," he said.

"What if he thinks we're bluffing, and he does something terrible? No, wait. I think he knows how much I want to see my kids again. He'll continue using them as leverage."

"You're right. It wouldn't work. If I were Pascal, I would imagine copies exist. We need the recording from Kate, regardless. We'll talk to her about that when she gets here. I'm gonna call her about something else first," he said.

He picked up the phone off the counter to call. She answered after a few rings.

"Kate, it's Shepard. Bea and I are here in your apartment. You're on speakerphone."

"How are you two doing?" she asked.

"We're fine, and we're trying to devise a plan. Do you have a moment to look something up for me?"

"Um, yeah, I was about to leave work, but I can help. What do you guys need?"

"Bea's therapist, Dr. Francis Summers. Have you heard of him before? We don't think he had anything to do with Pascal, but can you do a check into his extended family as well?"

"Sure thing. Hey, I'm not supposed to tell you this, but we acquired an art smuggling case a few weeks ago—some new player leaving signature initials 'F.S.' on every painting. They traced it to a storage facility in Brooklyn. You think it's the same guy?"

"Dunno. You think it might be a coincidence?" asked Shepard.

"It's a stretch, but anything's possible. And no one's seen this person. For all we know, the signature could be an alias of an alias. The last art heist like this was in France—Paris to be exact."

"Okay, thanks, we'll see you when you get here." He hung up the phone. Bea, do you think Francis stole those paintings?" he asked.

"No. Not a chance in hell," I said.

"How are you so sure? Did you know him well enough? Did you trust him with your life?"

"Yes, I trusted him, and he helped me. He never hung anything expensive in his office. Paintings weren't his thing," I said.

"I'm sorry I had to ask her about him, but someone knows something, and they're not talking. Kate doesn't have any leads on her end. It may take her division weeks or years to solve, if ever."

"So, we're searching for a ghost—someone like you. Great!" I said.

***

I sat with my arms crossed. Kate arrived about an hour later, opening the door.

"It's just me," she said. "No one saw you guys come in, right?"

"We were careful," said Shepard.

He sat behind the coffee table cleaning his gun. She walked into the kitchen to pour herself a glass of water before sitting down in the living room with her legs crossed. As our conversation progressed, we told her about Francis and our plan. Shepard shifted back and forth between cleaning his weapon, talking, and texting. Kate agreed that using the recording might backfire—and the smartest way to subdue him was by surprise. She didn't tell us where she hid it. I paced back and forth, eager to resolve my problems.

"We should just give Pascal what he wants to end all this bloodshed. Where's the recording, Kate?" I asked.

"I can't tell you that, yet. He'll hunt me down and kill me, regardless. Then he'll hunt you down and kill everyone you love, too. I'm sorry, but it's better you don't know."

"Fine, but this plan better work. Shepard, who are you texting?" I asked.

"Ace," he said.

"What if this plan goes sideways? Then what?" asked Kate.

"We have 'Ace'—a friend who'll be our eyes when we decide to execute. He says he's game," said Shepard.

"This... 'Ace' guy—you trust him?" she said. She sauntered about the room.

"Indefinitely. I got him out of a jam a few years back, so he owes me," said Shepard.

"He's here in the city?" she asked.

"In the neighborhood, sitting in the bodega across the street as we speak." His phone chimed. "Oh, just got his text."

"What does this guy do for a living? How's he gonna help us?" asked Kate.

"He does 'contract' work. That's all I can tell you."

"Okay, do we get to meet him?"

"I met him once at one of my past events. I trust Shepard, and Shepard trusts him, so... are we gonna do this or not?" I said.

"Use me as bait," she said. "Pascal won't see Shepard coming his way—doesn't even know he exists, I bet."

"Bea, are you ready to call him to arrange a meeting?" asked Shepard.

"Yeah... I think I am."

I took a deep breath, thinking of what Pascal might've said before I dialed. Either everything could've gone smooth, and I would garner a chance at a normal life—or everything could've gone south and lost my children. Scenarios of my future swam about my head—like being forced to live in a mental facility. If I killed Kate, I could persuade Pascal to clear my name—not a guarantee, but he had friends in high places. *What kind of life will my children* have? *I can't imagine their life being a terrific one with their father as an ally to my enemy. Screw it. Everything will be okay with Elizabeth's help.* I hoped for the best, and dialed him, anticipating his voice. He answered, but remained quiet.

"It's me. Bianca."

"I'm glad you're calling sooner than later. Have you found Kate? Did you do as I asked?" he said.

"Yes, I found her. I'm inside her place, searching for the recording as we speak before she gets home. I'll take care of her afterward."

"Okay, good. Two of my men are on their way up. I trust you'll cooperate. We're going for a ride."

20

Guggenheim

WHAT!? HE'S HERE? I CONSIDERED his ambush a game of sorts—unpredictable and forever-adjusting our arrangement. A mudslide of stress dominated my existence.

"Pascal's here! He's outside the building with two men on their way to escort me down!" I said.

"What? What do you mean he's here—like, now?" asked Kate.

"Yes! Now!"

Kate grabbed her gun from the coffee table and rushed toward the door, aligning her back and head parallel to the wall.

"How the hell did he find us, Bea?" she asked.

"I don't—I don't know!"

"Well, do you think he followed you guys here?"

"No, he must've followed *you*, Kate," said Shepard.

"Not possible."

"What do you meanly by that?" he said.

"Believe me, I'm the *definition* of paranoid," she said.

"Okay, let's think a minute. If he knew you were here—if he sensed I was lying, he would've confronted me. So no need to freak out. The plan is still in effect. We'll improvise," I said.

"...Wait, Bea. The gun he gave you—where is it?" said Shepard.

"There, on the sofa. Why?"

"Doesn't make sense how he found us," said Shepard. "What if he planted a tracker in the heel of your gun? Why didn't I think of this before?"

Shepard scurried across the room to dismantled my weapon, finding what he feared. Kate exhaled, closing her eyes and biting her bottom lip.

"F**k! He's been tracking you guys the entire time," said Kate.

"Okay, well, this doesn't change anything. Shep, I need to take that with me. I can't leave it behind or he'll send someone back here. His men will be here any moment. Hurry!" He re-assembled my gun and placed it in my hand.

"We'll follow you, but keep our distance," he said.

A heavy muffled pounding on the door resonated throughout the apartment. Shepard and Kate made themselves scarce, hiding in the bedroom. I grabbed my belongings, and opened the door, flipping the light switch to 'off.' They stood erect in posture—one on each side of the door in black, thermal coats, black leather gloves, and black pants. Neither one of them said a word while remaining inexpressive.

I closed the door before one of them patted me down for any weapons. They took my gun, having nothing to defend myself. Despite their intimidating demeanor, I didn't feel an ounce of fear in their presence. Confidence and bravery swooned through me, but I worried about the kids while walking to the elevator. We made our way to the lobby and headed outside. Pascal waited for me in a black Lincoln Navigator, idling in front of the building. He rolled his window down while smoking a cigar. "We found this on her, sir," said one of his guards. "Get in," he said. He smirked. A second identical Navigator pulled up, parking behind him. I wondered why he needed so many men for me. *I'm sure he's taking precautions, but what if Michael and Isabelle are in it.*

I couldn't show any signs of weakness while I assumed their nearby existence. He would've used it against me or to his advantage, somehow. I got in, sitting in the rear passenger side. We drove on to 6th Avenue, headed uptown. Pascal didn't say anything to me until we got close to Central Park.

"Two beautiful children is a lot to lose, Bianca. I trust you'll behave yourself, especially with Reinaldo behind you."

I turned my head to find him sitting in the last row of seats. He possessed a serial killer appearance you could spot a mile away, yet fear had no ownership of me.

"I want to see them—my kids. Are they in the car behind us?"

"No."

"Where are they? How do I know they're still alive? Show me proof."

Pascal glared at me, examined my eyes and facial expressions while smoking his cigar.

"Which one are you? The good one or the bad one right now?"

"I am who I need to be, Pascal."

He laughed at me in hysterics, mocking me as if my reply was the world's funniest joke. But I believe it was because I scared him—terrified of my unpredictability.

"You're afraid I might kill everyone in here, saving you for last."

"You're not that foolish, child. Why would you do such a thing with so much to lose? Indulge me."

"Go f**k yourself."

"*There's* that fire we talked about earlier. I *like* it," he said.

Elizabeth and I hated being mocked, but I bit my tongue, letting him have his laugh.

"You are *something* else, you know? As my niece, I can't tell which person you are, but I can *always* see through a poker face."

"Cut the sh*t. Show me my children are alive."

"Wow, I'm impressed. You speak as though you're holding all the cards."

Pascal tapped his guard on the shoulder, sitting in the passenger seat in front of him. He handed him a tablet, displaying video feed of Michael and Isabelle. They were in a bedroom with two beds—comfortable and taken care of.

"How do I know this is real and not looped?"

He smirked, delivered a heavy exhale, and retrieved his phone to make a call. Someone on the receiving end responded to his orders.

"Make one of them wave at the camera. Tell them their mother is coming to get them soon," he said. I readjusted myself in my seat.

"Can't blame me for not trusting you," I said.

Sure enough, a man entered the room before they waved. I smiled, and yes, missed them a great deal, but the need to be emotional didn't occur. Withholding emotions developed in an incredible span of time.

"Satisfied?" he asked. I nodded.

"Where are we going?"

"To visit one of the best museums in New York City. Guggenheim."

"It's after hours. They're closed."

"Always worrying, like your father. He worried about everything—which is why he drank so much. He owed *a lot* of people money at the time."

"I don't care to hear anything about him. He's been dead to me a long time."

***

The vehicle turned off the corner of Madison Avenue, through East 89th Street, and left on 5th Ave before coming to a halt. We arrived at the Guggenheim Museum, and Pascal walked in through the front door like he owned the place. His men stood outside, standing guard. Two wine glasses, a bottle of a 2002 Louis Roederer, and a Chateau Margaux sat on a table along the wall.

"What's all this for?" I asked. He handed me a glass of Chateau.

"You like expensive red wine. I can tell by looking at you."

He poured himself some champagne and walked across the lobby floor before heading up the ramp.

"Come. Join me," he said. I glanced back at the entrance before moving in his direction.

"I don't need my security. What is said between you and me is between you and me, Bianca. I'm sure you'll offer your undivided attention while accompanying me. And should anything happen to me... well... you know the rest. Cameras are located in every corner of this building. It would be a shame for you to be charged with another murder. You don't want your children suffering anymore for your mistakes."

I bit my lip, hating every moment I spent with him. He covered *every* base.

"Let's proceed," he said. He extended his arm.

"Why am I here, Pascal? You didn't bring me here for your amusement, and to drink a four-thousand-dollar bottle of wine."

"How does it feel to be the most wanted woman in New York, Bianca?"

"A nightmare. I want my life back—the one I had with my children."

"It'll be yours the moment you give me the things I want."

"Why should *I* of all people kill her? Why can't you or one of your men do it?

"You're a Gallucci—simple as that. It's in your blood to take lives. You only need some grooming. Deep down inside, being powerful *excites* you. You've proven yourself. You have what it takes, and we can accomplish *so* much together... as a family."

"You and I will *never* be a family. The blood we share means *nothing* to me," I said.

"I had a meeting with the man you tortured. He described you as, 'il Diavolo' and refused to look at your photo twice."

"So, you *did* send him after me!"

"Not at all. Why would I hire a hitman when I have what you want, and you have yet to fulfill my request?"

"So if you didn't, then who did?"

"I can't help you with that."

"*Why* not?"

"Do I strike you as a man who would sell out his associates?"

"How about Dr. Summers? Did you have *him* killed?"

"I have no dealings in that matter either. However, regarding your tortured assailant, nothing like that would ever happen, again. You have my word."

"Your word means nothing! You've already altered our original deal."

"Come. I want to show you something."

Frustration and mental exhaustion geared a considerable amount of weight for me. The answers I sought dangled in front of my face—unable to reach out and grab them. To me, Pascal was playing a game of chess I never wanted to play. He calculated every move and treated me like a helpless pawn.

I walked beside him down the hall, keeping my distance––waiting for him to surprise me with something outlandish. His snub demeanor and formidable mannerisms rubbed me the wrong way. He strolled in his black Dolce & Gabbana suit as if he had the world on a string. Wherever he was taking me, I was positive he didn't plan on getting his clothes bloody. I thought of all the possible exit routes—if anything were to happen, but I was willing to bet he guarded them.

"Where are we going?"

"Have a little faith," he said.

I, repulsed by his response, folded my arms and stood still while he called the elevator down. We entered, and I stood on one side, as far from his as possible until we got to the roof. The doors opened, and I stepped out into a frigid, dampened corridor. *Something's not right.* My hands trembled—not because of the cold air, but because of the dreadful swoon swiveling around in my stomach. Two large metal doors stood before us. I grew warier of Pascal's motives.

"After you," he said. He stepped to the side, gesturing I lead the way.

"Why are we up here? What's beyond those doors?"

"A test," he said. He drew his gun with ease from the inside of his coat.

"What test? I don't have a choice, do I?"

"In a moment, 'choice' will be the deciding factor in either life or death."

21

Do It for
Your Children

I PUSHED THE DOORS OPEN, AND the cold wind rushed into the corridor. Two large air conditioning units resided far apart from each other—one on my left and right. Shepard stood on the roof's edge beyond them with his hands tied behind his back, bloody face, and mouth gagged. He trembled, standing on the margin of death. Pascal's guard held a gun in his direction, ready to shoot upon command. My heart raced in fear. Uncertainty and despair emanated from within while I lunged forward. "Shepard!" I said. Pascal grabbed my elbow, refraining my advancement.

"What did you do to him?" I said.

"He's done this to himself. Is he not the man you hired to steal my painting?" he said.

"I don't know what you're talking about."

"*Allen Shepard*—the great art thief—the notorious *ghost in the wind.*"

"How did you—"

"How did I know where and who he was? It was by accident, no doubt. I kept my eyes on you the whole time, Bianca. Did you think I would've let you out of my sight? *Everyone* you associated with remained within my radar—even Ms. Kate Clarke, here," he said. He smiled from ear to ear.

Kate appeared from behind a large industrial air conditioner with a guard aiming a gun at her head. My eyes widened and my jaw dropped. Pascal laughed.

"Oh, Bianca, the look of surprise on your face is an amusement park of *thrills* for me. Priceless! I can only conclude you planned to follow me after I picked you up, ambush me, and then what, huh? If that was all, then you failed. Did you think you could all outsmart me? Did you think you could escape your duty of killing Kate?"

She didn't frown nor cry. I didn't expect her to. Her eyes said it all—the way she leered at him. I yanked my arm from Pascal's unnerved grip, plodding closer toward her.

"We've failed you," I said. "I... failed you."

I looked over to Shepard, pitying him, too. *I'm sure he put up one hell of a fight.* Pascal moved closer, standing face-to-face with Kate, glaring.

"Get on your knees," he said.

She refused to comply, spitting on his face. He wiped her saliva off with his handkerchief before glancing at his guard and nodding his head. The henchman punched her in the stomach, grabbed a fist-full of her hair, and kicked the back of her knees. His gun pointed at her skull while she glowered into Pascal's eyes. Shepard's fidgeting diverted Pascal's attention.

"If *he* moves, shoot him!" he said.

"*No!* Please, I'm begging you," I said. He paused, averting his airy gaze between him and me.

"You two are... Oh, you're in—you're in *love* with him. Does Lucas know?"

"Please, let us go. No one else has to get hurt here. No one needs to die. We'll leave New York, and you never have to see or hear from any of us again. I swear."

"Kate must die. She's like an untreated, festering wound that lasted two decades. Kate, finding you was like searching for water in the Sahara."

"*Go to hell. You'll never get your hands on that recording.* It's proof you're a pedophile and that you murdered my family like you did Bianca's."

"I barely remember," he said.

"*But I remember everything!*" I said. "I hid under the floorboards and saw your smug face when you killed my family. I *remember* hearing the gunshots that destroyed any chance of a future. You slaughtered them like cattle, but I got away. You're a low-life piece of sh*t, like my father. And I swear, if you ever laid a finger on Michael, I will—"

"I didn't touch your boy," he said.

"I'm going to make you pay one day. You took my mother and sister from me."

"I *saved* you from your father."

"You *stripped* me of everything good that was left!" I said. "You didn't have to kill them!" He pointed the barrel of his gun against my head.

"Enough! I had my reasons. Where's the recording, Bianca?" he said.

"It's safe," said Kate.

"Where?" he asked.

"I'd rather die. For all you know, I made copies and sent them to your competition."

"You're lying. You no longer have leverage over me." He removed a labeled DVD and portable hard drive from his pocket. Kate's expression transitioned from anger to despair. Pascal stripped her of all retribution in seconds.

"How did you get that?" she asked.

"Simple. I found it in a fire-proof safe, hidden in the wall of your apartment while you were playing in the woods with Bianca and Shepard. Some plaster, paint—voila! You never suspected any changes."

His sinister grin resembled my father's—like the Grinch concocting a new idea. I thought about Michael and Isabelle in that instant—their future without me, knowing Pascal got what he wanted.

"Pascal, please stop this. You made your point. Just let us go. Give me back my kids, and we'll *never* see each other again."

"You're right. This has gone on too long. It ends tonight."

He turned his attention to his guard whose gun was still pointed at Kate. Pascal pressed the barrel of his gun against her forehead, and she stared at him with malice glazed over her eyes. I begged and pleaded to let her go, but he disregarded my request.

"She's a loose end I should've taken care of a long time ago. She could bury me—destroy everything I built, but killing her is not my task. Bianca, your carelessness has led her to her shame," he said. He yanked my wrist, forcing me to hold the gun.

"A deal is a deal, Bianca. Her death in exchange for your little angels."

"No, I can't."

"You *can't* or you *won't?*"

I hesitated to respond. He guided my hand, pointing his weapon at her forehead, assisting my uncontrollable shaking. He whispered into my ear, "Do it for your children."

Breathe, Bianca. Breathe. Slow breaths. Inhale... and exhale. Kate's fear permeated the air. A daunting sense of terror lingered among us. I carried the burden of the world in my hand, contemplating every possible alternative.

"I never wanted this to happen, Kate. I'm *so* sorry."

"We tried. Save your kids," she said.

I cocked the gun, closed my eyes, and took a few labored breaths before placing my finger on the trigger. My heartbeat slowed to a normal, steady rhythm. My attitude changed, confirming Elizabeth's presence. I fought an internal battle with her, refraining from pulling the trigger. I only wanted to do the right thing.

"Lizzy, stop! We *can't* do this," I said aloud.

I opened my eyes. Kate and Pascal furrowed their eyebrows, bewildered by my random vocalization.

"You have to, Bea. There's no other way," Elizabeth said aloud.

To everyone, it appeared I was talking to myself. Pascal and his men repositioned their stance, glancing at each other. I closed my eyes and placed my finger on the trigger, ready to fire, but opened my eyes to the sound of someone gurgling. A guard clasped his hands around his neck. Blood gushed through his fingers, covering his hand. The tighter he squeezed, the more it oozed. His death, imminent.

Everyone ran for cover. Everyone except Pascal. He grabbed the gun out of my hand, and stood behind me, hiding with it pointed at my lower back. We witnessed his other guard—the one near Kate fall to the ground with blood pouring out of his chest. She didn't move from behind the air conditioning unit. Pascal and I were the only two standing out in the open where he held me against my will.

"You brought a sniper?"

"I didn't plan this, I swear! I don't know what's going on!"

"You're lying!" he said.

Kate couldn't help me in the least. Neither one of us knew what was happening.

"Kate, if you move, I'll kill Bianca. Now, tell me who's out there!" he said. She sat with her back against the dull, weather-worn unit.

"I don't know! I swear to God," she said.

"Wait a second. *Wait a second.* Cross, is that you? We had a deal. You won't get those kids by hijacking me!" he said.

"Cross? Who the hell is that? Who else is after my kids?"

"Shut up," he said.

No answer—only the cold, howling wind sweeping around us. Shepard set himself free and appeared from behind another air conditioning unit. Pascal kept his gun pointed at my lower back. "Another step and I'll kill her," he said. Shepard froze and Kate stared, breathing heavier by the second. Pascal forced me to walk backward with him. "Stay back!" he said to them. We made our way to the rooftop doors, but he didn't get too far. A third bullet sliced through the air, and a sharp pain pronounced itself in my left thigh. Pascal yelled, stumbled, and fell to the ground clenching his thigh.

I, too, fell before acknowledging I'd been grazed by the same bullet. He clutched his wound, attempting to slow the bleeding. The sight of his blood activated arousal of excitement. His suffering incited pleasure. Elizabeth spoke loud and clear to me from within, saying, "He deserves to die, Bea." I fought to suppress her hijacking. "*No,* we need him alive," I said.

Once again, Elizabeth's manifestation was subtle, yet victorious in her will to take full control. I closed my eyes and released my doubts and fears. My transition commenced in full.

"I'm the only one standing in between you and your children. You *need* me alive," said Pascal.

"Shepard! Kate! Give me a hand with him!" I said. I used his tie as a tourniquet. He yelled in pain and I smiled from ear to ear. "Bianca wants me to save him. We can't let him bleed out. Looks like he needs a hospital," I said.

"Liz, you've been shot. You're bleeding," said Shepard.

"Just a scratch."

Shepard turned around, waving to someone in the distance. A shadow-like figure waved back with what appeared to be a rifle by their side.

"That's him—Ace. He came through. Alright, let's get Pascal out of here! Liz, put his arm around your shoulder. Kate, grab his legs."

The three of us carried him to the elevator and did our best to get him past the front entrance. We faced the challenge of his other guards standing in our way. Shepard used his skill and tactics to clear a path for us with Pascal's gun, shooting anyone who stood in opposition. The psychopath, Reinaldo was the last to be eliminated.

***

We arrived outside, and headed toward the Navigator, demanding the driver hand over his gun and keys. Shepard knocked him out without a second thought. I slipped my hand into Pascal's pocket, recovering the disc and thumb drive in the height of the commotion. Getting him in the Navigator was a struggle while trying to minimize his blood loss.

We were on the move, and eager to get help. He couldn't speak much, due to his labored breathing, but I hoped he stayed alive. I sat on one side of the car with his head on my lap—and Kate on the other side with his legs on her.

"Take me here. He's a doctor," he said. He fumbled about his breast pocket, struggling to remove his phone. The number he speed-dialed resulted in a man clearing his throat before stating his name.

"Doctor Carter speaking."

"Dr. Carter, Pascal's been shot," I said.

"Where?"

"In his thigh. There's a lot of blood."

"Any exit wounds?"

"Yes."

"And is he conscious?"

"Barely."

"Put me on speakerphone," he said.

"On my way," said Pascal. He spoke with a faint, airy whisper before passing out.

"*39* Gramercy. Come immediately!" said Carter. He hung up.

"Shepard, you got all that?" I asked.

"39 Gramercy. Got it."

It took us minutes to get to the West Side Highway. He sped through traffic lights before an SUV tailed us within moments.

"Where did that car come from?" asked Kate.

"I dunno. One of his men must've called for backup. Liz, I'm gonna need you to get rid of them. Take the gun," said Shepard.

I climbed into the front passenger seat, checked the gun's cartridge, and rolled the window down, unloading five bullets toward our pursuers. I shot the driver, which resulted in his vehicle spinning out of control before crashing. I laughed.

"We're in the clear! Kate, how's he doing back there?" I asked.

"Not too good! His pulse is faint!"

"Shepard, hurry! Bianca needs her kids. We can't let him die."

22

False Memories

WE ARRIVED AT 39 GRAMERCY. SHEPARD slammed the
brakes before scurrying to the back seat. I ran to the front door of
the house, knocking and ringing the doorbell multiple times—
hoping Dr. Carter would hurry. *This is the right address, right?*
He opened the door.

"Quickly. Follow me," he said. He wore his surgical attire,
standing at average height, wearing a well-groomed salt n' pepper
beard. He and Shepard carried Pascal to the basement, placing him
on an operating table. We stood in a customized recovery room
with a surveillance camera mounted on the wall on the far end of
the room. Cabinets, sofa, and surgical lamps furnished the entire
area. Illegal operation? Likely.

"He gonna live?" I asked Dr. Carter.

"Too soon to tell. You. What's your name?"

"Kate."

"Grab an apron from that cabinet in the corner, wash your
hand, put those gloves on, and do as instruct."

"You're kidding me, right? No way. Not me. Let *her* do it! There's no way I'm gonna help save his life after I spent *my entire life* trying to destroy his."

"I have an obligation to this man—a Hippocratic oath, so whatever beef you two have, you need to put aside. Your hands are the smallest, so, I'll need you. Now, are you going to stand there and whine or help me?" he asked.

Kate glanced at me, taking a deep breath. Her reluctance suffused, thickening the air.

"Fine," she said.

"I need the rest of you out of here," he said.

"You got a medical kit I can use?" asked Shepard.

"You'll find one in the bathroom upstairs—first floor, make a left—second door on your right."

"Thanks."

Shepard sustained cuts and bruises—superficial wounds easy to bandage. I helped him clean up, and he offered to stitch my leg wound, but I insisted I do it myself.

***

He and I headed outside afterward to sit on the stairs, listening to the silence the city offered. The situation inside calmed down after some time, and we waited for a prognosis. He pulled his phone out, ready to call someone.

"Who you callin'?" I asked.

"Ace. I owe him a 'thank you' for saving our asses."

"Your sniper friend. Yeah, tell him I say, "Thanks.""

I walked away and sat in the driver seat of the parked navigator while he stayed behind. Something caught my eye, spotting a shiny black piece of metal wedged in between the seat and console. Pascal's tablet—the one Bianca viewed earlier.

"Shepard, look!" I said. "You can trace the video feed back to its origin, right?" He placed Ace on hold and approached me with long strides in his steps before I showed him the screen.

"What's are we looking at?"

"Live video of the kids. This is where he's keeping them. Can you trace this?"

"Holy sh*t. Yeah, shouldn't be a problem."

"Let's get your laptop at Kate's."

"You're driving," he said.

He scurried into the passenger seat, continued his call with Ace, and secured the tablet on his lap.

***

We arrived at our destination not too long after, and I stayed in the idling car while he returned a few minutes later. I headed off down the street—back to Dr. Carter's home. He plugged the device into his laptop and typed as if his life depended on it.

"How long?" I asked.

"Might take a while. Pascal's firewalls are pretty difficult to breach. It's like peeling layers off—one at a time," he said.

He shrugged his shoulders and resumed. Five minutes turned into ten, and ten into twenty. My patience grew thin until he exhaled, smiling at the screen.

"You found them?"

"We're in. We did it!" he said. He continued typing.

"What's the address? Where are they?" I asked. "Shepard, where are they?"

"Liz, would you... *give* me a second please?" My impatience and anticipation grew at an insurmountable rate.

"Got it. 314 Lafayette. Brooklyn."

I didn't hesitate to speed off in the direction of our destination, disregarding every red traffic light without drawing attention.

"Don't get pulled over. I'm gonna check the feed again— make sure it isn't looped or that we're running into a trap," he said. My phone rang. Lucas called.

"Not the best time right now. What do you want?" I said.

"Where the hell have you been? I've been trying to get in touch with you!" he said.

"Well, we're talking now, so what do—"

"I have them—the kids. They're here with me at the FBI headquarters."

"What? What do you mean they're with you? I swear to God if you're messing with me I'll—"

"Get your head out of your ass for one second. You're not listening to me. The Feds found them around an hour ago in front of their building. I called you a bunch of times, and left a hundred messages."

"I was busy."

"I'm really not supposed to be talking to you. You're still a fugitive. You need to turn yourself in—get some help—explain your side of the story."

"You and I both know they'll kill Bea for shooting that cop. They won't believe her," I said. "Gotta go."

I ended the call, and pulled over, trying to figure out Pascal's plan as my mind grew foggy. I placed the car in 'park,' sitting in silence with Shepard.

"That was Lucas, right?" he asked.

"The kids are safe," I said.

"What do you mean. Where are they?"

"*With* their father. Pascal must've organized their drop-off at the FBI building *after* he picked Bea up at Kate's. Why would he do that? What's he up to?" I asked.

"None of it adds up," said Shepard. "The video feed's a fake, by the way."

"Lucas says I should turn myself in, but *no way* am I doing that. We need to get back to Pascal and find out who this Cross person is. I'll do whatever it takes to make him talk. Do you remember what he shouted before the bullet to his leg?"

"Yeah, he called out to Cross saying they couldn't have the kids."

"Someone else was after them. But, why? What agreement did he make with this 'Cross' person?"

"I dunno, but I have a strong feeling that whoever visited Francis is affiliated with Pascal—might be Cross. Just a hunch based on how everything happened. I'll try hacking Francis' office building cameras, again."

I called Lucas back while I turned around, headed back to 39 Gramercy. He answered the phone.

"...What do you want?"

"*Something's* not right. It doesn't make sense—the kids being dropped off in front of the building like that. I remember you saying, "they're safe," to Bianca back in the cab a few days ago. You're involved with Pascal, and I'm gonna prove it. What are you not telling me?"

The line died, abandoning me with an annoying silence. He didn't call back. I called him again, receiving only his voicemail. *That a**hole is involved. I can't wait to interrogate Pascal.*

"Any progress on hacking the security feed from Francis' office building?"

"No. Nothing in the system," he said. His chest flattened. The air from his nostrils brushed the hairs on my arm.

"What do you mean there's *nothing*? How's that possible?"

"S*omeone* got to it first. It's been erased!"

Pascal held the answers I sought, and I drove back to Dr. Carter's house, white-knuckling the steering wheel with flames flaring out of my nose and smoke exiting my ears.

***

We arrived and Kate opened the door. Shepard headed straight to the couch. I paced back and forth in the living room.

"Where'd you guys disappear to?" asked Kate.

"I can use a nightcap," said Shepard. He yawned, covering his mouth before tilting his head back.

"We left to find the kids, but it turns out they're with Lucas. Something's not right, though. Pascal arranged for them to be dropped off at the FBI headquarters around the same time he took us to the roof. We need to find out who Cross is. By the way, how's that a**hole doing?"

"He's stable—lost a lot of blood, but he'll recover... unfortunately," said Kate.

"Thanks for help keeping him alive. He and I need to exchange a few words."

Dr. Carter appeared in the hallway with his laptop in hand.

"I'm afraid that won't be possible. I just finished stitching him up. He's exhausted, traumatized, and needs his rest. It might be another twenty-four hours before you're able to speak with him."

"Well, I guess we'll wait here till he wakes... I'm not asking, doctor," I said.

"Who are you, exactly?"

"Pascal's niece. Elizabeth. He's made my sister's life a living hell. He killed her family, kidnapped her children, and *forced* her into a position of doing things most mothers never experience. I need answers from him—Kate included."

"I don't give a damn *who* you are or what he's done. This is *my* home, and you don't come in here making demands. I don't like you, and if I feel the need to kick you out, I'll remove you myself," he said. Kate took a step forward.

"Dr. Carter, I'm sorry. We're *all* sorry. We've all had a *very* long night, and we're not thinking straight. I would be grateful if you let us...*them* stay here the night," she said.

"...Fine, but keep her away from Pascal for now. Don't allow her to do anything stupid."

"Got it. Thank you, doctor," she said.

He left the room, but not without a curt, berated glance my way. I didn't know what he was capable of and thought it best to not push my luck. Kate apologized again, relaxed her fist, and turned toward me.

"Do you know what happened to the disc and thumb drive? I couldn't find them on him," said Kate.

"I've got 'em and using it as leverage. I promise you'll get it back." I walked away toward the basement and traveled downstairs to visit Pascal. Kate didn't get in my way. I didn't let him out of my sight and needed to be close by, choosing to sleep on a small sofa located in the corner on the other side of the room next to a wooden chair. He slept in a transparent, vision-paneled, 10x10 isolation recovery room with the curtains drawn apart. I tiptoed in and checked his phone sitting on the nightstand. No other contacts besides doctor Carter were listed. Expecting more would've been foolish of me. I wanted to be the first person he laid eyes on when he awoke, but I needed sleep. I ambled toward the couch, laid down, and closed my eyes.

***

I woke up to the aroma of cooked food—dinner prepared. Pascal awoke moments after me. The clock on the pale, white wall read six o'clock pm. It appeared I slept all day. I didn't utter a word to him—for a while at least and assumed he'd been sleeping a long time, too. He glared at me, and I stood from the sofa, approaching him.

"You're a good mother," he said.

"The only reason I let you live is so Bea can be with her kids again."

"Hmm. You're *not* Bianca."

"And you're not dead, yet."

"Thanks to you," he said.

"You don't stop with the games, do you? What if I decided to end your life, today—right now, huh? You couldn't stop me."

"I've had worse people than you threatened my life. Besides, you wouldn't do it. Bianca *needs* her kids... and they need their mother."

"Wow, you are something else," I said. "You organized the kids' drop-off at the FBI building after showing Bianca that video. You *fooled* her into believing that killing Kate was her only choice. I'll admit that was tactful. However, the children are with their father, now—and don't deny it—I wanna know the deal you made with Lucas. I also wanna know who this 'Cross' person is, and the deal made."

"Don't be ridiculous. You know I won't talk. What are you gonna do—*chop my balls off?* Besides, Bianca can be with her kids, now, and everyone goes their separate way. I have what I want—wait, where's the DVD and thumb drive?"

"I took them while you bled. Let's face the facts, Pascal. You're either gonna die someday soon or you'll go to prison for the rest of your life," I said. I revealed the items, retrieving them from my pant pocket.

"Okay, let's make a *real* deal," he said. "A new one."

"Let me make this crystal clear to you. *I'm* God in this room, now, and the one making the deals here. Tell me what I need to know about Lucas and Cross, and I'll let you go. You can also have the recording back."

"You're bluffing."

"You're right. I am. I know you won't talk," I said. I walked toward a cabinet outside his room.

Dr. Carter housed a plethora of drugs—available but locked away. Breaking the lock was easy, and I had the pleasure of choosing whatever I wanted to inject into Pascal's body. I grabbed what I needed, hummed a lullaby, and strolled back in with a wooden chair to find him reaching for his phone placed next to his Zippo lighter and Rolex on the nightstand. I closed the door and jammed the chair against the handle, barring it secured.

"You think I'd leave it within reach for you to call one of your goons? I can't say I'm surprised you don't have any contacts listed in there—just a few incoming and outgoing calls. Yeah, I checked it. It's over for you, Pascal. You belong to me. So, tell me. Who is Cross, and why did this person want the kids? What's Lucas' involvement?"

"You women are never satisfied. You always have to win. Nothing will ever be enough, will it?"

"This *isn't* about winning. It's about payback, desire, and my pleasure in watching you suffer. So, tell me what I need to know. Consider this a warning."

"I'm a businessman. None of it was personal."

"Answer my questions, and I'll spare you," I said. I filled a syringe.

"You think you scare me?"

"I'm going to show you what real pain and fear is like, Uncle," I said. "Lucky for you, Bianca married an anesthesiologist."

The syringe contained a local paralytic called succinylcholine. He would be a vegetable—unable to move. I planned to paralyze his legs. Repeated injections were deemed necessary if he refused to talk. If I gave him too much he could've suffered from cardiac arrest, chest pains, progressive hypotension, visual and auditory hallucinations, and dementia—to name a few. I explained it to him, hoping he'd comply.

"Cross is not a friend, neither is she an enemy."

"That was quick. She? Where can I find her, and why does she want Bianca's kids?"

"I could tell you, but where's the fun in that?"

I forced the needle into his wounded leg without warning, administering the paralytic. He yelled at the top of his lungs, drawing attention to himself. Kate and Shepard rushed downstairs, standing in front of the recovery room's door. They pulled on the handle, and knocked on the glass, trying to derail my concentration.

"Liz, don't do anything stupid," said Shepard.

"Let's talk about this," said Kate.

"Who is Cross? Where can I find her?" I asked Pascal.

He leered into my eyes before lifting the corners of his mouth. I didn't hesitate to injected his other leg. At that point, the anesthesia took effect. He struggled to move.

"How does it feel to not be in control?"

"Relaxing. It's like I'm tanning on a beach."

I was running out of time. Shepard and Kate banged on the door without relent. I removed the linen from his bed and tore his sheet into long, manageable pieces. He tried fighting but lost while I fastened his left and right wrists to the bed's side rails. I grabbed his lighter from the nightstand and held it under his forearm.

"Who is she and where can I find her?"

"What are you going to do? Set me on fire?"

"... If that's what it takes, yes. I'll burn your arm, followed by your ears, and then your other arm. Last chance."

He refused to speak, so I ignited the flame, burning his skin. Dr. Carter ran downstairs, rattling the door. Kate and Shepard continued yelling and banging. Pascal screamed. The odor of his burning flesh ascended into my nostrils.

"You killed me and burnt my house to the ground. A part of Bianca died that day, too. I'll stop when you start talking." He wailed in hysterics, yet no surrender. Not a slight of remorse ran through my veins.

"I can do this *all* night till I see bone," I said. He struggled, yelled, and thrashed about before passing out.

"No! Wake up!" I said. I swung my palm across his face with the full weight of my arm. He slipped in and out of consciousness until I gained his undivided attention. His breathing labored. I lit the lighter again.

"Please stop! No more. I'll tell you!"

"Spit it out!"

"... Bianca's best friend, Cross. That's the only name I know of."

"What are you talking about? She doesn't have any friends by that name."

"Yes—the blonde. She sat at the diner with her. The one that helps her with her kids."

"Claire? Claire Benoit?" I said. "I don't believe you. She would *never* do that to Bianca. You're lying."

"It's her, I swear it! She and Lucas are together—a couple. When I found out it was Bianca who stole the painting, I approached Lucas about it at the St. Regis Hotel. Cro... Claire accompanied him, and he claimed to know nothing about my painting, but soon devised a plan—one which we would both benefit. The situation got out of hand, and kidnapping the kids didn't go as planned. We twisted Bianca's arm, so to speak. I knew about her personality issues and took advantage. Kate had what I wanted, and I used Bianca to get it from her. Getting close to Kate was extremely difficult," he said. "She's protected."

"Why did you think Claire was the one who shot you?"

"Because I got a glimpse of Bianca's kids—a photo in her wallet at the hotel. I believe those two had something to do with Francis' death. My men didn't do it."

"This is crazy. You're saying she and Lucas had Francis killed?"

"I believe he was killed because he couldn't keep his mouth shut. For the record, I never sent that mercenary after Bianca to the cabin. Someone tried making it look like it was me."

"Lucas wouldn't kill anyone. Why would he devise a plan to kidnap his own kids? It doesn't make sense."

"Why else. Money. He and Claire have their own agenda. Regardless of the reason, it worked out for all of us. I kept my end of the deal, and so did they."

"One more question—these gold cards. What are they?" He sighed, and laid his head back onto the pillow, remaining silent.

"New multi-functional technology. Bitcoin. Peer-to-peer monetary transactions can be made and exchanged and a way to bypass any red flags from the Feds. It was an incentive for them to keep their mouths shut, or I could've killed them, but I didn't. However, I found a way to make Bitcoin anonymous and untraceable. The Black Market is full of innovation."

"So the hotel key card you sent Bianca is also a credit card?"

"Don't be ridiculous. That was one of the master key cards. I modeled it to look the same. I own the St. Regis."

I turned my head, glancing at Dr. Carter, Shepard, and Kate, and advanced toward the door.

"Don't you want to know the truth about where you grew up?"

"Bianca and I were born in Naples, Italy. That's the truth."

"You know that story Bianca's proud of—the one she tells people about how she met Lucas?"

"Yes. They met in Naples."

"Never happened," he said.

"What are you talking about?"

"False memories. People who suffer sexual abuse can suffer from it—at least that's what Lucas said. He's *so sick* of her telling that story. Bianca, I *know* you're in there somewhere. Perhaps we'll speak again, soon."

"Why are you telling me more than I asked for?" I said.

"Maybe because I've lost the battle against you... for now, at least," he said. "Maybe it's because I care."

"Too late for that."

He was right about Bianca. She clawed on the walls of my mind as he delivered such news. She was in denial of Lucas' and Claire's behavior, but sometimes the truth is all we need. Sometimes, it destroys our world—and sometimes it's the light shining on the path, pointing us in the right direction.

23

Kidnapped

I REMOVED THE BARRICADE FROM the door. Dr. Carter ran in to his aid, rushing past me with an ugly leer to follow.

"Shepard, I need your help," he said. "Give me a hand with him." I made my way toward the stairs. Kate followed.

"What the hell happened in there?" she asked.

"I got the answers I was looking for."

"What did he say?"

"A lot."

Kate lingered inside while I left the house—outside to call Lucas. *Pick up, Lucas. Pick up you prick!* The never-ending ring drove me to frustration. I paced back and forth, hung up, and dialed again. *Come on! Answer the pho—"*

"Turn yourself in," he said.

"What's your involvement with Pascal?"

"You keep going on and on about him!"

"Unbelievable. You might as well tell me before I find out because when I do, you'll regret everything you did."

"Look, I'm not hiding anything. The kids are happy to be home, and they miss their mother. The sooner you surrender—the sooner they can see you. Let's meet at Friedman Carousel tomorrow at noon to talk—just you and me."

"Okay, but I swear you better not bring the police, or I'll kill you myself, Lucas."

"No cops. You have my word."

I hung up. The unsettling notion of trickery lingered like a dense fog. Shepard and Kate walked out the front door, standing at the top of the stairs.

"You could've killed him in there!" he said.

"But, I didn't. He'll live."

"What the hell did you two talk about?"

"Everything. Lucas and Claire are lovers. Here's the best news, yet. Claire goes by the name, "Cross.""

"What? You gotta be kidding me. Just "Cross?"" said Shepard.

"Pascal swears by it. I just got off the phone with Lucas and agreed to meet him in Central Park—Friedman Carousel tomorrow at noon. Says he wants to talk, but it's a trap of course."

"Definitely," said Kate.

"Pascal told me everything, but clueless as to Lucas' agenda. They had an agreement, and it's obvious they met a couple of times. Claire's role in all this is still unclear to me. I don't doubt they share the same motive. Hey, I got an idea. Why don't we get ahead of the game—ambush him tonight? Shepard, can we take him back to your place for questioning?"

"I'm more than happy to help."

"Good. Lucas is a creature of habit. He *should* be home, and won't see us coming. We'll ambush him inside the house. I have the keys."

"What about the doorman?"

"Approach him with a fake law enforcement badge. Knock him out or something—I dunno. We need him out of the way for a while. He's the only employee manning the desk in the evenings."

"Alright, but we need to follow Lucas—make sure he isn't being tailed," said Shepard.

"I'm game."

"What about Pascal? He's *not* getting away. What if Dr. Carter decides to move him?" asked Kate.

"I placed a tracker in his watch while he and Liz slept. We'll know if and when he moves. You can go home if you want. You'll bring him to justice soon enough."

***

Kate left without rebuttal or reluctance. Shepard and I performed a stake-out thirty yards up the block from Bianca's building, later that day. We sat in the Navigator and kept our eyes peeled, observing everyone who walked in and out. A silver car pulled up in front of the entrance. *Claire's* car. Lucas exited while the kids remained in the back seat. The urge to confront those back-stabbing a**holes swelled within. Shepard placed his hand on my wrist, deflating my hot-tempered impulse.

"We can't mess this up," he said. "Gotta stick to the plan."

He was right. I was a bit too eager and decided to stay put. She drove away, dissipating into the distant city traffic. I redirected my attention toward the building, craning my neck through the windshield, waiting for the living room lights to turn on. Shepard stuck his head out his window and opened his door the instant the room illuminated.

"Time to go. I'm headed upstairs," he said.

"Okay, here are the keys. Use the service elevator to exit."

"Got it. Wait for me at the back entrance. I'll call you before I come down." I hopped into the driver's seat the moment he stepped out and started the ignition, making my way to the end of the street and around the block.

***

Ten minutes passed and he didn't call. I worried about his safety. Another ten minutes passed before he contacted me. "I'm on my way down," he said. *Perfect. Everything's going as planned for once.*

I waited at the service entrance, eager to do something— anything while the engine ran idle. I texted Kate, asking her to send audio and video-recording law information to my phone. I was thinking of a plan, one I thought would come in handy later. My impulsive urge to somehow hurt Lucas—choke him, stab him, beat the hell out for him for his conniving behavior toward Bianca unleashed its fury. My attention soon diverted to the loud, squeaking metal hinges of the back door swinging opening. Shepard exited with an unconscious Lucas hanging over his shoulder, like a sack of potatoes. He laid him on the back seat.

"Let's get out of here," he said.

"What did you do to his face?"

"He put up a fight. Chloroform did the rest."

We left and headed to Shepard's place in Brooklyn. Traffic remained minimal. When we arrived, Shepard parked the Navigator in front of his home, and I got out with the intent of transporting Lucas into the house with haste. I held his legs. He grabbed his torso, heading inside. One misstep on black ice cost me my balance and a bump on the back of my head. A full head of hair under my ball cap helped cushion the impact.

***

I woke up on Shepard's couch an hour later and called out to him. No answer. The door opened behind me.

"Hey, you're awake. How does your head feel?" he said.

"Uh, a little hazy, and a bit of a headache again, but I'm alright."

"Why am I here?" I asked. A flashback of recent events projected.

"Good to have you back, Bea. You took a pretty heavy fall earlier. We spent the last day or tw—"

"Lucas. He's here, isn't he—in that room you walked out of, right? I remember, now... I remember everything we did. I wanna see him. I want him to look me in the eyes an—"

"Bea, wait. You should take it easy—get yourself re-orientated. Look, you understand there's no turning back once we go through that door, right? Unorthodox methods might be necessary... if you get what I mean."

"... Whatever it takes," I said. "Trust me, I'm fine. I'm ready."

I stood from the couch and walked toward the door. A sense of fear and desolation lingered in the room upon entering. It was cold, low-lit, and soundproofed with about two inches of styrofoam covering every inch of the walls and ceiling. Lucas sat in a metal, industrial chair fifty feet in front of me—his ankles tethered to the legs, and his hands tied behind his back with zip ties. He slept. *Exhaustion must've taken over.* It was difficult seeing him like that at first, but my thoughts of his deceit superseded any feelings of pity, remorse, and reserved affections. It was as if the 'apathy light switch' turned on inside me. Shepard walked to the other side of the room to retrieve his leather gloves sitting on an old, pale-green, metal desk. His gun remained tucked into his waist behind his back.

I slapped Lucas across the face. "Wake up," I said. He awoke in a confused, disoriented state of mind. His breathing staggered and his eyes widened upon seeing my face.

"Bianca? Honey, what's going on? Where am I?" he asked.

"Don't 'honey' me. You're *exactly* where you belong."

"You're crazy. They'll put you both away for a *long* time when they catch you."

"You have a lot of explaining to do, Lucas. I *want* answers. The man you made a deal with—Pascal, sold you out. He told me about you and Claire—about how he used my illness to his advantage. Oh, yes, I know everything, Lucas—everything except *why* you arranged to have *our* kids kidnapped."

"You don't want the truth, Bea. You can't handle it, but I guess I'm as good as dead," he said. He glanced at Shepard and cried. "Please don't kill me."

"We're not gonna kill you, but I *will* do whatever it takes to clear my name."

"They'll lock you up for killing that cop, and then throw you in a mental institution."

"Not unless I can prove it was self-defense. You three set me up. Coercion. I *can* prove it with a good lawyer. Everything I did was to protect our children. Now, tell me. What was so important you had to put our children's lives in danger for?"

"Go ask Pascal," he said.

Shepard glanced my way with a raised eyebrow before inching closer, standing in front of Lucas. I glanced back, lowered my eyes, and delivered the calloused nod of approval to inflict pain. He clenched his fist, exaggerating the friction of his rubber glove before swinging his arm. Lucas yelled, groaned, and spat blood. His ragged breathing didn't incite pity.

"This can all stop if you tell the truth."

"Leave it alone, Bea."

"*Leave it alone*? My kids are out there with a woman who claimed to be my best friend, and you expect me to *leave it the f**k alone*?"

Shepard punched him in the face again, causing him to bleed out his nose. Still, no pity. I repeated my questions, asking him multiple times, yet he responded with silence after every blow to his face and body. Anxiety and frustration stifled my soul. I was running out of patience, and my blood boiled to a catastrophic level. I placed my hands around his throat, squeezing it with his blood trickling in between my fingers. My desire to hurt him peaked, wanting to somehow transfer my emotional agony into his physical pain. I squeezed harder as the seconds passed. He gagged, choked, and convulsed in his chair, trying to inhale. I allowed my duressed mind and unhinged rage to take over before closing my eyes.

I soon opened them, and Elizabeth stood behind him. She lifted the corners of her mouth, showing off her plump, rosy cheeks—her eyebrows unmoved, sitting relaxed above the small wrinkles on the corner of her eyes. The transference of her emotions grew, delighting in his suffering. I released my grip and ran out of the room in a hurry, shocked to have seen her without warning, and scared that I almost killed Lucas. Shepard rushed after me, locking the door behind him.

"Why didn't you try stopping me?" I asked.

"Because you're not your sister. You weren't going to kill him," he said.

"He won't talk. We *need* a different method."

"You know him better than anyone else. What's his worst fear?"

"Uh, I dunno. He's prideful and has a God complex. Um, he's afraid of losing in life and also afraid of drowning, heigh—"

"That's it. Drowning."

"What are you talking about? What, are we gonna hold him down in bath water or something?"

"No, we're gonna make him feel like he's drowning."

"So, we're gonna water-board him."

"I was thinking of using the car battery and cables before, but drowning him will work. You okay with this?"

"Yes."

"Are you su—"

"Let's do it."

"Okay, gimme a hand with this old bench I have in the other room. We'll strap him to it."

We walked back in. I was more than willing to help but more desperate for answers. I re-entered the room to find Elizabeth smiling and running her fingers through his hair. She gazed at me, and I understood the vacancy in her eyes. I embraced the next step. My future and the future of my kids hung in the balance. A sense of pride projected from her while Shepard and I were setting up. I looked back over my shoulder. Liz disappeared. Shepard and I set the stage soon enough, strapping Lucas to the bench after filling two plastic gallons of water. He was too weak to fight back but terrified the moment he put two-and-two together.

"Bianca, don't do this to me!" he said.

"You married a woman who knows your deepest secrets. You brought this on yourself," I said.

It took some strength, but we managed to elevate him on to a forty-five-degree angle—his feet pointing toward the ceiling.

"Shep, give me the gallon of water," I said.

He held a towel over his face, adding pressure to stabilize his head. I took my time pouring the water, forcing it into his mouth and nostrils. He struggled to breathe, gurgling. His body convulsed and thrashed about until Shepard gestured to stop with a nod.

"You gonna come clean, or should I continue? The choice is yours," I said.

Elizabeth appeared again, standing beside me, smiling. I poured another gallon on his face until he begged me to stop.

"I'll tell you!" he said. He expelled a violent cough. Shepard sat him upright. Mucus dangled off his nostrils.

"Give me the truth," I said. I removed my phone from my pocket, pressing record.

"…It started with your uncle looking for his painting. He was convinced you took it—*swore* it was you... and he was right. I had no idea what he was talking about, but he showed me proof. He approached me first because prying it from you wasn't going to be easy. There was truth in that, and I thought, 'why not force her to give it up.' The only thing you love as much as the kids is your art. Even *I* came in last. You were so involved in yourself and that *damned* gallery you didn't notice I hadn't loved you anymore."

"…I see. So what was the agreement you two made?"

"I received a fee of fifty grand from Pascal on that gold card you saw with an offshore account—the works. We agreed that... he would conduct a fake kidnapping of the kids and keep them safe. With that in play, I figured your life would end sometime in all that mess, but I also knew you'd fight anyone to protect them—*especially* after you turned into that monster."

"Why would you want me dead, Lucas—the mother of your children? Why would you do such a thing?"

"…Because we're broke. I'm about to lose my medical license in a malpractice suit. I owe people money—important people—the kind you can't reason with. I borrowed to stay afloat but was unable to pay back. As the beneficiary of your life insurance, it would've solved all my prob—"

"And you and Claire would live happily ever after…"

"It was her idea, I swear, Bea. I swear. Filing for divorce means I wouldn't get a cent. You had the policy for ten years—always paid it on time."

"Oh, my God, I can't believe this—always about the money. My life is worth ten million dollars to you, Lucas? Look me in the eyes and tell me I'm worth ten million." He turned his head away, shifting his focus into the harsh, cold cement.

"You can't. When did you two start seeing each other?"

"... A year."

"*All* this time. You took advantage of my illness with the hopes I would get killed so *you and Claire* would collect... *ten million*? Pathetic. You should've told me you were having money problems, Lucas!"

"What good would that have done, huh? I owe three million. The people I borrowed from threatened to kill me! What else was I supposed to do? It's not like you can cash out on the policy whenever you feel like it!"

"That insurance money was for you to take care of Michael and Isabelle—God forbid I died, but you were gonna use it with your slut!"

"I'm not proud of it, Bea, but that's everything. Please untie me. I told you everything."

"We're not done. You need to explain why you had Francis killed."

"What? I didn't have him killed. I mean, he found out what Claire and I were doing, so I threatened him and his family—forced him to shut up."

"So why did he die?"

"It was an accident," he said.

"What do you mean it was an accident? ... Oh, God, that bullet was intended for me? Who took the shot?"

"Some guy—an old Military friend of Claire's. He called her "Cross." She sent the first guy—the one at the cabin, and when he failed, she sent another who killed Francis. Bea, I f**ked up. I really f**ked up. Please forgive me. Oh, God, I'm sorry, Bea. I'm so sorry." I punched him in the face.

"I'm not, you piece of sh*t."

I threw the metal chair across the room, screaming at the top of my lungs. No tears, only anger ravaged me. Disappointed? Yes. I wanted to confront Claire. I wanted her to look me in the eyes and tell me our entire relationship was a lie. I wanted the truth, and as luck would have it, Lucas' phone began buzzing on the table nearby.

"Who is it?" asked Shepard. I glanced at that caller I.D.

"His lover," I said. We walked toward him. "Lucas, why is she calling you?"

"I dunno," he said. Shepard drew his gun, pressing the barrel against his temple.

"We captured you before you turned me in to the FBI and you *don't know* what she wants?" I said. Shepard cocked the hammer.

"Alright! If I don't answer after the third ring it means I'm in trouble, and she should call the FBI!"

It stopped and rang again. I stared at it, contemplating what I'd say to her—thinking of the damage she caused. She betrayed my trust in the worst way possible. She exploited me. She *used* me. After a flow of heightened emotions, the only question I was most interested in asking rolled right off my tongue upon answering.

"Where are my kids, Claire?"

"…They're safe. In fact, my angels are asleep."

"*Your* angels? I know what you did, and I want them back. I swear, if—"

"No need for threats, Bea. You know I wouldn't hurt them. We should talk—you and me. Meet me at Au Bon Pain down the street from the 17th Precinct tomorrow at eleven o'clock. Take a cab, and let it drop you off in front of the Precinct, then make your way to the café. I'll be watching."

"You *gotta be* out of your mind."

"If I catch a scent of anyone with you, you'll regret it. Do you understand? I need to hear you say, "I understand," Bianca."

"Yeah. Tomorrow at eleven o'clock," I said. I hung up.

"What did she say?" asked Shepard.

"She wants me to meet her at Au Bon Pain near the 17th Precinct."

"The one a few blocks from St. Patrick's? You might as well turn yourself in if you're gonna go there."

"Right. She's got something planned, and I have no choice. She didn't even ask for Lucas."

"She suspected he talked. You answered instead of him, and that's a signal—a red flag. Their Plan B."

"I can be arrested, but if I'm found guilty, the insurance money disappears—from what I remember. Lucas gets nothing. That's the agreement, so if she's not trying to get me arrested, then what's she trying to do—kill me herself? I'm gonna need your eyes and ears tomorrow while I'm there, okay?"

"Absolutely. So, what about Lucas?" asked Shepard.

"What about him? Chain him to the pole and leave him. We'll get to him when I feel like it."

24

Café

I TOSSED AND TURNED THAT NIGHT, waking up on occasion, thinking of Claire and the trap I'd be walking into. I figured, as long as she wanted the money, she couldn't have me arrested. My only conclusion for meeting at her requested location was to rattle my cage, so to speak. I grew exhausted—tired of running around, and desired some peace of mind. It was time to listen to her version of the truth roll off her tongue. That morning, Shepard and I got ready to leave, but not before verifying Pascal's whereabouts. *He's still on Gramercy.* I also received a text message response from Kate about the audio and video recording law information I inquired about.

"Any activity with Pascal?" I asked Shepard.

"Nope. Hasn't moved, yet. My tracker will notify us if he does."

"Good. It's a relief knowing we have that situation under control, for once."

"We're making progress," he said.

We left Lucas chained to the metal pole, locked up, and headed outside to hail a cab. "17th Precinct, Manhattan," I said. Getting there took a while—roughly forty-five minutes from Brooklyn. I still wore my disguise. The driver eyed me twice in his rearview mirror. Innocent glances, perhaps. I suppose I either appeared to be familiar or crazy. I prayed he perceived the latter.

The last thing I wanted was to threaten him, and I would've, had his behavior altered. A small television remained attached to the back of the passenger seat in front of me. ABC7 Eyewitness News broadcasted a profile picture of me with the headline, "Still at Large." Shepard turned his head away and held my hand to help keep me at ease. I didn't want to draw attention to myself. I turned my head toward the window and stared outside.

***

We arrived at my destination. "You can stop here," I said. I gave him fifty dollars. Shepard continued, exiting the cab one block from the café. Police cars remained stationary in front of the precinct, and I walked along the building, knowing Claire watched from afar. I maintained a serious, unemotional expression, and strolled through the pen of swine undetected until I approached the intersection. I stood relieved and smiled—proud of myself for slithering through danger unscathed. The adrenaline alone eradicated my need for caffeine, inhaling the lingering aroma of bravery and defeat. I crossed the street, ready to dominate Claire's world. The café resided before me, and I made my way in at ten-thirty a.m. I searched for her and scanned the room, but there was no sign of her. I found an empty table in the corner, approached it, and sat, staring at my phone—keeping my head down. I glanced upward, and she sat at a table across the way with her legs crossed. A set of salt n' pepper shakers, sugar, and two cups resided on the table. My eyes met hers, and she stared at me, smiling until I claimed the chair across from her. I assumed Shepard toddled along into the cafe, headed toward the back.

"Good seeing you again, dear friend," she said.

"What's with all the theatrics? I'm sure you enjoyed watching me walk down that way."

"The Bianca I knew wouldn't have done that, so I had to witness it for myself. I had to gauge the type of person I'd be dealing with, today. The old you would've been crying on the phone last night, pleading and begging me to return the kids. You've changed. You're different, although, ending a life would change anyone. I remember being with Francis when you admitted to killing that cop."

"You took advantage of that so you could always be one… step… ahead. You just sat there and pretended to care about me. What kind of friend does that? Never mind. Don't answer that. Where are my kids?"

"Bea, they're fine... and safe. You need to trust me."

"*Trust you*? I'm their mother. They need me! You're delusional and psychotic."

"And you're a dissociative b**ch—an unfit mother. I mean, look at you. Look at the mess you made. The FBI has a pile of evidence against you. Your face is everywhere. Sad. The reality is you're going to die trying. Oh, by the way, I got you a cup of your favorite coffee."

"F**k your cup of coffee."

"Bianca, how rude of you to refuse my kindness. Here... accept it as a nice gesture between old friends."

"Do you take me for an idiot? Rat poison could be in it. Listen, I know everything, Claire. You hired someone to kill me... twice and failed. The bullet meant for me killed Francis instead, right?"

"Hmm. You wouldn't be sitting in front of me if I had you in my crosshairs," she said.

"…Ah, hence the name, Cross."

"A nickname from back at the academy. I never missed a shot. But why would I hire someone to kill you, Bea?"

"Money. Lucas told you about my life insurance policy. You thought my resistance toward the police would get me killed––in which Lucas would collect a payout, but when that failed, you sent someone after me at Lake George. I traced your gun for hire's number back to Francis' office where you misplaced your phone. I saw the security footage of you."

"Liar. I confiscated that before anyone else got access," she said. She tapped her finger before folding her arms.

"You sure about that? I have a copy of it on a thumb drive. You got careless, Claire. Your fingerprints are on the phone you left in Francis' office. I was also able to view your text message correspondence with your mercenary. I also have Pascal in custody, as well as Lucas' full confession. He says it was *all* your idea."

"No. No way. He wouldn't do that. He loves me too much."

"Open your eyes, Claire! He *cheated* on you with my old assistant. You didn't know that, did you? Look what he's done to me. What makes you more special than me?" She took a deep breath and exhaled before lifting her chin and lowering her eyes.

"We love each other, you know. He got tired of you—tired of your obsession with that *stupid* gallery—tired of your postpartum, and *tired* of the same old story of how you two met. He was *dead* last on the list of the people you loved. I was there for him when you weren't. You didn't even meet in Italy. It was Naples, New York. I knew something was wrong with you when he showed me your birth certificate. Your childhood abuse gave you false memories."

"Was it all worth it, Claire—to strip my family from me and try having me killed?"

"I loved Lucas the first day I met him. He was so kind and made me feel like part of the family. And when you gave birth to Michael and Isabelle, they opened my world. The love I had for them forced me to view life from a new perspective—especially when reciprocated. You bore the sort of children my broken womb could *never* have. My hysterectomy and the military *f**ked me* for life! So, I envied you, but they all love me, so yes... it was worth it. They're better off with me."

Patrons glanced our way, and I trembled at her response––appalled and mortified. The veil lifted from my eyes, learning the origin of her two-faced, lackluster loyalty and delusion. I thought we were family, but the truth proved otherwise. Our friendship derived from jealousy, deceit, and lies. I put too much trust in her over the years.

I could tell she trusted some information I divulged about her fingerprints earlier, regardless of her poker face. As you imagined, I lied, telling her I owned those prints, text correspondence, and video footage. Throwing in a few concrete facts about Lucas and Pascal with a lie made it plausible. What she didn't know was that I recorded Lucas' confession as well as hers, too, at the table. It was enough to absolve me of any crimes. I hated her at that moment but was more than pleased to witness her facial expression after playing back a segment of our conversation from my phone.

"What did you do?" she said.

"What do you think?"

"You think you're smart, huh? Recording without my permission is inadmissible in court in New York." I leaned forward.

"Not unless it's in a public place. I can prove coercion and use it to keep you, Lucas, and Pascal away from me and my kids––thanks to my friend, Kate who sent me the information," I said.

"I still have Michael and Isabelle. If you submit that to the authorities, I swear you won't ever see them again."

"It's over for you, Claire. Nowhere to run."

"Bianca, you're considered armed and dangerous. I'm sure the law wouldn't hesitate to eliminate you on sight if I yelled, "gun."

She shoved a 9MM in my hands before throwing her hands in the air, shouting, "Don't shoot!" She acted scared, staring above my head. I turned around. Two officers stood near the register with their hands placed on their holstered guns.

"She's got a gun! Please don't hurt me!" she said.

I turned back around, leering at her. The room's indistinct chatter subsided. I became the focal point of everyone's attention. People stared in terror—their fear breathing hot air down my neck. The cops withdrew their guns. Goosebumps surfaced on my arms, straightening their hairs. I sensed the officer's careful advancement. Men, women, and children removed themselves from my presence in haste. A single voice projected toward me a few feet away.

"Ma'am, I'm Officer Lopez. I'm gonna need you to place the gun on the table and put your hands in the air for me," he said.

My heartbeat slowed. The ringing in my ear didn't commence, yet, I closed my eyes, allowing Elizabeth to take control of the situation. A seamless transformation. *Deep breaths. I've got this.*

"Hey! Put your hands up... right now!" he said.

Claire's Oscar-winning performance fooled everyone, yet I remained the culprit with my palms resting on the table. I was running out of time, and had no plan, but assessed my options without delay. Lopez stood behind me to my left, and the other advanced to my right. The gun sat in-between my hands close to my chest—clear as day for everyone's viewing. Not a morsel of compliance existence within. Bianca did nothing wrong. One of them called for backup on the radio. The small bell above the front door sustain a never-ending ring, as people evacuated, transitioning to the sidewalk and street. Claire, the 'acting' victim removed herself from my sight with ease, slithering away like a snake. Stopping her proved to be impossible.

"This is your last warning! Show me your hands!" said Lopez. I used the reflective silver salt and pepper shakers in front of me to approximate the officers' positions.

"Hands! Now!"

"This isn't mine," I said.

Cornered and out of options, I relied on Shepard—my only hope. He showed up in time, edging from the far end of the café, blurting out a fake name.

"Officers, I'm special agent Daniels approaching you from behind. My weapon is drawn, and I'm on your side. What's the situation here?" said Shepard.

"We have a non-compliant female—armed and dangerous," said the officer to my right.

"Holster your firearm and show me your badge, sir," said Lopez.

"No can do. That woman's wanted and dangerous. *I'm on your side.* Keep eyes on her."

The agent to my right swapped positions with Lopez. He approached Shepard with caution, inching toward him to view his credentials. *Perfect timing.*

"Alright, I'm putting my hands in the air now," I said.

I stood and turned around. My eyes fixated on Shepard. He gazed at me, displaying a succinct, sly smirk. I reciprocated, and he threw a brisk, unexpected punch at the officer's face, attempting to disarm him. His assault didn't knock him out, so they continued fighting, causing a big commotion. Officer Lopez turned his head to catch a glimpse of the action before turning back around. I, too landed a punch, breaking his nose before gripping his gun. He took a swing at me, and one I couldn't escape, but I refused to release his weapon. He placed his hand around my jaw, squeezing with tremendous strength. Blood from my nostrils ran down his hand. I placed my hand on his throat, clenching without a glimmer of remorse. Neither one of us dared to yield.

Bang. A shot fired into the ceiling. He gasped, refusing surrender, banging my skull against the painted drywall. My grip on the gun and his neck weakened. *Thud.* He bashed my head once more, impacting my ego.

"Enough or I'll shoot!" said Shepard. He scurried toward us, pointing his gun against the back of his head. The officer released his grasp from my jaw. "The gun, too." Lopez paused, reluctant to comply. "Do it!"

"Okay, okay. Don't shoot. I have a family."

"Put your hands behind your head and turn around. Walk to that corner."

"You don't have to do this. Please don't kill me."

"Shut up, face the wall, and handcuff yourself to that pole. Move the wrong way and you'll be full of holes. You got it? Don't make me repeat myself." He nodded and complied.

"What about my partner? He alive?"

"He'll be fine. My friend and I are leaving, now," said Shepard. He peered into my eyes, knowing my identity. "Liz, are you okay to walk? Let's leave before more come. Hurry." I struggled to stand, making my way to the front door.

"Claire—where's Claire?" I asked.

"I don't know. She must've left before I showed up."

"We can't let her escape."

"Don't worry. I put a tracking device on her car before I walked in. You okay?

"Peachy. Let's go after her."

"Are you sure you're okay?"

I nodded, regaining my balance, wit, and vigor as those precious seconds passed. We made our way through the bystanders outside the cafe. Some people cheered. Others, angry. We ran down the street as fast as possible. Claire outsmarted me, and my insatiate thirst for revenge endured. I turned around to find people staring from afar—pointing in our direction.

"Hurry," said Shepard.

The police sirens wailed from afar. Several officers ran toward us with their hands placed on their holstered weapons. Shepard hopped on a black Royal Enfield motorcycle a few feet away from the curb. He turned the ignition, revving its engine.

"Where'd you get the keys?"

"You know the answer to that. Hop on."

The officers got closer, almost within firing range. Some of them removed their guns. We raced off, making our way to 3rd avenue. Traffic soon made us halt, and I continued glancing backward, hoping the officers kept their distance. Shepard advanced, squeezing in between cars.

"Construction ahead," he said.

"Jump the curb!" I said.

I turned my head around again to discover 'the boys in blue' running after us with vigor. Every second we stayed put was another second closer to either being shot or apprehended. The temperature decreased as flurries sifted through the air. Adrenaline coursed through my body.

"Liz, hold tight!" said Shepard.

He accelerated, turning onto the sidewalk, riding as fast as he could without running anyone over. A dark-haired woman and her two young children jumped out of our way. I couldn't help but turn around to look at them. They reminded me of Bianca and the kids. The police were almost out of sight, and we arrived at the end of the sidewalk, getting back on the street.

"One more street 'till we drive down Park Avenue. Hold on!"

It was deemed to be the more viable option, and yet the best route in our attempt to make a clean escape. Our desired street was less congested than the others, so we made the left turn. I glanced to my right, and discovered Claire beside me, riding in the back of a cab—not in her car. *What?* Call it fate, coincidence, or whatever, it was as if Shepard was guided in the right direction.

"Claire!" I said.

Her eyes widened the instant we made contact. She pulled out a gun, pressing it against the back of the driver's skull, shouting at him. He white-knuckled the steering wheel and accelerated. We pursued. The police caught up with us, and their sirens blared, slicing through the thin, icy air. Apart from them, our only other problem was the traffic light ahead.

"They're not stopping!" I said to Shepard.

The chances of them making it without a scratch—well, the odds were not in their favor due to the impatient nature of New York City drivers. The opposing traffic sped off, darting through the intersection the second their light turned green. *Wham.* A Honda collided with the tail end of the cab, causing it to fishtail onto the concrete median. Traffic halted in both directions. Claire opened the passenger door with her gun in hand, striding toward two curious motorcyclists from a nearby lane.

"Hey, lady, are you alright?" one motorcyclist asked.

She pointed her weapon at his head. "Move!" she said. He backed away with his hands in the air. I stood two cars behind. "Claire!" She mounted the red Kawasaki, disregarding my existence. *She knows how to ride?* Police sirens grew closer. She sped off, leaving the biker in disarray.

"We can't let her escape, Shepard!" I said. I unmounted the bike, headed toward the bikers.

"Where are you going?" he asked.

"To borrow a bike," I said.

"You barely know how to ride!"

"Believe me, Bea remembers."

I *had to* chase her myself. My impatience got the best of me.

"I need your bike," I said to the biker.

He extended the kickstand, stepped away from his fluorescent green Kawasaki, and displayed his palms at shoulder-length, walking backward.

"Don't have to tell me twice," he said.

"You hear those sirens? Tell 'em everything that woman did."

I drove away. Claire sped down Park Avenue toward the MetLife building, weaving through vehicles. I did my best to move through the congestion with little concern for traffic lights. Shepard followed while I blazed through. It wasn't long before I caught up to her. She took advantage of the green lights and glanced back before making an abrupt, last-minute maneuver— making a quick right turn on to 44th street. I hoped to cut her off, so I stopped a moment to converse with Shepard.

"What's wrong?" he asked.

"I've got her. You go that way. Cut her off on Vanderbilt and 42nd. Hurry!"

We sped off, riding as fast as possible. Shepard disappeared around the corner and I continued tailing her through 44th street. I was positive Shepard would catch up to her sooner than me, but I was wrong. Blaring horns ricocheted off the building walls, traveling down the street toward me followed by a crash. It appeared she slowed down, approaching Vanderbilt and 42nd street. I approached the scene to find Claire's bike parked near the curb, and Shepard lying on to ground covered in the shattered glass behind a Ford Expedition. His bike laid wedged under the rear. I caught a glimpse of Claire running into Grand Central Terminal.

She disappeared into the busy crowd by the time I arrived at the door in pursuit—gone with the wind. I turned my attention toward Shepard lying on the frigid asphalt. Strangers surrounded him. Sirens wailed.

"Nobody touches him!" I said. "Hey, you okay?" I knelt beside him. He winced, gnashing his teeth.

"No, I think I cut my leg pretty bad."

"We need to get out of here," I said. I used his belt as a tourniquet. "Stand to your feet. C'mon, we gotta go."

"Ouch! Damn, that hurts."

"Let's stitch you up."

"I'll be fine. I've had worse."

"You're not fine. You're bleeding! I'll find us a ride," I said.

The driver of the Expedition stood nearby, holding his head in his hands, staring.

"This your car?" I asked.

"Oh, sh*t. Yeah. Hey man, you 'ight?" he asked Shepard.

"He look alright to you? It's freezing and he's in pain. Open the door and let him lie down on your back seat till the ambulance arrive."

" 'Ight lay him down, but don't get no blood on my seat," he said. Shepard winced, mounting into the vehicle.

"Help me remove the bike out from under here. You'll have to maneuver it while I move your car up. We're blocking the intersection."

"Yeah, no problem."

I climbed into the driver's side, accelerated, and drove away with Shepard. The owner yelled in the distance as I leered, watching him get smaller in the side mirror.

"How you holdin' up back there?" I asked.

"I'll be fine. Nothing a drink or two can't fix," he said.

"You rode that bike like a natural, by the way." He chuckled.

"We'll get you stitched up and everything else you need soon enough. We're almost at the drug store."

I clutched the steering wheel, anticipating the surprise arrival of the police… and noticed my bloody hands. Bianca started surfacing. She grew strong enough to distort my thoughts, but I sustained consciousness. She evolved and morphed, elevating herself within me. I stopped at a traffic light, and my once-benevolent sister took complete control.

More capable, more intelligent, and increased self-awareness, these qualities stole the limelight. I glared into the visor mirror with clarity of mind, viewing a woman fueled by love, driven by instinct, and shaped by circumstance. However, I adored the power and dominance I possessed, flowing like a current of unconstrained electricity stirring within. I tapped my fingers on the wheel.

"There's a pharmacy a few blocks from here," I said. "Hang in there."

"No, don't stop. I'll be fine, Bea," he said.

"We're going to Dr. Carter's."
I sped off, aware of the possibility of being spotted by the police. Claire's escape fueled my infuriation and weaved Elizabeth's egregious, inauspicious behavior deeper into compartments of my disfigured psyche.

25

Finding Claire

I DROVE THROUGH RED TRAFFIC LIGHTS with caution, all the while conversing with Shepard, trying to keep his mind off the pain.

"How's it going back there?" I said.

"I think I'll live. Carter's got no reason to help us, but he's a reasonable man, but not fond of Liz."

"I'm aware, and ready to make it up to him."

"We need to find Claire, though," he said.

"We *need* to get you stitched up, first. You're lucky you didn't cut your femoral."

***

We arrived at the house. Dr. Carter didn't hesitate to treat Shepard. He welcomed us inside, leading us to the dining room.

"Hey, clear the table, so I can lay him on it," he said. "Wait here."

He returned with a few items, ready to suture Shepard's leg. Apologizing about Elizabeth's conduct didn't come without some embarrassment.

"I'm so sorry for my sister's behavior earlier. Although, I appreciate you helping Shepard, here."

"I shouldn't be doing this—especially after what happened. If Pascal finds out, I'm a dead man. Do you hear me? My loyalty is to him, but my conscience won't allow me to neglect my oath."

"Get me some water, will you, Bea?" asked Shepard.

"Sure. Be right back."

I moved away, walking toward the kitchen, and returned with some tap water in a cup.

"You mind if I use your bathroom, doc?" He squinted, hesitating to give a response.

"I won't cause any—"

"Top of the stairs, on the left. Don't touch anything."

Shepard held a conversation with him, one long enough for me to slip away, so I could sneak a peak of Pascal. The door to the basement was open—enough to wedge myself through without making it squeak. I chose my steps with care, hoping my footsteps wouldn't re-direct his attention. I didn't have to walk down the full distance to see him—only halfway to catch a glimpse of his pathetic self, sleeping. He appeared to be a prisoner in his state of being, confided to his inability to recover sooner than later. I tiptoed back upstairs to the second floor, entered the bathroom, and flushed the toilet. Dr. Carter continued attending to Shepard upon my return.

"So tell me, doc. How long do you think Pascal will be down there, for?"

"After what your crazy sister did to him... days—weeks, maybe. Why?"

"Damn—just wanted talk to him, is all—with your supervision, of course."

He finished suturing Shepard and carried his supplies into the basement. I grew eager to converse with Shepard—to tell him we needed to leave. Lucas was on my mind. I left him chained to a pole all day. *He must be in a lot of pain.* No food, water, or sunshine the whole time... *Eh, so what. He'll live.* I sensed Elizabeth had a serious question for him—one a man under duress might answer in haste.

"Shep, I went downstairs and saw Pascal. He was sleeping or maybe unconscious. I don't think Carter's planning on moving him anytime soon. We need to get back to Lucas. He'll know where Claire is. Are you okay to walk on your own?"

"No, but some painkillers would be amazing right now."

"I'll ask Carter. Be right back."

He walked back upstairs with crutches in one hand, and a few pills in the other. Shepard swallowed them, chugging the water to follow.

"Thank you, doc," I said.

"Yeah, and thanks for sewing me up. We'll get out of your hair, now." He handed me two small unlabeled orange and white bottles.

"Here. Take as needed. Also, do yourselves a favor and don't ever come back to this house. I won't be able to help after today, and it won't go well for me if Pascal learns what I did for you."

"Got it. Thank you for everything," I said.

We left the house and made it to the corner of the sidewalk with a bottle of painkillers and antibiotics in my pocket. I hailed a cab, abandoning the Ford Explorer. Shepard viewed his phone, trying to track Claire, but her car remained stationary near the café. "She won't go back for it," he said. He also struggled to stay awake, and I dozed off a portion of the ride to his place.

***

Our driver stopped at a traffic light. "We'll get out, here," I said. He let us out one block away. I hated myself for waking Shepard, but couldn't risk allowing anyone to know his location. After helping him inside, I got him undressed, removing his bloody clothes and shoes before he laid to rest on his bed. I showered, borrowed some of his clothing, and went downstairs to visit Lucas with a glass of ice water in hand.

"Wake up," I said.

I launched it into his face. He jolted out of his sleep, breathing heavy—frightened out of his mind.

"Bea! *Get me out of here, please!* Un-cuff me. My arms are cramped."

"Good. You deserve it."

"Oh for God's sake, you just can't leave me here, tied up."

"I don't see why not."

"Can you be a decent human being and give me some water?" he asked. I walked away.

"Don't go anywhere," I said.

***

I returned with two ham n' cheese sandwiches and bottled water. Elizabeth appeared in an elegant, black dress when I sat down on the stool in front of Lucas. He needed to be hand-fed, finishing it in no time at all. Liz didn't say a word the entire time, but paced about the room with poise and grace, humming 'What a Wonderful World.' She soon sat on the chair nearby and crossed her legs, divulging scenarios of his demise.

"A man's gotta eat—even the disloyal ones, I guess? He's so pathetic-looking," she said. She tilted her head and lifted the corner of her mouth while delivering a long, malevolent glower.

"Now's not the time, Liz."

"No food. No water. No sunlight. My idea of a party."

"Who are you talking to, Bea?" asked Lucas.

"Shut up," I said.

"He'll never understand us," said Elizabeth.

"He will when he's locked up."

"There's no one else here," he said.

"Lucas, shut up!"

"I wish we could kill him," she said. Her tongue browsed her bottom lip.

"Well, we need him alive. He'll die a slow death behind bars, one day soon."

"You should ask him about the house in the Poconos."

"Our vacation home? Why?"

"Because I bet he and that b**ch spent weekends there. The kids are probably there, as we speak. She's familiar with the area. That's where I'd go if I were her."

A recollection of Claire mentioning my vacation home dawned on me. It made sense she'd go there, and probable the twins resided with her. I yearned to hold them in my arms again while Lucas held a bewildered gaze, desperate to be free.

"You're bat-sh*t crazy, now, aren't you—talking to yourself?" he asked.

"Just imagine what I'd do to you if you lie to me. I'm gonna ask you this once, and only once. The kids... are they currently in our vacation home with Claire?"

He wept, nodding his head—pouring his regrets onto the cold cement. Elizabeth was right. She relished in the presence of his anguish and basked in the reality of his distress. She sat about thirty feet away from me on the chair when a tingling sensation rippled from the center of my chest. Her emotions channeled in transference. She smirked—and as fast as she appeared, she disappeared the instant I turned my head.

"How long are they staying there for, Lucas?"

"Three days. We agreed that if anything were to happen to either one of us, we'd stay there for three days to sort things."

"I ran into Claire a few hours ago. She *believes* in you, and is kinda obsessed, too. She wants the ideal family—*my* family. It breaks my heart that she wanted me dead as much as you. You know, her ex-husband left her because she couldn't have kids—around the time Michael and Isabelle were born. She stuck to me like glue, pretending to be a loyal friend. I see why, now. It all makes sense, and I've been a fool the last seven years. Not anymore. If I go now, I can make it to the house in about two hours."

"Wait, please don't leave me here. Let me come with you. I wanna help you make this right."

"Oh, you gotta be joking." I walked away without looking back.

"No, Bea. Don't leave me here! Bianca. *Bianca!*

I closed the door and listened for his yelling, but couldn't hear a pin drop. Judge me however you like. I settled part of a score. Wouldn't you have done the same?

Shepard was in no condition to leave with me to Pennsylvania—so I wrote him a note and placed it under his medication bottles along with the thumb drive and disc I took from Pascal. Apart from, "I miss you, already" and "Get better soon," I offered the details of my plan and future location. My gun, disguise, and Shepard's car keys were all I needed before walking out of his place.

***

I left Manhattan, exiting the Holland Tunnel, and stopped at the gas station before the Pulaski Skyway bridge. I filled the tank, opened the car door, and sat down. Elizabeth appeared, sitting in the passenger seat with her legs crossed, wearing a black satin dress under a white fur coat.

"You're nervous, Bea," she said. "I can feel it. What do you plan on doing with Claire?" I squeezed the steering wheel.

"I don't know," I said.

"You gonna have to shoot her if you wanna stop her."

"Not unless I feel like my life or the kids' lives are threatened."

"Hmm. It's almost over, Bea. We'll get them back."

"Tell me something. There's something Pascal mentioned to you earlier about where we grew up. Did we really grow up in Naples, New York, and not Naples, Italy?"

"Oh, Bea. Is it *that* important right now?"

"We have a two-hour trip ahead of us."

"Well, if you insist—yes. He's telling the truth. You blocked out so much to preserve your sanity. We dreamed of going to Italy when we were kids, and *you* fantasized about your future husband, children, and the perfect life. I mean, we were young, and I never cared about those things. You were always the dreamer. I was the doer."

I had no memory of being a native New Yorker. Elizabeth reclined in her seat, closing her eyes.

"Shh. Close your eyes," she said. "Relax."

I complied and experienced an instant flashback of us on a beach. The way she reclined reminded me of our mother reclining in her chair the day we visited Jones Beach Island—Wantagh, N.Y. The memory only lasted a few seconds—the only recollection of a life I lived in New York. Elizabeth and I were happy. It was a time we used to play in the sand with our mother before life became horrible. Our mother, Ismarelda, told us she grew up in Italy before migrating to the states with the hopes of a better life. I opened my eyes. Elizabeth did, too, smiling at me.

"How'd you share that memory with me?" I asked.

"We'll always have that special connection," she said.

I started the ignition and removed my phone from my pocket to brief Kate via text message, saying, "I found Claire and the kids. Send everyone to 1076 Greenbriar Dr., Skytop, PA. Someone's dying tonight." I accelerated, leaving the gas station to drive on to Route 80.

***

Some time passed and Elizabeth spent the whole ride with me until I got to the house. She disappeared in the blink of an eye, again before I approached the gravel driveway. The presence of despair lingered in the dense, surrounding wooded air. The snow-laden evergreens hunched forward in the darkness while the atmospheric fog impaired my vision. I switched the car lights off, parking alongside the thickened bushes before making my way to the front door. I kept my distance, waiting for movement inside the house. No activity.

I decided to approach the house and found a car in the rear driveway. It belonged to Claire. *Probably a rental.* Visibility increased the closer I approached, hoping not to be seen or make any alarming sounds. My heartbeat accelerated and my jugular pulsed, like it wanted to burst out of my neck. I stood with my back hugging the wall of the house—left of the door, leaning over to stay undetected while reaching for the doorknob. Locked. I kept a spare key hidden in a fake rock pile under the wilted shrubbery and used it to enter the house, advancing without making a sound. The kid's sneakers sat near the door, bringing me some relief. Claire's shoes were present, too, and her purse hung on the wall-mounted coat rack.

It was late in the evening, and I was sure the twins fell asleep in their rooms. I checked every room on the first floor before the basement, submerging into its depth. Claire wasn't anywhere to be found until creaking and humming resonated from above. I tiptoed upstairs hiding behind the crackling, two-sided fireplace with my weapon drawn. An empty bottle of Risperidone (an antipsychotic) sat on the mantle amongst other medications. She ambled toward the kitchen, headed in my direction.

I had one of two options—confront her and wait for the police—or wait for her to fall asleep before evacuating the kids. I leaned forward for a better view of her. Muffled, succinct thumping vibrated above us. She turned around, sauntering toward the bottom of the stairs.

"Go back to bed. We've got a long day tomorrow," she said.

She made her way back past the fireplace, still humming a tune. I maneuvered to the other end, hiding from her view while she walked to the sofa with her cup and phone in hand.

She lifted her head, tilting it after gazing out the window––and noticed something, judging by her obscure body language. She stood, approached the living room window, and exhaled. *Something's not right.* Claire held a distinct walk when upset—one where her heels impacted the floor hard enough for you to feel the vibrations across the room. She spotted something in the distance, craning her neck forward before making her way to the front door. She looked down, clicking her tongue. My faint, dissipating footprints trailed into the house. I made myself visible with the inevitability of being found and extended my arms with my gun pointing at her face.

"Sloppy work with the trail, Bea. You should've walked around back if you didn't want them to be seen."

"I'm here to see my kids and to talk to you."

"Bea, we *talked* about this. They're better off with me."

"Claire, you can never be their real mother. Even Lucas knows this."

"Where is he? He should be here with me."

"Like I said, he sold you out and told me your location. How else do you think I found you? Claire, you may never see him again. You understand, right?" She elevated her eyebrows.

"You need to leave or I'll end up killing you," she said.

"I don't know what's gotten into you, but the police and FBI are on their way. They'll find my body and a pile of evidence against you if you kill me."

"You'd be dead... and my little angel wo—"

"Would be in foster care. We don't want that to happen. I only wanna see them. That's all."

"You think I'm gonna roll over and *let* you take them from me, Bea?" She removed her gun from her purse, hanging near the door.

"It's over Claire. Let's stop this nonsense."

"No. Those are *my* kids!" she said. "The kids *I* was supposed to have."

"Alright! Yes, I'm sorry. I'm sorry. Now, put the gun down and just… talk to me, okay?"

"I'm not giving up on them. They love *me*, and Lucas, he loves *me,* too," she said. She readjusted her aim, bending her elbow before extending her arm. I paused but soon stepped toward her.

"Claire, I love you... so much. You've been the only real friend I ever had my whole life. Why don't you set that down on the floor and let's talk about this?"

"Stop it. You're just saying those things to soften me up." Her voice cracked and her eyes welled up. "Bea, *stop* moving or I *will* shoot you," she said.

"It's not so easy to pull the trigger when I'm right in front of you, is it?"

"Don't make me do this. Step back!" she said.

"Alright! Alright, I'm not making you do anything, Claire. I'm sorry. Please put it down. No one needs to get hurt. I've been doing a lot of thinking about you and Lucas. You two can be together, and the kids can live with both of you. I want to turn myself in and terminate my parental rights. You're right. I'm unfit to be their mother. I just want to see them one last time."

"What? Don't f**k with me. You really mean it?" she said. She cried while I placed my gun on the floor before advancing with caution.

"I wanna hug you, Claire. We're family, and I loved you since the day we met. We've been through so much together," I said. "Haven't we?"

She allowed me to embrace her, lowering our guard. Elizabeth appeared, standing behind her, smirking and applauding my performance. She raised her eyebrow and whispered, "It's time." Killing Claire would end it all. Yet, deep inside I knew she acknowledged her actions. A surge of hate and revenge brimmed.

"I'm sorry, Bianca. I'm so sorry," she said. "I made such a f**king mess of us."

She fell to her knees with her gun clutched. I knelt with her, holding her in my arms while she cried.

"It's okay, hon. We'll sort this out," I said.

She hugged me tighter, displaying true remorse. I soon found myself in a position where I no longer had eyes on her weapon. She whispered into my ear, "I'm sorry, Bea," and yanked my hair, exposing my torso.

BANG. I couldn't believe she pulled the trigger, shooting me in my stomach. Red and blue lights flashed a few seconds afterward. We stared into each other's souls, where I couldn't find a morsel of regret in her eyes. She panicked, standing up before grabbing her purse and running out the house through the back door. My hands shook and heart raced. I stumbled to the floor, trying to add pressure and close my wound. I shouted the kids' names to find them hiding around the corner. I was ecstatic to see their faces, crying tears of joy and pain. My breathing increased, but I managed to prop myself upright against the wall. Blood poured out, claiming the wooden floor. The kids ran toward me, hugging me tighter than ever before.

"Michael, baby. Get mommy the blanket on the couch, please? Isabelle, the police are here. I need you to let them in so they can take me to the hospital, okay?"

I didn't want to die in front of them like my parents died in front of me. Hell, I didn't want to die at all, but my love for them kept me alive, I suppose. Their love for me helped me stay awake until the ambulance arrived.

***

Kate and her colleagues showed up minutes before I laid on a gurney. The medic prepped me for departure, but she asked for a moment with me. I was conscious, handcuffed, and smiling.

"How's it feel, taking a bullet?" asked Kate.

"It hurts like hell," I said.

"You'll live. It was a 'through-n-through,' missing your major organs. You got *very* lucky."

"Shepard's hurt. He was in an accident."

"Is he okay? Where is he?"

"He'll be alright. He's stitched up, drugged, and sleeping it off. I took his car, so he's home. You should call him and tell him where to find me later. By the way, thanks for the information you sent, earlier. Both confessions are recorded on my phone."

"Good, I'll take care of those. What about Pascal? He's still at the doctor's house?

"Yeah, he's all yours. Oh, Shepard has the footage, too, by the way."

"Thanks so much, Bea. Wait, what about Lucas? Where's he?"

"He's tied to a pole in a padded room at Shepards. Hold your breath before walking in. He hasn't seen a bathroom in almost forty-eight hours," I said.

"Hey, try not to worry about Claire. They'll find her. Oh, and don't worry about your kids. I'll look after them while you're away. You'll be in police custody a while until your preliminary hearing. And be at ease about any of the evidence. I think the judge will find it in his or her heart to be lenient, based on the extenuating circumstances. Either way, we both have Shepard to help. I'll pay him a visit in the morning, collect Lucas, and work on getting you acquitted."

"Thanks for everything, Kate."

We departed minutes later. The ambulance hauled me away, but not before I kissed my kids goodbye. Elizabeth showed up, sitting next to me, holding my hand. She held it the entire ride. I dared not acknowledge her for fear of appearing crazy in front of the medic. She had a one-sided conversation where I nodded or shook my head without being seen.

"I wonder where Claire is headed. You think she'll ever show her face again?" asked Elizabeth.

I lifted my eyebrows, folded my lips, and shrugged my shoulders, hoping she'd keep her distance from the kids. The act of crossing my fingers wasn't good enough to keep her away, but I'd soon find out that my enemies were a little more difficult to track down.

26

'201119'

I WOULD'VE BEEN A FOOL TO EXPECT anything more than a comfortable bed and room service at Lehigh Valley Medical Center. Surgery for my wound commenced where I thought of my children before being 'put under.' Yes, it hurt like hell—being shot, but I was more worried about surviving for them more than anything else. Thank God the ambulance arrived in time. I 'toughed it out.'

***

I woke up to two police officers outside my door with automatic rifles, a nurse inside my room named Jackie, and handcuffs around my wrist.

"You're awake. How are you feeling?" she said.

"Groggy. Where am I, exactly?"

"You're at Lehigh Valley Medical Center's Recover Room. I'll fetch the doctor."

Special Agent Gerald Hall entered the room with his colleague the moment she left. He wore a smirk, puffing his chest and raising his chin. Sure, the possibility of running into him again was likely. Thrilled? Not in the least. The last time I saw him, well, he pointed a gun at Liz at Rockefeller Center.

"Well, well! Look what our 'boys in blue' dragged in. I bet you're happy to see me," he said.

"Nothing but cartwheels on the inside. That being said, I'm going to walk away from this, Special Agent A**hole."

"Really, now? You sound pretty confident, Bianca—especially after *murdering* that officer. There's no walking away from that."

"Self-defense—and protecting my kids from a compromised officer of the so-called law."

"So, you're admitting to killing him," he said. He placed his hands inside his pant pockets.

"I'm only admitting to exercising my rights as a U. S. citizen. Nothing else."

"What about the man you held at gunpoint at Rockefeller Center?"

"Who? I don't remember any of that."

"Oh, come on, Bianca. The insanity card won't work."

"I don't know what you're talking about, but the evidence will speak for itself. Everything will be made right."

"What's that supposed to mean? You plannin' somethin'?"

"I wanna call my lawyer, now, if you don't mind. Maybe I can use your phone?"

"Funny. A hospital phone will be brought to you. We'll be listening."

"And where will I be transferred?"

"We're taking you to Metropolitan Correctional Center in a few days," said his colleague.

"Where's that?"

"Downtown Manhattan," said Agent Hall.

I dialed my lawyer, Jennifer Bailey. We spoke for about five minutes and hung up. Shepard appeared out of nowhere, dressed as a patient—like an apparition from a haunted house, strolling past my room window. He smiled, glancing my way—and up to something, no doubt. I smiled, diverting my gaze toward Mr. Hall and his colleague.

"This conversation is over. You've got nothing. Get out," I said. They stormed away, slamming the door shut.

***

My recovery lasted about a week. Kate and my lawyer were the only two allowed to visit. I hadn't seen Elizabeth during my stay. The drugs I took suppressed her, I suppose. Kate entered with a sheet of paper in hand and told me Pascal and Dr. Carter disappeared. The entire house had been cleaned out, and after further investigation, they found it belonged to my despicable uncle. I asked about the tracker Shepard placed inside his Rolex.

"The only thing left in the basement was his watch and the tracker lying next to it on the floor, Bea," said Kate.

"You're kidding, right? Son of a—he did it to tease us," I said.

"We underestimated him."

"I'm so sorry, Kate. He'll come back. I know it sounds crazy, but my gut tells me he'll pop up. You know, I wouldn't be surprised if he made a grand entrance, unannounced at the Gala. Everything will blow over by then."

"I've got the recording of Pascal to show the judge. The sooner they review everything, the sooner you're released. It's all substantial. Don't worry. You'll be taken care of, okay?" she said.

"What about Lucas?" I said.

"He confessed to everything. He folded—couldn't take it anymore."

"And what about Claire? Did you find her?"

"She's gone, Bea. A wanted woman. She'd be a fool to risk coming back. The evidence against her is overwhelming."

Disappointment settled in, realizing they could emerge from the shadows at any time.

"Oh, I almost forgot. This is for you," said Kate. She handed me the sheet of paper she walked in with. "We found it under Pascal's watch." I viewed a copied, archived newspaper article entitled, 'Family Brutally Murdered'—The Naples News. It dated back to June 12, 1990.

"It says you went missing after the murder," said Kate.

"I thought he'd find me. Did what I had to until I felt safe, and ran into an old couple somewhere who took me in as their own. I didn't say a single word for about a year, suffering from Selective Mutism—and when they died, child services came. Even then, I kept running. The rest is history."

Kate held my hand, trying to console me, experiencing similar circumstances.

"We'll get him. I'll never stop," she said.

***

It was time for the officers to transfer me to the correction center that afternoon. I didn't want to go. I mean, I didn't know what to expect—the process, the rules, but my lawyer said, "You'll be alright. We'll figure this out." I held on to those words but had more faith in Kate and Shepard. Liz found a way through to me in the elevator.

The guards shackled my legs with restraints, and Elizabeth's presence lingered, keeping me calm the whole time. Shame and remorse eluded me while I walked through the halls with my head held high until we made our way outside. Three guards exited their SUV. One, the driver, and the others, armed with assault rifles, ready to eliminate me if I tried anything stupid.

The ride to the facility had taken two hours, and within that time I did nothing but enjoy the scenery, imagining I was on a road trip with the kids. I reminisced, cherishing the moment I held them in my arms a week ago, yearning to be with them again.

***

Time flew by, and we were back in Manhattan. I exited the vehicle, ready to face the paparazzi and ABC7 Eyewitness news standing in front of the facility. They were hungry for answers, swarming me—asking multiple questions all at once. Reporters and journalists took pictures.

Guards escorted me to a room where two female officers performed a *complete* body search about twenty minutes upon arrival. Humiliation dampened my soul—never experiencing such nakedness to that degree. Fingerprinting commenced, followed by an issued inmate number, 201119. A glamorous, orange outfit completed my processing. The corrections officers didn't like me much, exhibiting gestures of contempt. I soon learned through word-of-mouth I could've been thrown to the wolves, but was ordered to be placed in isolation. They escorted me down the hallway to my cell—too small for performing jumping jacks.

***

Dinner time approached. No steaks, pasta, or a glass of wine, but a half-hour to swallow the slop they called "food." The obliteration of my freedom started the instant I walked into that building. I experienced the expanded reality of isolation from the world. Disconnected. Lucky me, Elizabeth resurfaced.

"They expect you to eat that sh*t?" she said.

"I don't have an appetite for garbage. Wait, is that what I look like in orange?" I said.

"I don't think we'll be wearing it much longer. So, when do they let us out of here?" she asked.

"I'm counting on Kate and Shepard to make something happen soon."

The guards came by every fifteen minutes to check on me. The intermittent jingling keys bounced off their hips as my constant reminder that I had no freedom, whatsoever. I anticipated some news from my lawyer every time they visited, and yet, I remained disappointed. I grew antsy—unable to make a phone call until the following day. The night was long—void of the life and the comforts of life I once knew. Breakfast time—four-thirty a.m. I didn't get much sleep at all—three, maybe four hours, tops, and later received word of a visitor. *Kate? Shepard?* Conversing with either of them would've been fine, but I wanted to see Shepard the most.

"Who's here for me?" I asked the guards.

"Turn around, place your hand behind your back and walk backward to the tray slot," said the mean-looking one.

I complied and walked down a long, narrow hallway with one officer on either side. Neither one uttered a word until we approached a door labeled, 'Visitation Room.' He guided me inside, un-cuffed me, and sat me down in front of Shepard.

"Ten minutes," said the guard.

He strolled away. Shepard sat on the other side of the bulletproof glass partition, smiling. We reached for the phones at the same.

"Oh, my God, I'm so glad to see you!"

"Me, too! So, are they treating you well in here?"

"No complaints. How's your leg?"

"Doing a lot better—like new," he said. "So how long are they gonna keep you in here?"

"Not sure yet. I'm waiting on my lawyer, and hoping she'll visit me today."

"I asked because... I don't think it'll be much longer, Bea. They won't have enough evidence to hold you," he said. He winked.

I was overjoyed to learn such news—relieved more than anything, and I couldn't wait to speak with my legal counsel. Shepard worked his magic, although he was unable to give details over the phone. I assumed he either hacked the FBI and police database, erasing the archived traffic cam footage—or walked into the precinct as an undercover cop and stole it. I was certain Kate lent a helping hand, too. Shepard and I parted ways where I went back to my cell. Jennifer Bailey contacted me with news of my preliminary hearing being fast-tracked.

"There have been some interesting developments regarding your case, and you're scheduled to appear before a judge in three days—maybe sooner. These things usually take longer, but with the lack of sufficient evidence at hand, there's no point in keeping you here much longer," she said. "I don't understand *what happened* or *how* the evidence went missing, but I'm not complaining. In regard to the other charges against you such as holding the civilian, Mr. Gilbert Watson hostage, having possession of an unregistered firearm, resisting arrest, and evading law enforcement, you'll have to pay the price for those."

"What does that mean?"

"It means you'll have to agree to a two-year probationary period, and within that time—given your documented mental history—you'll have to undergo mandatory psych sessions."

"Are you serious? That's *all*? Yes, I'll take it! Thank you!"

"I cashed in a bunch of favors and deals to make it happen with the D.A.'s office. It's the best I could do, considering…"

"We get what we pay for," I said.

***

It was the most exciting news of my entire life. I stood before Judge Pratt two days later, agreeing to the charges. I was a *free* woman afterward! "Insufficient evidence," the court ruled. Those words were like music to my ears. Shepard arrived to pick me up, and we made our way to Council of Family & Child Care in Manhattan for my kids. I'd never been so happy and grateful to see them in all my life.

"You ready to go home?" asked Shepard. My heart exploded with joy.

"I'm dying to get there."

27

Well Done

TWO WEEKS PASSED. I SPENT MOST of my time painting and playing with my kids. It was three days before Christmas, and the roller coaster of events we all experienced took a toll. Quality time with them was of utmost importance with the transition of an absent father. As ordered by the court, I reported to a shrink, Dr. Taylor Obel twice a week. Keeping Elizabeth suppressed was an undesirable of mine, however, staying out of trouble behooved everyone. I struggled to digest being told, "Your sister isn't actually real." Francis believed she was a part of me in some way. I'm stronger and survived because of her. She's the reason I hold my children in my arms, today.

Lucas remained in a jail cell, waiting to be sentenced. Claire disappeared—fallen off the grid. I kept an eye out and an ear to the ground concerning her. My children didn't leave my sight no matter where we went. Any short-haired, blond, Caucasian woman who crossed my path caused me to cringe. Living in fear of her surprise return etched paranoia into my daily life, but Shepard's presence allowed me to feel more at ease. He was the new man in my life—the man I grew fonder of—the one who cared for me.

The Bianca I used to be almost diminished in full. I transitioned into a new version of myself, completing my metamorphosis. My newfound independence took a platform of its own, regarding emotional strength. Elizabeth and I fused in mind and heart. I attributed my perseverance and will to my children—the thought of their faces, fragrance of their hair, and warmth of their embrace. It brought me happiness and kept me moving forward. *Who would I be without them? Where would I be without them?* They were the light of my life *every* day of the week. We played at the park, spending countless hours creating arts and crafts, as well as our evenings' paintings together.

Oh, speaking of painting, the Gala fundraiser event took two weeks to prepare and finalize. Hiring an assistant proved to be a challenge, but not impossible. Shepard and I performed an *extensive* background check before I coasted back into the swing of things. I also changed my personal and business lines, hoping the media would stop calling me. Pesky reporters leached onto me with questions of recent events. A young Asian female journalist approached me outside my workplace, asking about the Gala and my expectations. She claimed to work for the New York Times. Jennifer Bailey coached me on delivering a brief response. "*I've been acquitted of the allegations against me, and as a partner of MoMA, the Gala will commence, as it does every year.*"

"It's best we get ahead of this. Staying quiet would only make you look guilty, and raise speculation," said Jennifer. It was only a matter of time before the reporters stopped harassing me. I followed her advice, but the truth is I wanted to lash out and swear like a sailor. *Restrain yourself, Bea. Stay calm.*

I forced myself to 'play the part' for the sake of the Gala. Embarrassing MoMA any further would've cost me. I wanted people to attend. Past events proved that guests have always enjoyed themselves. I expected artists, gallery owners, auction houses, journalist's and many more to make an appearance. I chose to display a piece of art I completed a few weeks ago, right before I met Pascal. I named it, 'La Geminae,'—a Latin derivative of Geminae Superia, meaning, 'twin guardians that accompany the Living Saint Celeste.' Like Elizabeth, they are protectors and defenders. It remained in the studio area of my home, untouched. I considered its excellence, but it lacked something I couldn't place my finger on. Ah! It needed a hint of—a mere splash of red. Claire thought of it as dark-spirited weeks ago. I sent a photo of it to a trusted local art expert and auctioneer, Anton, in search of a second opinion. He described my work as "Marvelously Eccentric."

La Geminae was decided to be displayed at the fundraiser. I crossed my fingers, hoping it would've been the talk of the evening. Anton agreed, too, and soon after speaking with him, I went about my day to run errands. Friends and acquaintances stared at me. Some wished me well. Others pretended they hadn't seen me. I understood some thought of me as guilty, but I didn't care. I viewed myself as a lioness, disregarding the opinion of sheep.

A few guests had fallen off my guest list, canceling at the last minute. No surprise there. The rumors about my ordeal spread like wildfire. I always looked forward to the big event, but never to run into Claire or Pascal.

The thought of bumping into them on the street crossed my mind from time to time. I often saw men who resembled Pascal from afar—impacted with brief flashbacks of his face. The trauma played with my psyche, regardless of how hard I tried leaving my trauma in the past. I declared that my peace of mind could only be attained by either the confirmed death or capture of my adversaries.

***

It was time for me to prepare for the Gala. I had a multitude of tasks to accomplish and couldn't get it all done in a day. Friday moved along, and before I realized it, six o'clock pm came around. Although my piece, La Geminae had been deemed finished, I believed it still needed that touch of red. *I need to re-paint it on a larger scale.* The blank canvases at home were too small. I desired for my painting to own a sense of grandeur in style and size. My large, blank ones resided in the gallery—which is where I went to paint my replica around nine o'clock in the evening. Shepard agreed to babysit the kids at my house for a while.

Music, solitude, and a bottle of red wine, sitting on my art cart solidified 'the perfect evening.' Hours passed. The atmosphere remained quiet. Having a relaxing night all to myself felt awkward, but soon subsided due to a calming glass of Gagliole Gallule Chianti Riserva. *I should order something to eat.* I ordered takeout from a local Italian restaurant a couple of blocks away and waited for the delivery. I stood, staring at my half-painted canvas, trying to discard my memories of the past few weeks—but I was soon interrupted by someone knocking on my main entrance door. "One minute!" I said. I got my food and walked into my office, placing my phone on the edge of my desk.

The overhead music helped cancel out the loneliness while a few good tunes kept me company. It freed my mind, diminishing the mesh of entangled thoughts I wished subsided sooner rather than later. *You can beat this, Bea.* I soon finished eating and re-focused, exiting my office. Elizabeth appeared, leaning against the door, drinking the wine I bought from the bottle.

"She's coming," she said.

"Who's coming?"

"You know who. She won't ever give up, Bianca. Do what's best for the kids. You know that feeling in the pit of your stomach—the one that's been gnawing at you? Don't ignore it. You'll *never* feel safe until she's dead. You said so yourself."

All the doors were locked. I contemplated her words and my reality. She was right, and if I ever saw Claire again, the police and FBI would be notified. A part of me wanted to end her life. The other portion of me wanted her to rot in prison, but I couldn't have both... and I needed to stay out of trouble. I strolled out of my office, down the hallway, and toward my painting. Claire stood in front of it wearing a black unbuttoned pea coat, admiring it with great interest. *You got to be kidding me.* I paused next to my art cart, unable to move a muscle, scanning my surroundings in search of anything else out of the ordinary. My breathing increased, and I held a firm stance, anticipating the unexpected.

"You should stay away from all that takeout. It isn't good for you, Bea," said Claire.

"How'd you get in here?"

"Back door. The code is Michael's birthday. I thought I'd drop by and say hello."

"You're here to finish what you started. You're *not* getting my kids!"

"Oh, Bianca. You don't have to be so dramatic. Don't look so scared. I won't hurt you unless you're uncooperative."

I glowered at her, wanting to obliterate her existence. She stared at me before admiring my painting again. I reached for the eight-inch pair of scissors sitting amongst the ceramic cup full of paintbrushes, and placed it in my back pocket before she provided her full attention.

"I should've known you were a crazy, back-stabbing b**ch the whole time."

"...But you didn't because you were too wrapped up in your *own* life. With the gallery, Lucas, kids on your mind and daily routine, you were too blind to notice anyone else's life," she said. "And you were so busy stealing paintings and lying to the FBI, you never quite saw the *true* me—even before Pascal showed up in your life. He was the *perfect* distraction and his presence made it easier to maneuver around you."

"You need to leave," I said.

"We need to have a conversation."

"There's no conversation to have. Get out of here before I call the police." I searched my pockets for my phone, but couldn't find it.

"You don't wanna do that, Bea," she said. She revealed a gun from inside her coat, ambling toward me.

"You're gonna drive me to your house, invite me in, and I'm gonna walk away with—"

"The hell you are! I'd rather die than give them up."

"Bianca... I'm not asking. I'm simply doing what's best for them."

"And I'm not moving. You're gonna have to kill me right here."

"We're *going*. Now!" she said. She pointed her gun, holding it an inch from my face.

"No!"

Elizabeth appeared beside her, staring at me. She lifted her eyebrows with a compelling succinct nod.

"It's time," she said.

I understood what I *needed* to do in that instant. I thought about my kid's safety and their future in her hands.

"She'll never stop, Bea. Even if she kills you now, Michael and Isabelle will *never* be at peace," said Elizabeth.

I closed my eyes and listened to my slowing heartbeat. A sense of calm descended over me before opening my eyes again. An internal switch flipped in my mind. I reached for the scissors in my back pocket, gripping the handles. My arm lunged forward, thrusting the pointy pair into her gut while clasping her gun away from my face. A single shot fired before she released her grip. Her eyes widened, and I gazed into them while the blades skewered against her ribs multiple times. Her hands quivered as she spat blood. It rushed to soak the fibers of her beige sweater. She staggered, struggling to maintain her balance until falling to the floor. I walked over and stood above, enraged.

"It's the only way," I said.

Moments passed. My attitude subsided, transitioning into uncertainty. Specks of doubt ascended, wondering if stabbing her was of my own volition. Elizabeth grinned before gulping the wine from the bottle.

"Well done," she said.

28

The Gala

OH, GOD, WHAT HAVE I DONE? You did what you had to," said Elizabeth. A sliver of guilt migrated from hell and forced its way into my derailed mind. I stood in my gallery not knowing what to do while her blood crept toward my feet like cough medicine crawling out of an open, toppled bottle. *Step back.* I dropped her .38 revolver from my hand while holding scissors in the other. Blood proceeded to claim the marble floor, following me. My thoughts whirled into a scattered frenzy. My cuticles dampened and my clenched grip, unable to release the scissors. They bonded to my hand—tethered by the crimson saturating my pores. *Take a deep breath, Bianca.* My heart slammed against my ribs. A devilish chill conjured its way to my skin's surface, skewing my grip on reality and immobilizing my legs. Nothing but time could stop my unnerved, bloody hand from shaking and drops claiming the floor.

My intermittent, pounding chest forced me to my knees. The adrenaline surged through my veins and a feverish sweat claimed every inch of my face, neck, and forearm. *Breathe,*

Bianca, breathe. The shock alone restricted my movements until I was capable of uncurling my fingers. I stared at my hand with a catatonic glare, as if afflicted with Locked-in syndrome. Nausea increased while I conceded second-degree murder. My eyes drowned in regret, knowing the likelihood of prison. No forced entry and or signs of a struggle. My prints resided on the gun and scissors. *I had motive.* I allowed the scissors to fall to the floor and acknowledged blood splatter on my gray shirt—the one I deemed worn-out and old. I rubbed it with the cuff of my sleeve, eager to vanquish the undeniable proof. *What am I doing? It's getting worse.* I contemplated my situation while wiping my cheek, smearing blood on my face.

Think, Bianca. Think. Calm down. Rationalize your thoughts. A small sense of relief permeated the air while I justified my actions. "I did it for the kids," I kept telling myself until I gained the strength to stand. My arms rested by my side while Claire surveyed my presence with furrowed brows. Although she didn't say anything, her eyes spoke to me. They displayed emotions of regret and sorrow, asking for forgiveness. No one witnessed my crime. *No one needs to know. Don't freak out, Bianca. Don't freak out. Think. Think. Think.* No alibi. No one to corroborate my story. *Did anyone see her enter?*

Claire tried speaking with an abundance of blood flowing out of her mouth. Her body sat upright a few feet from me, as I paced back and forth. I was afraid to touch her, petrified to dial the authorities, and terrified to leave. *I need to call Shepard for help. Oh God, where's my phone?* I searched the front desk after scouring my office and found it in the wastebasket. 'What a Wonderful World' played overhead.

Elizabeth took over one last time, merging herself into my body. My pounding heart accelerated before slowing down, and I existed in a world of complete peace while listening to the melody. *This song—oh, I love this song.* The music grew faint, dissipating with every note that followed. I smiled, closing my eyes—ready to bask in the ambiance of my surroundings.

The walk back to Claire appeared timeless, and the closer I got, the more I enjoyed watching death devour her. I smiled while kneeling to caress her pale, saddened face. Her breathing labored.

"You deserve this. You should've stayed away. Now, you'll be gone forever. Time to clean you up," I said. I elevated to a superior version of myself. Rejuvenated. Renewed.

"I promised to keep Bianca and the twins safe, and that's what I'm going to do. She *will not* rot in prison because of you. We're ready to do what's necessary," I said.

I knelt over her almost-dead body, placing one hand over her mouth while my other pinched her nostrils. It was only a matter of time until she stopped struggling. She convulsed. *Shh. Be still. It'll be over soon.* She ceased to budge, and the power I possessed from taking her life exalted my superiority. Claire was no more.

The radio continued playing in the background, cradling my core while I sat next to her lifeless body. I contemplated disposal of her corpse and Bianca's unfinished painting. The hint of red she desired laid within my reach, and I fell intrigued by the color before me.

I painted, finishing what she started. *Ah, yes. More.* I dipped my brush into the pool of blood, smearing it onto the canvas. *There. Perfect.* The mixture of her blood and the paints gave it an astonishing, robust hue. *Beautiful.* One hour turned into two, as I continued making her work of art a masterpiece. Bianca deserved to shine. Her true talents needed to be showcased. *Hide the evidence in plain sight. No one would be suspicious.* I took a few steps back to admire our achievement. *Perfect. This is better. La Geminae will be the talk of the city.*

Claire's body and our finished masterpiece sat side by side. My adrenaline wore off around one o'clock in the morning. Time flies when you're having fun, right? *What do I do with her, now?* I grabbed Bianca's opened bottle of wine, sat down on the floor, and admired our work in a different perspective—adjacent from where it stood. I relished in the achievement of our accomplishment, gesturing a toast before drinking. My eyelids soon grew heavy, consumed by sleep. *I'll deal with the corpse soon.*

***

Another day commenced. I awoke confused from my bed at two o'clock in the afternoon in pajama pants and a t-shirt. My alarm clock kept buzzing. I shut it off, remembering Claire's body in the gallery. *How the hell did I get here?* I jolted out of bed and sprinted to the children's room. "Michael! Isabelle! Shepard!" Silence sustained. I grew concerned about my kids more than ever and ran back to my room for my phone. I dialed Shepard's number. He answered on the fourth ring.

"Shepard!"

"Bea, you okay?"

"Do you have the kids with you?"

"Yeah, of course! We're having lunch at the diner down the street, now. We had breakfast earlier, too." I exhaled.

"You should've woken me up or left a note or something."

"I did. It's taped to your bedroom door."

"Oh… sorry."

"You had a rough night, Bea. Liz took over."

"I dunno. I was holding a pair of scissors, but I can't remember anything else. I have a feeling I did something terrible."

"Don't worry. It's taken care of. We'll talk about it some more when we get back, okay? We'll be back soon."

"Okay. See you guys in a bit."

Flashbacks haunted me the moment I hung up. A shot of tequila helped me relax. Shepard reassured me I was 'in the clear,' but I still worried. I surfaced from overthinking too much and needed to be patient with their return. A wave of memories overwhelmed me, projecting Elizabeth's actions as well as my own. I had clarity—knowledge of the murder I committed. The revelation spoke so profoundly, I dropped to the floor, trying to catch my breath. *Calm down. Everything will be okay.*

***

My kids soon showed up, greeting me with hugs and kisses. I held them close. Shepard sat me down at the kitchen table, telling me his side of the story.

"It seemed odd you didn't contact me till one o'clock this morning. I figured something went wrong when you didn't return any of my calls, so I visited while the kids slept," he said.

"Where was I? What was I doing?" I asked.

"You laid next to her body with blood and paint all over you. I almost couldn't tell you two apart. I cleaned up, brought you home, changed your clothes... and here we are."

"Oh my God, Shep, how could I ever repay you?"

"It's what we do for the ones we love."

He smiled and leaned forward with an extended hand. I did the same, and held his hand in mine, reassured he covered my tracks. The children played in the living room.

"What about my clothes?" I said.

"Incinerated," he said.

"... And what about—"

"It's better you don't know. Plausible deniability."

***

Another day passed and I hadn't heard from Kate, nor did I learn of any updates on Pascal. He didn't make the news, which struck me as 'odd.' This made me a little nervous. Looking over my shoulder was a hard habit to break. Claire being gone from our lives was a partial relief. I was able to let my guard down a bit, but my gut instinct leaned toward my uncle's return someday. Each day took a lifetime to end. Perhaps that was due to the psychological impacts of Claire's absence, or maybe due to experiencing the essence of her life slip away by my hand. Regardless, I chose to rise above my feelings. I received an anticipated call from Kate early that morning the instant I decided to relax my nerves.

"Hey, I'm downstairs. Just thought I'd drop by."

"Hey! What are you doing here? Everything okay?"

"I have something important to tell you."

"Come on up."

Her words diffused anxiety within me. I thought she wanted to confront me about Claire—to tell me someone found her body. Shepard was the only one who knew what happened to her, and I planned on keeping it that way. Kate wore a black coat with a blue Yankee's hoodie, sunglasses, and blue jeans. We sat down at the kitchen table.

"So, how you been?" she said.

"Umm, I've been okay the last couple of weeks. I'm so glad to be home with the kids, you know?"

"Yeah, I can imagine how grateful you are. I'm sure everything's somewhat normal, and I bet readjusting took some time."

"Things are definitely starting to feel a bit more normal around here."

"I'm so sorry to spring this on you like this, but, I'm here because my team and I devised a last-minute plan to capture Pascal. It's a risky one, but we have reason to believe he's still in New York. We wanna flush him out—bring him out into the open, but we can't do it without you.

"How so? What's the plan?"

"We didn't allow his face to be shown in the media. You and I both know he still wants the footage we confiscated. The only way for him to get his hands on it, now is if news stations declared me dead. The files haven't been uploaded anywhere online, and he *doesn't* know whether or not I have it, at this point.

"So, if you're dead, he'd contact *me,* looking for it."

"That's right. We need him to think you have it in your possession, willing to be done with him once and for all."

"And when he has it, he'll have no reason to come after me and my kids. But wait, you won't give it to him…"

"Correct."

"So how do we go about this?"

"You'll hear about my death in two days. It'll be in the newspaper, the news—everywhere. You *must* attend my fake, closed-casket funeral, which will happen the day after. Once he verifies my death, he'll call you, hoping you'll hand it over. Play hard to get, but not too hard. Steer him into approaching you. Make him think he's choosing a safe place to collect. With my death, the ceremony the next day, and your Gala the day after, he'll most likely choose to meet you there. A lot of people will attend, and you won't risk embarrassing yourself—and he knows this."

"He *does* like to show off—display his power."

"You see. *Perfect.* I'm confident this will work, but we need your cooperation to pull this off."

"He'll be skeptical—very cautious, even."

"And we don't anticipate him being alone. I really do hate to raid your special night, but it's the *only* window we have where we might be able to catch him."

"I'm in. I'll do it, and you'll get your retribution. So, where's the thumb drive and DVD?" She removed a manila folder from her coat pocket.

"In here. It's a replica, but empty. Guard it with your life."

"Will do."

"I placed an encrypted phone inside for us to communicate the night of. Text, "Go," before he verifies its contents. We'll be disguised as staff. Oh, I almost forgot to ask you. Have you heard from Claire at all?"

"…Um, no. Nothing at all."

"Well, I hope you don't. I *still* can't believe she shot you."

"I think it's better than being stabbed in the stomach. My bullet sliced right through."

"Hmm. Yeah, the thought of a blade slicing through flesh creeps me out. Anyway, again, I'm sorry for showing up, looking like a bum, unannounced. I had to take precautions. You understand. Oh, and by the way, I want to apologize in advance for Agent Gerald Hall."

"That a**hole's been a pain in the ass since day one!"

"I know. I know... he's a piece of work and still thinks you're guilty, so if he approaches you with any questions, just... be yourself, alright?"

"Of course," I said.

I smiled before she stood to leave. I wanted nothing to do with Pascal, but if seeing him in a controlled environment one last time was the way to lock him up for life, I was all for it.

***

Two days later, Kate's picture appeared in the newspaper. "FBI Agent Brutally Murdered," headlined. *"FBI Agent, Kate Clarke recognized for her bravery in the attempt to saving Dean Anders, a New York City politician caught in the crossfires of a downtown robbery."*—The New York Times. I attended the funeral the next day to pay my respects. Shepard met me at my place afterward to hang out—and I received a call from a blocked caller on my new cell number the instant I stood from my sofa.

"Hello?"

"It's a shame what happened to Kate." I cringed, recognizing the raspy, airy voice.

"How did you get this number?"

"Why would you go to the funeral of the woman who slept with your husband?"

"The hell you put us through made us closer, but now she's…gone. You're happy about her death, aren't you?"

"Best day of my life. Now, let's talk about—"

"About the recording. God, you never stop. You wanna know if I have it. She's dead, and you think she could've left it with me. Why didn't you contact me sooner?"

"Not everyone recovers as quickly as you, Bianca. No thanks to that *f**king* sister of yours."

"Hm. Maybe I *do* have it. If I threatened to use it against you, would it keep you away from me and my family?"

"You give me what I want, and you'll *never* see my face again."

"And if I ever do, I'll send all the copies I made to every major news station in the country, including posting it to every social media platform. *Every* soul on earth will witness the crimes you committed."

"Fair enough. Meet me to—"

"No. I have my Art Gala to host, and much to do before then."

"Ah, yes, the Gala. You know how much I appreciate the arts. I expect to be on the list."

He hung up the phone. Kate was right. I stared at Shepard, sitting right across from me with the realization Pascal's end drew near.

"He took the bait," I said.

"He won't be alone. If I were him I'd have at least five or six men keeping guard."

"Should I expect him to cause a scene?"

"*I'd* make a scene if I felt cornered."

"Kate and her team know what they're doing. It'll be okay."

***

Time moved on. The day transitioned into the night and the Grand Ballroom at the Plaza Hotel is where the event took place. The doors were open to all guests at seven o'clock, and I greeted them as they walked it. I also made my way around the room, mingling with colleagues I hadn't seen in an entire year. The ballroom lived up to its name, decorated with fresh flowers and linen on every table. The detail of its interior remained exquisite, possessing an early 1900s French Renaissance chateau style. A marble floor, stage, ambiance, live music, and all-adoring guests added to and filled the atmosphere. The works of art displayed— La Geminae, included—completed the night.

I kept my eyes peeled for Pascal—positive he'd make a grand entrance. Shepard, dressed as wait staff wearing eyeglasses, kept me company from afar for some time. We met in the kitchen to rendezvous.

"Any sign of him?" I asked.

"No. Nothing yet."

"He's a pompous prick. I'm sure he'll walk right through the front door."

He and I parted ways, and someone bumped into me—a beautiful woman I never met before. She apologized several times. Her long, dark hair flowed like waves of an off-shore sea, and her smile radiated, brightening the room.

"It's fine, really—a silly mistake. Are you enjoying yourself this evening, Miss..."

"Burke. Marcella Burke. Wait, you're Bianca Gallucci— the gallery owner in Chelsea, right?"

"Guilty as charged," I said.

"So nice to meet you! You *have to* meet my husband, Rafael. He's a landscape and portrait artist and *loves* the painting you have displayed tonight. *All* the artwork is wonderful, of course, but yours is truly inspiring."

"Thank you! I'm flattered." She waved, motioning a Spaniard to come closer.

"Hon, come here, quick. This is Bianca Gallucci from the Gallucci Gallery. She painted the one we were talking about," she said.

He smiled and shook my hand. "It's a great pleasure meeting you Ms. Gallucci. I adore the tones of red you've incorporated as well as your technique," he said.

"Oh, you're too kind. I'm glad you admire it! Sweat and blood went into that piece," I said.

"I can relate," said Emilio.

"Perhaps I can take a look at your work sometime," I said.

"That would be an honor."

We exchanged business cards, said our farewells, and parted ways. They reminded me of Lucas and myself when we were younger, but I grew antsy wondering *where* or *when* my adversary might show up. Shepard and I regrouped in the kitchen again, but he soon retreated to the restroom. "I'll be back. Text me if anything happens," he said. I walked back to my table.

Pascal waltzed through the front door with a wooden cane and a limp about one minute later. Elizabeth also showed herself, sitting on the chair beside me, wearing my identical black gown, but in white. She smirked.

"Wow. I'm so proud of us. Look at him," she said. I sipped my champagne.

"I'd do it again," I said.

I sent Shepard a message with discretion, saying, "He's here. Keep your distance." Pascal made his way to me and sat down. I folded my arms and re-crossed my legs. His existence, vexing.

"Ah, we meet again," he said.

"Unfortunately. I want you gone as fast as possible," I said.

"This is only a quick business transaction."

"You left your men at the door."

"I have men everywhere. Besides, you wouldn't do anything to jeopardize such a lovely evening."

"We should kill him," said Elizabeth.

"You have sixty seconds to say what you came to say before you disappear from my life, Pascal."

"I believe you have something for me, first."

"I have it, and it's all yours as long as you keep your end of the bargain."

"Very well. I assume you have copies."

"Perhaps, but you'll find out if you come near me or my kids, again."

"Touché."

"You know, I wondered why you would come here. I mean, why take the risk? What's the real reason you're here, Pascal?"

"When we first met, I hinted that Lucas was a bad seed. Do you remember?"

"I replay it in my head every day since we met. Why'd you do that?"

"To gain your trust—or at least some of it. The least you can do is thank me." I glanced at my wristwatch.

"Thirty seconds remaining."

"The thing about trust is it must be earned, but I'm here to show you this," he said. He reached into his left breast pocket.

"What is it?"

"Just watch," he said.

I viewed a recording of myself breaking the neck of the corrupt police officer on the West Side Highway on Pascal's cell phone. The footage came from the officer's dashcam across the way on the median. Pascal and I had leverage over each other. He smiled, placing it back into his pocket. I removed the manila folder from my purse. He looked over my shoulder, delivering a nod. I handed it to him. A stranger dressed as a cocktail waiter walked up to our table and retrieved the package.

"Make sure it's all there," he said. "You know I can't leave here without checking its contents. I know who you *really* are, Bianca, but don't worry. You can rely on me to keep your secret as long as you keep mine."

"You sick bastard," said Elizabeth.

"Your sixty seconds are up. You got what you came for, and we're now considered even. See yourself out," I said.

"I *trust* we have an agreement, then. By the way, that look in your eye will *never* part from you. You're a killer, and can't change what you are, my sweet niece. You will *always* be a Gallucci."

"F**k you. See yourself out."

I pulled my phone out to text. Pascal stared at me with suspicion.

"Don't bother making a face. You of all people know how much I worry about my kid's safety. That's all I'm doing."

I lied. I sent Shepard a text message saying, "Phone. Left breast pocket," before Pascal's tech guy could return.

***

Shepard approached the table minutes later and bumped into Pascal, spilling a few glasses of champagne on him.

"What the hell! Watch where you're going, you idiot!" he said.

"Oh, my God. I am *so* sorry sir. My deepest apologies," he said. He attempted to help clean the mess, applying light pressure to his lapel with a white dinner napkin. Shepard slipped his hand into his breast pocket, confiscating his phone.

"Get out of my face, you fool!" he said. He snatched the cloth from him.

The following text I sent was to Kate. It said "Go," while he cleaned up. She and six men dressed as staff surrounded him with guns pointed, shouting, "FBI!" She smiled, reciting the Miranda rights while handcuffing him. His crew, too. Shepard handed me Pascal's phones, and I smiled from ear to ear at his dumbfounded reaction.

"Pascal. Trust must be earned," I said. I waved his phone in the air.

"How did... When did...?" he said.

I walked away, knowing my children and I were going to live our lives in safety and peace. It was over. Kate got her revenge, and everything worked out as planned. Other than that little hiccup with Pascal, the event was a success, and I arranged to have my painting delivered to my gallery the next day.

***

My new assistant began the day with a pot of fresh coffee and a warm smile the instant I walked through the front door. It was time for me to make room for my La Geminae on the wall— in the exact spot Claire died. The moment appeared surreal, and the spotlight cascaded its beam onto it like a vibrant ray of sunlight. I marveled at its beauty with every glance. Evidence hung in plain sight. Daring? Yes. Foolish? Maybe, but a part of me enjoyed the thought of standing on the edge of danger. It was perfect. The authorities would continue their search for Claire, and no one suspected her to be dead. In a way, a part of her would always be with me. I carried mixed feelings about her—her betrayal and deception. I wondered if I could ever forgive her. Maybe someday. Lucas? Possible with a chance of 'maybe' in my forecast. I know I should, but my callousness fortified my heart. I figured time would do all the healing I needed, and I wasn't in a rush. I inhaled the sweet aroma of my coffee in hand and the freedom I enveloped. My kids were safe and, although life would never be the same, I had the chance to make it better for me and them. One more glance at my work satisfied my urge to embrace it once more.

"Wow. Exquisite," said Elizabeth.

She stood by my side with her hair styled in a bun, white blouse, and gray trouser pants, admiring our work. She reached for my hand and interlaced our fingers before resting her head on my shoulder.

"I wouldn't have survived the last few weeks without you," I said.

"We make a great team, but deep down inside, it was all you, Bea. Deep down, you *know* I'm only a construct of your mind. I love you, sis."

"I love you, too."

She completed what she pursued to accomplish, and I held on to her words, contemplating them the rest of the day, and into the night. Elizabeth struck a chord within me—one that reverberated from the inner lining of my core. The longer I reflected upon my arduous experience, the more it became apparent that her words couldn't be farther from the truth.

Acknowledgments

Thank you, Yasmine and the artist of New York City for your inspiration.

ABOUT THE AUTHOR

Richards visits Manhattan's art scene often. The Gallucci Gallery is his first novel. Follow along on Instagram: @kemrichards or visit www.kbrichards.com and submit your email to the eNewsletter for future updates!

Made in the USA
Middletown, DE
23 April 2022

64629522R00154